SUMMER ON THE FRENCH RIVIERA

JENNIFER BOHNET

Boldwood

First published in Great Britain in 2023 by Boldwood Books Ltd.

Cover Design by Debbie Clement Design

Cover Photography: Shutterstock

A CIP catalogue record for this book is available from the British Library.

Paperback ISBN 978-1-80162-282-0

Large Print ISBN 978-1-80162-284-4

Hardback ISBN 978-1-80162-283-7

Ebook ISBN 978-1-80162-285-1

Kindle ISBN 978-1-80162-286-8

Audio CD ISBN 978-1-80162-277-6

MP3 CD ISBN 978-1-80162-278-3

Digital audio download ISBN 978-1-80162-280-6

Boldwood Books Ltd
23 Bowerdean Street
London SW6 3TN
www.boldwoodbooks.com

Once again this is for you, Richard, with love xxx

Once again this is for you, Richard, with love xxx

PROLOGUE

Gabriella Jacques was more tired than she'd care to admit. All through the months of January, February and into March, sheer adrenaline had kept her going and boosted her flagging spirits when she wavered with the effort of organising the move to France. It would, she knew, be worth it in the end, but selling and moving house for only the second time in her life was far more stressful than she'd anticipated. There were so many bitter-sweet memories of her time living in Dartmouth, the town that had adopted her as one of their own, her life with Eric and, when Harriet was born, their happy family life. Until it all changed when Eric died. Not that she wasn't looking forward to returning to her childhood home in Antibes Juan-les-Pins, she most definitely was. The chance of a proper family reconciliation, with no more broken promises, had to be seized and brought to fruition if at all possible. Elodie, her twenty-four year old granddaughter, had carried her along on a wave of hyper-energetic enthusiasm as well as practicality, although even she was starting to flag this last week of February.

Since their return from Juan-les-Pins in France two days after New Year, with the decision made to move there permanently, the two of them had gone through the long, and continually evolving, to-do list that had been the first thing Elodie had started writing, sitting at the breakfast table, the morning after they had arrived home. Every time they ticked something off as done, another job invariably took its place.

'So much to do. I suppose it will all come together in the end,' Gabby sighed.

Elodie glanced at her grandmother. 'Are you sad about selling this house? We could rent it out instead. Give you an income.'

Gabby shook her head. 'No. A clean break is better. We're going to be too far away to be able to keep an eye on things, so it would mean the hassle of getting an agent to handle things – and I'm a bit anti agents at the moment, as you know. I'd just not realised how much was involved. When your grandfather and I bought this house, I remember it being a lot simpler, but then, in those days, we didn't have so many things.'

Having to go through the contents of a house that had been her home for over three decades and share unwanted, unneeded, possessions between the local charity shops before consigning the rest as rubbish to the bin had been unsettling to say the least. Everything Gabby had picked up seemed to taunt her with some unspoken memory demanding attention before she disposed of it.

Elodie gave her grandmother a concerned look. Gabby, more her mother than grandmother if the truth be told, had been the one constant presence in her life since she was four years old and Harriet, her mother, had forsaken them both for Australia. At New Year, Gabby had celebrated not only her seventieth birthday but also their joint decision to move back to the villa of her childhood that she'd inherited from her father Hervé. When Harriet's unexpected decision to join them for New Year in Juan-les-Pins had culminated in Gabby inviting Harriet to move into the villa with them, Elodie had been both shocked and wary of her mother's acceptance. She had the feeling that adjusting to having the stranger who was her mother living in the same house was going to take some time.

'Has Harriet given you a date for when she is coming?' Elodie asked. The original plan had been for Harriet, who was currently renting a small cottage on the outskirts of Bristol, to join them within a fortnight of their return from France and help with the packing up of the house. But she'd rung Gabby to say it would be the end of the month before she could make it, if not later. It had proved to be later.

'The day after tomorrow.' Gabby said now.

'Cancelling at the last moment seems to be a habit of hers,' Elodie said with a sceptical look. 'Let's hope she doesn't cancel for a second time. I suppose she could have changed her mind about moving with us?' She glanced at her grandmother.

'I'll ring her again this evening.' Gabby gave an inward sigh. She too worried about Harriet cancelling again, but the last time they'd spoken, she'd insisted that she was on board with their future plans for a life together on the French Riviera. All Gabby could do was to hope and pray that she meant it. That Harriet wouldn't be the reason for her family falling apart again. She wished for nothing more than that both her daughter and her granddaughter would eventually form a conventional loving mother-daughter relationship. After all she, Gabriella Jacques, wouldn't be around for ever.

1

No matter how well organised a house move is, something always goes wrong on the day. Things get broken, empty rooms show their desperate need for decoration, boxes are dumped into the wrong rooms, and moving-in day invariably descends into a chaotic shambles. Which is when the conscious thought, why on earth did I think moving here was a good idea, becomes lodged in the brain.

For Harriet Rogers, standing in the room that was to be hers in Villa de l'Espoir, that moment came as she watched the removal men drive away, leaving herself, Gabby and Elodie facing a veritable pile of boxes that would, once unpacked, become a recyclable mountain in its own right. The fact that, for once, the sun had hidden behind a sky full of grey clouds had added to the frustration of the day. Now, as the time approached six o'clock, the sun had finally decided to shine on this their first evening in Antibes Juan-les-Pins.

Gabby was in the kitchen going through various boxes with the word 'kitchen' written on them in red that had actually reached their correct destination. Thankfully, the kettle and the microwave had surfaced early on, largely, Harriet suspected, due to the fact that the removal men needed copious amounts of tea and biscuits to keep them going. Elodie had done a dash to the nearest boulangerie at midday, buying freshly filled baguettes for them all and a tarte tatin to slice up.

Harriet ran her hand through her hair and sighed. This last week had been difficult. When she'd finally arrived in Dartmouth to help pack up Gabby's house, Elodie, in particular, had made it clear to Harriet that she'd let them down by not coming to help earlier, adding to the guilt that Harriet already felt. The tentative relationship that had started to develop between the two of them over Christmas and New Year had proved to be a fragile bond that needed more nourishing, not the neglect that had occurred over the last couple of months. Now they were all actually together in Villa de l'Espoir, all Harriet's doubts broke through her carefully constructed mind barrier and rushed to the surface.

How could she explain how terrified and anxious she'd felt at the thought of returning to Dartmouth and potentially meeting up with people from her past? The less time she spent there limited the likelihood of that happening – particularly if she stayed in the house and didn't venture out. She eased her guilt by making a secret pact with herself that she'd work extra hard in France to help to get the villa straight.

By arriving so late to help, Harriet's plan had almost worked, but then on their last evening, Gabby had insisted on treating them all to fish and chips to be eaten on Bayards Cove. 'I want to make a new happy Dartmouth memory for the three of us,' she'd said.

The late March evening air had been cool but with a welcome feeling of spring all around, with daffodils in the various planters on the embankment. The town had been quiet as they'd walked through and bought their supper from Elodie's favourite fish and chip shop, before making their way to Bayards Cove. Glasses of wine were bought from the pub, The Dartmouth Arms, and sitting on a bench on the cove overlooking the river the three of them had tucked into their fish and chips.

Eating her supper, Harriet had watched the activity on the river. The lower ferry, with its tug alongside, didn't look a lot different to the one she'd grown up with, the one she'd routinely jumped on to go to Paignton or Torquay. The ramp had still clattered and jarred its way down noisily onto the access slope as the ferry had motored in far enough for the two to fit together safely for vehicles to drive off and those waiting along the embankment to board.

Gabby had been the first to finish her food and as she had screwed up the packaging she'd started to reminisce. 'I remember sitting here so many times with Eric, and the two of you at different times when you were younger. And now here we are a three-generation family, making a Dartmouth memory to take with us into our new lives.' She'd been silent for a moment before turning to Harriet. 'Do you remember coming here with your dad?'

'Of course. Our Sunday mornings together were special. He'd buy a pint of beer for himself, a lemonade for me and we'd share a large packet of crisps.' Harriet had smiled at the memory. 'The times I tried to get him to buy me a proper drink. I was eighteen before he'd even buy me a lemonade shandy.' She shook her head. If he'd ever heard about the cider she and her friends downed on a Saturday evening, he'd never let on. Screwing up her own empty packaging, she'd held out her hand for Gabby's and Elodie's. 'I'll go put these in the bin.'

'I'll take the glasses back to the pub while you do that,' Elodie had said.

Walking across to the rubbish bin, Harriet had smothered a sigh, remembering how numb she'd felt for months after her dad had died, unable to process her grief about the loss in her life or cope with the huge cavity it had created. Saying she was devastated didn't come close to how she'd truly felt. She might have been almost twenty years old but, child-like, she'd assumed that he'd always be there; to interrogate her boyfriends, to tell her off when she did something stupid, to finally walk her down the aisle when she married the love of her life and, later, to bounce his grandchildren on his knee. He and her mum had been such a perfect fit, the yin and yang of her life. She loved them both dearly and had promised her dad she would look after her mother. A promise she was aware she had spectacularly broken with her actions after his death. Thankfully, he had never known how badly she had behaved, how promiscuous she'd been or the selfish way she'd left the two most important people in her life and fled to the other side of the world.

Now she was back from Australia and the three of them were reunited, she intended to do everything, everything, in her power to make amends to them both. Gabby, who'd greeted her return without voicing any recriminations she might have harboured, had accepted her return with a true mother's love. Elodie, though, had taken a while to come to terms with her mother being back in her life. Her wary reconciliation at Christmas in Antibes Juan-les-Pins had shown that it wouldn't be easy establishing a mother-daughter relationship after an absence of twenty years, that it would have to be worked towards. Bridges between them needed to be built, old wounds needed to heal and, at the very least, a tentative trust had to establish itself. Healing the breach with Elodie was the most important of several problems that Harriet needed to address to regain her own self-respect.

'Hattie? Is it really you?' A woman's voice had broken into her thoughts. Her fear of being seen had been realised. And, of course, of all people, it had to be her best friend from Torquay.

'Lizzie. Fancy seeing you.' Despite herself Harriet had found herself smiling at her old friend, as Lizzie had started to chat away excitedly.

'How lovely to see you after all these years. We must have a catch-up. Are you back for good?' Lizzie had asked.

'It's lovely to see you too,' Harriet had said, starting to try and to explain that she was back in Europe for good but about to move to France when an excited Lizzie had interrupted her.

'D'you remember my daughter, Kelly? No, of course you won't. She was a baby when you left. Kelly, this is my best friend, Harriet, from years ago, she's been in Australia for years.' Not waiting for an answer, Lizzie had babbled on. 'We're all so thrilled – you must remember Jack Ellicott? American, came here the year we started college, before he disappeared back to the US unexpectedly. Well, Kelly is marrying his son next month, would you believe? She went to the US for work experience – she's a video game designer and it's the place to be, apparently – and met Nathan. We couldn't believe it when he turned out to be Jack's son, such a small world these days. You must come to the wedding. I'll send you an invite – your mother still lives at the same address?'

'Same address,' Harriet had said, telling herself it still was, until tomorrow at least, so not a downright lie. Besides, Gabby had arranged for the post to be forwarded to France, so the invite would reach her eventually. She'd turned to Kelly. 'Congratulations.'

'We need to catch the next ferry so we can't stop and chat right now,' Lizzie had continued. 'But it's been a lovely surprise bumping into you. We'll have a proper catch-up at the wedding. Come on, Kelly.'

Harriet had watched the two of them walk along the quay towards the ferry before she rejoined Gabby and Elodie.

'Was that Lizzie?' Gabby had asked.

'Yes. She hasn't changed a bit.' Harriet had laughed. 'I didn't do much talking. I'd forgotten how she used to gabble away. It's not until she draws breath that you can get a word in. Right, shall we go home for that early night we promised ourselves? Busy day tomorrow.'

And the three of them had left Bayards Cove and started to walk homewards.

Harriet had kept the news that she'd been invited to a wedding to herself, thankful she had a cast-iron excuse for not attending. She'd be out of the country. Meeting Lizzie unexpectedly had been lovely, but it was enough. The thought of meeting other people from her past en masse at a wedding reception terrified her.

Even now, a day or so later, standing in her new bedroom in the villa and remembering that evening, Harriet felt a wave of anxiety seep through her body. People had long memories for juicy gossip and hearsay. The hope that they would show understanding and compassion if they heard the truth was not something that Harriet had ever thought likely. Thankfully, she was in France now, where nobody knew or cared about her past.

A past where she'd selfishly screwed up her own life, not caring about how much her actions affected others. It was time to try to redeem herself in Gabby and Elodie's eyes and pray they would both give her the second chance that deep down she'd wanted for so long.

Crossing over to and opening the French windows of her bedroom, Harriet pushed back the shutters and stepped out onto the small balcony. Her bedroom at the back of the villa overlooked the garden and the pool, both of which looked in need of some loving care.

For the first few weeks here in France, she'd concentrate on trying to break down the barrier that she sensed Elodie had erected around herself, whilst helping Gabby sort the villa before starting to think about what she was going to do. She didn't need to work, as money wasn't an issue. The amount of Todd's life insurance coupled with his investments had come as a welcome surprise. She could live anywhere and do pretty much what she wanted. What she couldn't do was sit around for the rest of her life. Was she brave enough to try to pick up that long-ago dream to make a name for herself as an artist, but, more to the point, had she left it too late? Surely she at least owed it to herself to find out.

Harriet pulled the box marked bed linen towards her and took out sheets, pillowcases and a duvet cover. She'd make up both her bed and Gabby's before going downstairs to help with whatever else needed doing this evening. Having her bed ready for her to collapse into at the end of the day would be good. After all, tomorrow was, as the old cliché put it, the first day of the rest of her life here in France. And it was a life that she intended to make the most of from here on in. If it wasn't too late, she wanted to become part of a family again, to build a proper relationship with Elodie, to say sorry to Gabby for her behaviour. To ask their forgiveness for her past actions.

If it did prove too late to mend the past and move forward together, she'd leave and try to accept the fact that sometimes it was impossible to right a wrong and that all those years ago she'd irrevocably screwed up her life forever. She would have at least tried.

2

In the middle of all the chaos of helping her grandmother organise the move to France, Elodie had also been busy trying to put together a plan for her future freelance writing life. She was so looking forward to living in France, getting away from her dead-end life in the UK and writing about things she was passionate about.

Since returning from France in the New Year, she'd turned down new copywriting commissions from the advertising company which had been her main source of income, to concentrate on finding new outlets for her own writing. She hadn't closed the door totally on the copywriting but had explained she needed a few weeks to help her grandmother move. Secretly, she was hoping not to have to do any more work for them, that her features about her new life and interesting places on the French Riviera would earn her enough money. She realised it wasn't going to be easy setting herself up as an ex-pat journalist trying to sell features to the UK media about life in France. People who were already established were struggling to find outlets for their work as print newspapers and magazines disappeared, so she had to find new outlets and offer editors something different.

So, as well as helping Gabby sort everything out as they had prepared to leave Dartmouth, Elodie had been busy pitching her ideas to magazines

and newspapers about writing travel and lifestyle features. Philosophi-
cally, she accepted that it was a hard market to break into, but she
intended to do her utmost to find a niche in it somewhere, somehow.
She'd already secured a year's contract for a monthly column of five
hundred words about 'My New life on the Riviera' for their local paper in
Devon, the *Dartmouth Chronicle*. The pay was minimal, but it would be
syndicated in the publisher's other papers along the south coast and get
her name out there on a regular basis. The first column was due next
week, so she needed to think about starting to write it.

And, of course, the added bonus to living down here was that she had
a new man in her life, Gazz. Elodie smiled to herself as she thought about
him. From the moment they'd been introduced at his parents' Christmas
aperitif party, there had been a connection between them – despite his
friend, Fiona, laying a possessive hand on his arm at every opportunity.
Gazz had assured Elodie they weren't officially an item, despite Fiona
trying to show otherwise, and she'd believed him.

Seeing Gazz standing next to Philippe, his grandfather, waiting to greet
them in Arrivals at the airport early this morning, ready to drive them to
Villa de l'Espoir, had made her heart skip a beat, as had the welcoming
kiss he'd given her. She knew too that Gabby had been more than happy
to see Philippe waiting to welcome them.

Now, as Elodie set up her computer on the desk in front of her
bedroom window, she glanced out at the view over the front garden and
the green in the middle of the cul-de-sac, remembering the first time she'd
seen the villa back in December. Gabby had told her that it had been the
Jacques family home since the end of the nineteenth century when it had
been built by her great-great-grandfather. Unusual in design for its age, it
was a sprawling villa built of the warm-hued local stone, the terracotta
tiles of the roof bleached to a pale pink by the sun over the last century.
Elodie had fallen in love with the place that first time she'd seen the villa,
feeling as if she'd come home from the moment she'd walked in through
the front door.

Elodie had been shocked to learn on that first visit that Gabby had
owned the house since the death of her estranged father ten years ago.
Since then, the villa had been rented out and Gabby had told Elodie that

the rent money had been put into a savings account for her which she would gain access to on her twenty-fifth birthday.

But the happy surprise of learning about the villa and what she'd laughingly called her unexpected trust fund had been buried by the Christmas surprise to trump all surprises. Whilst the news about the villa had been a good one, full of possibilities for the future, the news that her long-lost mother wanted to be back in her life had not been so welcome.

Elodie sighed. Even now, months later, if she put her hand on her heart, she couldn't honestly admit to being happy about the reunion. Sure, overtures had been made, regrets acknowledged, hopes for the future voiced, but there was still a tentative nature to the relationship between herself and her mother. Walking on eggshells, Gabby called it.

Harriet had even expressed the hope that time spent together in Dartmouth packing up the house would help her and Elodie get to know each other before the move. Hadn't happened though, had it? Harriet had only turned up when most of the work had been done, leaving no time for any real mother and daughter closeness to establish itself. It was all very well saying she wanted to be reunited with the family, but being with them all the time already seemed like a step too far for her.

Harriet had also told Elodie privately that she'd give living 'en famille' in Villa de l'Espoir a three-month trial. If she felt it wasn't working at the end of that time, then she intended to move out. Something which Elodie knew would upset Gabby, especially if Harriet not only left the villa but moved away from France as well. That was something which Elodie didn't want to be responsible for.

Remembering the scene in Nice airport as the three of them had spent time in duty-free before flying back to the UK, Elodie gave a wry smile. She had been the one to liken Harriet's unexpected arrival to a Christmas present they would never forget. But, she couldn't help worrying, what if their fractured relationship remained broken? Would it turn into the proverbial poisoned chalice with every Christmas from now on being remembered for the failure of that particular year?

There was so much that needed to be asked, talked about and to come to terms with before they could all move on. Once all the facts, the misconceptions, everything, was out in the open, who knew whether that would turn out to be a good or a bad thing?

Elodie groaned. Now they were all together in Villa de l'Espoir she would have to try to graciously accept the fact that Harriet was back in her and Gabby's lives, whilst deep down she was still aggrieved with her mother for leaving her twenty years ago.

There were still so many unanswered questions about the past buzzing around in her brain. Questions only Harriet could answer. Questions she sensed that Harriet was reluctant to divulge the answers to. Gabby would probably advise her to let sleeping dogs lie – no point in dragging up the past when it was the present and the future that truly mattered.

The last thing Elodie wanted to do was create a situation that would hurt Gabby, but deep down she knew that, come what may, there was one question in particular that she had every intention of pressing Harriet for an answer on. Who was her father?

And once she knew his name, the next two questions would need answering. Why wasn't his name on her birth certificate and, importantly, why had he never been in her life?

3

Downstairs, Gabby was gazing around distractedly, wondering where on earth she could put things in this kitchen with its limited number of units. In her mother's day, it had been a real family kitchen – large enough for free-standing cupboards, a long pine table and chairs and a big old-fashioned range-type cooker. Gabby smiled to herself as the memory of the day their first ever fridge arrived popped into her mind. Her mother had been beside herself with delight as she planned where in the kitchen it should go.

Today, the big American-style fridge they'd brought with them was plugged in, albeit on an adaptor for the English plug, in the same place. The one length of working surface under the window had the kettle, the microwave and the remains of the makeshift meals – sandwiches, crisps and tea – they'd eaten today. The bowl in the sink was full of dirty mugs and plates. Piles of crockery, cooking utensils, saucepans and cutlery were all piled haphazardly on the kitchen table they'd brought over from Dartmouth. Flattened empty cardboard boxes were stacked in a corner. Sorting the kitchen would have to be their first priority, Gabby decided. Turning it into a kitchen that was at the heart of the home she and her family were sharing.

Gabby smiled – her family. Having her daughter back in her life, as well as Elodie, was something that she'd long given up even dreaming about. Now it had happened, she was determined to do everything in her power to make it a success so that Harriet would never want to leave again and, importantly, she and Elodie would form a proper mother-daughter bond. The last twenty years of caring for Elodie alone, trying to be a mother as well as a grandmother hadn't been easy but the love she had for Elodie had carried her through the difficult times. These days she and Elodie had a close, loving bond but Gabby knew that nothing could take the place of a real mother-daughter bond like the one she sensed still lurked in the shadows between herself and Harriet. They'd been so close once upon a time. Gabby smothered a sigh. She could only hope and pray that the fractured family bonds between the three of them would all heal in the coming months.

Gabby began to pick up the cardboard. Tonight, they were eating out, so she'd leave trying to sort the kitchen until tomorrow and take the cardboard to the garage out of the way. Opening the internal door to the garage in the hallway, Gabby stood at the top of the flight of steps that led down and threw the cardboard onto the garage floor below. She remembered how easy the steps were to fall down and there was no way she was going to risk the descent with her arms full. Coming back up empty-handed would be fine.

Once down in the garage, Gabby picked up the cardboard and placed it near the closed garage doors, ready to take to a recycling point when they found one, before looking around. The small window on the side had thick iron bars fixed to the outside, something she didn't remember being there before. The garage was empty, save for the large box Gabby had remembered at the last moment being in the Dartmouth house attic and one of the removal men had peevishly climbed up to fetch it. A floor-to-ceiling unit of wooden shelves was in the centre of the back wall.

Absently she ran a finger along one of the empty shelves, cutting through a layer of dust. In the past, they'd held a diverse collection of what her mother had always called utter 'déchets', in a disparaging tone of voice. Tins of half-used paint, grease guns, spark plugs, nails, screws, brushes, broken tools. Like the kitchen was her mother's domain, the garage had been her father's, although rarely used for its original purpose back then, as he always parked outside on the drive in front of the double doors. It was only when he acquired a Renault 4L in the late sixties that he started to park the car in the garage, but even then there was always lots of boxes filled with the next dodgy business opportunity to come his way.

Now, standing in what had been his carefully guarded empire all those years ago, Gabby stifled a laugh as she realised something for the first time. Her father, Hervé, had been the French equivalent of Del Boy from the English sitcom *Only Fools and Horses* that Eric had loved to watch. It was only now she realised why she hadn't shared her husband's love of the programme: in many ways, it had unconsciously reminded her of her father.

Hervé had inherited the house from his father, who, following the family tradition of being a successful businessman, had left Hervé not only the villa but a substantial fortune in the bank as well. Sadly, Hervé did not follow in the businesslike footsteps of his forebears. Instead, he flitted from one business to another like a moth around a flame, blaming everyone but himself when he failed yet again. If only he had been more like the lovable rogue that was Del Boy, instead of the man he was, her life might have been different.

Gabby pushed the memories of her father away. It was all too long ago to have any bearing on her life now. She might be living back in the house she'd been born in and where she'd spent her childhood, but it was a new beginning. Past memories would not be allowed to surface and spoil things.

Crossing the empty space and moving towards the stairs, she wondered about getting a car. Would they need one? Public transport in Dartmouth had always been somewhat hit-and-miss, making a car essential. Here on the Riviera, there were trains and buses running inland and along the coast all hours of the day. Harriet and Elodie might decide a car was needed, but she was quite happy to catch a bus or train if where she wanted to go was too far to walk. Besides, Philippe had a car and she knew he'd be more than happy to drive her wherever she wanted.

Gabby smiled to herself. Dear Philippe. Both in their seventies, both single, there had been an instant bond between the two of them from the moment they'd met last Christmas. Jessica Vincent, owner of the apartment Elodie had found for them to rent over Christmas and the New Year, had invited them to a festive drinks party. When they arrived Jessica had immediately taken Elodie off to meet some of the younger guests, including her son Gazz, whilst Mickaël, her husband, had taken Gabby to meet his 'reprobate' of a father. Gabby had found Philippe, still a handsome man with more than a touch of the French actor Jean-Paul Belmondo about him, to be delightful company that evening and in the following days.

This morning at the airport when she'd walked into Philippe's open arms and received a tight welcoming hug, she'd felt an all-enveloping sense of relief and of being exactly where she wanted to be and, importantly, where she was wanted.

As Gabby reached the top of the stairs and stepped into the hallway, Harriet appeared from upstairs.

'I've made up your bed, Mum, so you don't have to worry about that before or after we go out. Anything interesting down there?' she asked as Gabby closed the door to the garage.

Gabby shook her head. 'Nothing. Shall we call Elodie down and go find somewhere to eat? I'm quite hungry. I've decided to leave the kitchen for now.'

'No need to call, I'm here,' Elodie said, running down the stairs. 'I'm starving and ready to go.'

* * *

Twenty minutes later, they were sitting at a table on the pavement outside one of the restaurants they'd discovered at Christmas in the heart of Juan-les-Pins, a bottle of rosé on the table and their food order – moules and frites for the three of them – given to the young waiter. Around them, there was a buzz of chatter as locals were joined by early holidaymakers enjoying their meals sitting out in the warm night air.

Elodie sighed happily as she picked up her glass. 'Santé. Here's to us and our new lives.'

The three of them clinked glasses and took sips.

'I can hardly believe we've made it to France,' Elodie said. 'I am so looking forward to living here.'

'There's a lot to sort out,' Gabby said. 'Starting with the kitchen. First, the walls need painting and we need to find either some units or some standalone cupboards that we can put things in. Goodness only knows where everything is going to go in the meantime.'

'No worries,' Harriet said, sensing Gabby was feeling overwhelmed. 'I'll get some paint tomorrow and make a start on the walls. Once they're done, we can decide whether we want a fitted kitchen or a more traditional one – in which case, we'll pay that brocante Elodie discovered at Christmas a visit and see what we can find. We'll fill the fridge with salads and charcuterie, and eat croissants from the nearest boulangerie for breakfast. If we eat out a couple of evenings, use the microwave and order in takeaways occasionally, we can exist for a few weeks without doing any real cooking. Think that's a plan?'

'Definitely,' Elodie said, for once in total agreement with her mother.

4

Elodie woke with a start the next morning as the alarm on her phone buzzed into life with a rousing chorus of 'La Marseillaise'. She'd decided to use the French national anthem as a wake-up call to remind her she was now living in France. As if she'd ever forget.

She lay there for a few moments before flinging the duvet aside, getting up and making for the shower in her en-suite bathroom. Half an hour later, she was showered, dressed and heading out of the front door for the nearest boulangerie she could find, to buy the baguette and croissants ready for their first breakfast out on the terrace overlooking the pool.

At Christmas, when she'd regularly done 'the breakfast run' to the boulangerie, her route had taken her along the Promenade du Soleil for several metres before needing to turn down one of the small streets leading into Juan-les-Pins centre. Today, because the villa was set back inland from the seafront, Elodie found herself in the centre of Juan within minutes, the tantalising smell of freshly baked bread drifting towards her from a boulangerie she recognised.

Both the croissants and the baguette were still warm and Elodie was glad she'd remembered to bring the canvas shopping tote with her. Leaving the shop, she hesitated before turning for home. Part of her longed to wander along the bord de mer first, see if Gazz was on the beach early, preparing for a busy day with the holidaymakers. Much to the worry of his parents, Gazz had decided at the end of the previous year that living and working in Paris was not for him and he was now the new owner of a jet-ski and paragliding beach business in Juan. But another part of Elodie was worried that she'd be a nuisance if he was busy. Yesterday, when he and Philippe had driven them from the airport to the villa, he'd said he was expecting a delivery today of some new paddleboards.

Elodie gave a sigh. It would be better to go straight back to the villa with breakfast just in case. Maybe she'd wander down to the beach later in the day.

* * *

Back at the villa, Gabby was in the kitchen organising coffee, while Harriet was out on the terrace arranging the small garden table and a couple of outdoor chairs they'd brought from Devon.

Elodie, placing plates and the croissants on the table, glanced at her mother. Was the time right to start asking questions? Or should she leave it until they were all more settled into life here? As she finally decided she would say something and opened her mouth to speak, Gabby appeared with the coffee and Elodie knew the moment was lost, her questions would have to wait a little longer.

As they ate breakfast, the three of them began to plan their day. Harriet wanted to buy some paint and make a start on the kitchen walls. Gabby said she'd potter around the villa and unpack some more things. Yesterday, Philippe had promised he'd pop in during the morning to give her a hand if she needed it, and she was looking forward to that. Elodie loved how Gabby's face lit up these days whenever she mentioned Philippe.

'I need to take a few photos for my first column in the *Chronicle*,' Elodie said. 'And I thought I'd find the brocante again and see if they have a dresser and possibly some outdoor furniture.' She looked at Harriet. She had to make the effort. 'Shall we walk into town together?'

'Why not.'

And the two of them left for town as soon as breakfast was finished.

As they walked to the end of the impasse and reached the bigger road that would lead them into the centre of Juan-les-Pins, Elodie sighed happily. 'I'm so happy Gabby decided we could come and live here.' She took a deep breath. She'd be even happier when she had the answers to the questions she was determined to ask Harriet and now seemed like a good opportunity. 'You told me at Christmas that you loved me and hated leaving me behind, but you still married Todd and went to Australia without me.'

Harriet tensed. She should have realised Elodie would seize the opportunity to probe into the past, particularly her past, she just hadn't expected it this morning.

'You also said it didn't take long for you to realise you'd made a huge mistake. But you did nothing to change things. To come back.' Silence followed Elodie's words as she looked at Harriet.

'It became impossible to leave,' Harriet said eventually. 'My pride wouldn't let me admit to Gabby how things were. She'd never really taken to Todd and had urged me several times not to marry him. She always thought, apart from being too old for me, that he wasn't the right man for me. I decided I had to stick it out and try to change things. Basically I determined to change Todd's behaviour towards me. I naively thought that was a real possibility,' Harriet shrugged. 'Never believe that loving someone will be enough to change them. People have to want to change themselves. And Todd liked me being under his control so was never going to change.'

'But even when you finally returned to Europe last year after being away for twenty years you didn't seek us out immediately. You went and lived in Bristol and it was months before you contacted Gabby. You also promised you'd help with packing up to move here, but you were very last minute, so in the end not much use at all.'

Harriet gave a rueful nod, hearing the accusatory note in Elodie's voice. 'I know. I'm sorry. Stupidly, when I first came back, I was terrified that neither of you would want me in your lives again. And then when we did get together, down here over Christmas and the New Year, Gabby welcomed me back with open arms. But you, you had to make more of an effort, true?'

Elodie pulled a face, acknowledging the truth of Harriet's words. 'Yes. I found it hard to trust or accept you the way Gabby wanted me to.'

Harriet gave her a look. The unspoken question 'you still don't totally, do you?' somehow manifested itself in the air, and Elodie looked away.

'It was difficult for me too,' Harriet said quietly. 'When we all returned to the UK and I left you at Bristol airport, I started to worry about it all going wrong, that the apparent success of the Christmas get-together was merely an illusion, all down to the fact that Christmas is always tradition- ally supposed to be a happy time and reunite families. I became convinced it was all bound to fall apart again. That's why I kept putting off joining you. But I am here now.'

In the silence that followed her words, the two of them continued to walk, their pace slower, both deep in thought. It was Elodie who broke the silence a couple of moments later.

'Yes, you're here now – will you stay though? You need to think about Gabby. She loves the fact that we're all living here together. She'd be heart- broken to lose you again. So please make it work for her sake – she's mourned your absence for years,' she said. 'Our relationship has time to sort itself out, reach an even keel, if we work on it, you just need to tell me the truth.' Elodie stopped and pointed down a side street. 'Not sure where you are headed, but I think the brocante is down there. I'll see you later back at the villa. Hope you find the paint,' and Elodie strolled off down the street.

Harriet stared after her for several seconds before pulling herself together and continuing on her way to the centre of Juan. There was no doubt about it, Elodie was going to keep probing. One day soon, Harriet would have to sit down with her and answer her questions as best she could. But if there was to be any hope of them bonding in the future, maybe it would be best if she told Elodie an edited version of her past.

5

Making her way through the town looking for a hardware store where she could buy paint, Harriet passed several art galleries and stopped to have a quick browse at the window displays of one or two of them. Seascapes, street scenes of old Antibes, belle époque villas and portraits of local characters seemed to be very popular, with the occasional modern piece in clear homage to Pablo Picasso and Marc Chagall thrown in to the mix. One of the galleries also sold artist's materials. Easels were lined up against the wall and a bureau with numerous shallow drawers evidently held small tubes of oil paint. Harriet made a mental note to return and check it out another day, buy a sketchpad and some pencils, perhaps even some brushes and oil paint for when she felt ready to tackle an actual canvas.

A woman pulled open the gallery door and disappeared inside. Before the door closed behind her, Harriet smelt the air, filled with the mixture of paint, turpentine and the soft smell of the gesso primer used for preparing the canvas before painting. It was a perfume that transported her back to the heady days of working in her studio at the top of the Dartmouth house. The studio her dad had lovingly created for her in the attic, with two large Velux windows that flooded the space with light.

Her dad had been so proud of her artistic talent, convinced that one day she would be world-famous. Harriet had always gently laughed at his ambitious belief in her. If only she'd had such strong belief in her talent. Besides, she'd always known just how difficult it was to survive in the art world. Her dad's answer to that was as long as she made the best art she could, had more faith and, importantly, kept trying, she would succeed. Instead, she'd given up as soon as things became difficult.

Early on in their marriage Todd had started applying subtle pressure, with phrases like, 'For me, it's not quite there yet, you'll have to try again.' Which she did once or twice, but it wasn't long before she realised that however many times she tried again, Todd could never see any improvement in her painting.

Before their first wedding anniversary arrived, Todd had convinced her she'd never be good enough to earn any money with her art. 'But don't let that stop you. If you enjoy it, by all means carry on.' And then he'd proceeded to keep her so busy looking after his needs that she rarely had time to think about painting anyway. She still painted though. Apparently her painting was more than good enough to paint the walls of their house. 'So much better and cheaper if you do it, darling,' Todd had said. 'And you enjoy painting, so it's a win-win.'

Harriet lost the will to argue that painting walls was a totally different experience to painting art. She'd tentatively asked if she could paint a mural on the sitting-room wall. The answer to that had been a definite, 'Oh, I don't think so, darling. You're not exactly Picasso, are you?

The stupid thing was, she'd allowed him to diminish her self-worth, barely noticing and without protest until it was too late. Life with Todd was easier when she didn't protest or, heavens above, dare to argue with him.

Standing there, staring unseeingly into the shop window, Harriet swallowed hard. Todd was dead. She was back in Europe living with her mother and daughter, how she lived now, whether she painted again or not, was up to her. The few quick sketches she'd been inspired to attempt at Christmas had ignited a small flame of latent creativity in her that she was determined to fan, to see if her passion for art was still as strong as ever it had been, despite its neglect over the last twenty years. Yes, she'd definitely be back to buy some art supplies from this gallery, but now she needed to find a DIY store.

The hardware store she found a few moments later a street away had a sign displayed over the top of the door proclaiming it had opened back in the 1950s. A bell tinkled overhead as Harriet opened the door and stepped inside. The shop, with its original dark wood fittings still in place and a counter behind which two men stood poised to serve customers, could have been a film set from the mid-twentieth century, it was all so old-fashioned.

Harriet looked around her, wondering where the paint was hidden, when she realised it was definitely customer service all the way. No stumbling around finding things for yourself in this store. Standing patiently waiting to be served, she saw a cork board with a miscellaneous collection of business cards and other notices pinned to it. Various tradesmen offering their services – decorators, electricians, plumbers. Other cards offered IT help, cleaners for holiday rentals, kittens looking for homes and in the top right-hand corner a picture of a dog with 'Très Urgent' written across it. Helpfully, the writing below was in both French and English. 'Lulu, a Tibetan terrier, two years old seeks a new home.' Quickly Harriet took a photograph of the details with its telephone number.

'Bonjour, madame.' One of the men behind the counter was looking at her expectantly.

'Bonjour,' Harriet said. Realising she was going to struggle with her French, she decided to go the simplest route with the minimum amount of words she could. 'Peinture blanche s'il vous plait.'

Ten minutes later, Harriet left clutching two tins of white paint, two brushes and a bottle of white spirit. The appearance of the brushes and the white spirit, both placed alongside the paint tin with a questioning smile, had been a relief as Harriet knew she needed them but was struggling to remember the French words. Walking home, Harriet resolved to make an effort and do something about improving her French. Gabby, she knew, would willingly help her with that.

6

Gabby was emptying a box of books and placing them on the shelves in the sitting room when the gate buzzer sounded and Philippe's voice came over the intercom.

'Gabriella, are you there?'

Her heart lifted and she hurried to press the door panel by the side of the front door in the hallway to open the electric side gate. 'Philippe. Come on in.'

She opened the front door and stood on the top of the steps to greet him.

'I wasn't expecting you so early – it's so lovely to see you.' That feeling of tenderness mixed with happiness that had flooded through her yesterday as he'd hugged her to him at the airport swept through her again. She was so lucky to have this wonderful man in her life.

'And me you, *ma cherie*,' Philippe said, placing gentle greeting kisses on her cheeks, before holding out the bunch of flowers – a mix of daisies, poppies and white rose buds – he was carrying, towards her. 'I hope you have a vase?'

'These are so beautiful. Thank you,'

'I am so happy you are here, the months have gone so slowly since you left. I wish my time away wishing you were here. I forbid you to leave again,' Philippe said. 'Unless you take me with you.'

Gabby smiled and shook her head at him. 'I'm not going anywhere now I'm finally back. I think there should be a vase in the kitchen somewhere. Would you like a coffee?'

'Please, and then you put me to work. I help you sort things? Where are the others?'

'Elodie has gone to the brocante to see if they have some kitchen furniture we need to buy and also to take some photographs for a feature she's written. Harriet has gone to buy paint for the kitchen.'

'How are things with you all?' Philippe asked, concern in his voice.

Gabby had told Philippe when they met how she had brought Elodie up when Harriet took off to Australia all those years ago, and how she hoped things would work out for them all, living once again 'en famille.'

'The air is a little tense, shall we say? It's going to take some time for us all to adjust to living together, but I'm sure we will adjust,' Gabby said with determination in her voice. 'Let's take our coffees out to the terrace.'

Sitting there, listening to the rasping noise of the cigales in the oak and pine trees that edged the garden on three sides, Gabby sighed as she gazed at the green water in the pool.

'Not very inviting looking, is it? I must find a pool man to come and sort it out. Elodie is longing to swim.'

'I give you the name of a good man,' Philippe said. 'Joel. He is a gardener also if you need help.'

'Thank you. I love gardening and I'm really looking forward to getting this one back in shape. I remember the roses my maman had everywhere, the blue of the plumbago bushes and the cherry tree that stood over there,' Gabby said, pointing to the right of the pool. 'Sadly, the cherry tree seems to have disappeared totally, but the olive tree in the front is thriving.'

Philippe took her hand as he gently asked, 'How are you feeling living back in a villa that has bad memories for you? It is difficult, *non*?'

Gabby shook her head. 'Surprisingly, it's fine. The memories are all around, yes, but time seems to have diluted them somewhat. They no longer hold me in their thrall. I seem to be able to regard them stoically and accept they are part of what shaped me and my life. The three of us being here is a new start for all of us.' She gave Philippe a pensive look. How could she possibly explain that her thoughts these days were such a jumble of complex memories from a long ago life – childhood, her maman, Colette, her best friend, her first job, her papa's anger with her. These were all now mixed in with the events of the last six months that had changed everything and brought her back to France.

'You are happy to be back then?' Philipps said.

'Oh yes,' Gabby answered with a happy smile. 'It feels right for the three of us to be here together.' She hugged the thought to herself, *And one of the best things about being here is I have you in my life.*

'Good.' Philippe stood up. 'Come on. I'm here to help. What would you like me to do?'

'There are a few boxes left in the sitting room – books and ornaments,' Gabby said. 'How about we finish unpacking those.'

* * *

An hour later, the bookshelves were full, cream rugs had been unrolled and placed in front of the two settees now covered with throws and resplendent with several cushions. Ornaments and framed photos stood in the little shelved nook beside the fireplace and a trio of white porcelain owls stood to one side of the wood burner. A vase containing the flowers Philippe had brought sat in the centre of the coffee table. Gabby gave a soft sigh. It looked homely and welcoming.

'There's just this now,' Gabby said, pulling bubble wrap off a framed picture. 'I thought maybe in the middle of the chimney breast?'

Philippe took the painting of a barn owl looking out from its nest high up in a barn from her and studied it thoughtfully. 'This is beautiful. Is it one of Harriet's?'

'Yes. A birthday present for me before she left. I love owls and I can't begin to explain what this means to me.'

'I'll need to make a hole for the hanging,' Philippe said. 'I'll bring a drill and a strong fitting next time I come. In the meantime, it will be safe leant against the wall here, out of the way.'

As they stood there together looking at the result of their hard work, Elodie rang to say she was on her way home and should she buy some of the local delicious onion tart, *pissaladière*, for lunch?

Gabby turned to ask Philippe if he'd like to stay for lunch. When he nodded, she said, 'Please. Philippe is here for lunch too.'

As the call ended, Philippe took hold of Gabby's hand. 'Now, you walk me around your garden. You have to decide where the lemon tree is going to live. Mickaël and Gazz they talk of bringing it over now you are here.'

To Gabby's delight, the Vincent family had given her a lemon tree in a beautiful pot for her seventieth birthday on New Year's Eve promising to take care of it until she was once again living in the villa.

'It is thriving on the balcony,' Philippe continued. 'But it needs to come to the garden now you are living here.'

Gabby looked around. 'Maybe best to leave it in the pot for a few more weeks until the garden is a bit more organised and weed-free? I definitely want to place it somewhere I can see it from the terrace.'

'In that case, why not put the pot near the back right-hand corner of the pool. It will be visible, not in the way there and will have the benefit of sunshine but also some shade.'

'Brilliant suggestion. If it likes that position we can plant it there and, in time, it could replace the cherry tree,' Gabby said.

'I ring Mickaël and tell him it is good for this afternoon to bring the lemon tree, yes?' Philippe said. 'I also ring Joel for you, d'accord?' Gabby nodded.

'Thank you. Ah, Elodie is back,' and she smiled as her granddaughter joined them in the garden.

Harriet arrived back shortly after Elodie and the four of them enjoyed a picnic lunch out on the terrace, balancing plates of food on their laps. 'The quicker we get a proper table, the better,' Elodie said. 'I saw one at the brocante this morning that would be ideal.'

After lunch, Harriet prepared the walls before starting to paint them, Elodie disappeared up to her room to send her feature with its accompanying photos, while Gabby and Philippe started to clear a space for the lemon tree in its pot before Mickaël and Gazz arrived. Philippe, looking at the field beyond the overgrown hedge, said, 'So that's the land Jean-Frances Moulin was after. How far does it stretch?'

'Not sure. I think it's just over a hectare,' Gabby said. The mention of Jean-Frances Moulin was an unwelcome reminder of the meeting she'd had with the man in the New Year when he'd tried to bamboozle her into selling the villa to him. 'I know I used to cut across it to get to work at the Provençal.'

'Ah, Hôtel Le Provençal. The hoarding is coming down soon and I hear the first apartments go on sale this summer. A new era begins.'

Gabby smiled. 'Luxury apartments to carry on the glamorous Provençal name. I must take a wander down that way and have another look at the outside. I doubt that I'll ever see the inside of the building again.' She knew just looking at the renovated outside of the hotel would be enough to bring up bittersweet memories again, Christmas had shown her that. Memories of how life had been for her back then, working in the Provençal, thinking she was in love, becoming pregnant, her world collapsing, leaving home... She pushed those memories away. She was ready for them this time. Any bad memory that sprang up uninvited would be dealt with and pushed back down. Living here at this stage of her life was going to be so different to what had gone before.

Mickaël and Gazz arrived just then and the two of them manhandled the large terracotta pot into position on the cleared space before accepting the offer of a coffee.

* * *

Elodie heard Gazz and his father arrive and quickly saved and sent the finished feature to her editor before running downstairs to the kitchen where Gazz was drying his hands after washing the soil off. He quickly turned and enveloped her in his arms. 'I am so happy you come to live here. I missed you,' and he gave her a gentle kiss. 'Welcome to your new life in Juan.'

Elodie gave a contented sigh. 'I can't believe it's finally happened. Living down here, I want to pinch myself.'

'How is Harriet?'

Elodie shrugged. 'As unreliable as ever. I don't think she really wants to be living in the villa with us. I know it's early days, but I fully expect her to move out at the end of summer.' Not wanting to talk about her mother when she was only metres away, Elodie changed the subject. 'And you? How's the new business going? Or is it too early to tell? Did the new paddleboards arrive?'

'*Oui*, they arrived. We're ticking over with early holidaymakers, finding our feet really,' Gazz said. 'Easter will be the first big test. Be able to judge then, but it's looking good. You must come down. I'll treat you to a paraglide.'

* * *

It was late afternoon before the three Vincent men left, having spent the rest of the afternoon drinking coffee and helping the women move some of the furniture around.

Harriet's suggestion that she'd make supper was greeted with enthusi-asm. And early that evening they ate in the garden, balancing the bowls on their laps.

'Philippe organised a pool man for us, earlier,' Gabby said, helping herself to some baguette to soak up the sauce remaining on her plate. 'Joel. He's calling in tomorrow morning between jobs, to dose the pool with some chemicals and then he'll be back in a day or two to backwash the filters. So it will be a few more days before we can swim.'

'Brilliant. I can't wait to have a swim,' Elodie said, looking at the pool with its pea-green water in front of them.

'As well as doing swimming pool maintenance, Joel is also a gardener. We definitely need him for the pool, but the garden? Do we manage it ourselves?' Gabby glanced at Harriet. 'I like gardening and I remember you used to like helping me.'

Harriet smiled. 'I do enjoy gardening. I'm no expert but happy to help you.'

'I'll help as well,' Elodie said. 'But I can't promise to be much use. I know a dandelion when I see one, but other than that,' she shrugged. 'What time is Joel coming? I was hoping to drag you both out to the brocante. There are a few things that I think we should get for around the pool.'

'Joel is coming between nine and ten o'clock,' Gabby said.

'I want to finish painting the kitchen walls tomorrow,' Harriet said. 'I'm happy to stay for the pool man while you both go to the brocante. Between the two of you, I know you'll make good choices. Oh, I've just remembered,' and she took her phone out of her pocket. 'Buying the paint this morning, I saw this.' And she handed the phone over to Elodie.

Elodie took one glance and looked at her mother. 'How could you forget her? She's beautiful. Have you phoned about her? No? Please do it now.' She passed the phone over to Gabby. 'It's a female dog looking for a home and she looks perfect for us,' she explained. 'And we did say we'd get a dog when we moved here, didn't we?'

'We did,' Gabby agreed as she handed the phone back to Harriet. 'And I have to agree she looks beautiful in the picture, but it's a big responsibility. Still, between us, we should manage. And she'll have plenty of space to run around in, the garden is quite secure.'

Elodie gave a happy laugh. 'Sorted. I for one can't wait to meet her and bring her home.'

7

After breakfast the next morning, Elodie and Gabby left for the brocante, leaving Harriet painting the kitchen and waiting to let Joel in. The sun was shining in a cloudless azure blue sky and Elodie almost skipped with happiness as they walked. She loved everything about Juan-les-Pins – the smell of the Mediterranean drifting in the air towards them, the narrow streets, the individual shops, the locals hurrying past clutching boxes of cakes from the patisserie and calling out jaunty 'Bonjours' as they greeted friends.

'Someone is happy to be here,' Gabby smiled at Elodie affectionately.

'Oh, I am,' Elodie said. 'I can't believe I'm actually living here – that all this will become familiar and I get to call it home. You must be happy too. You are, aren't you?' she added anxiously.

Gabby nodded. 'Yes, I'm happy.' She didn't add that her own happiness was tinged with worry over the past. It was too late for those kind of thoughts. 'Not sure about Harriet, though. She was quiet when we left.'

Elodie shrugged. 'I didn't notice, to be honest.'

Gabby sighed. 'I don't think she ever envisaged living in France when she left Australia,' she said. 'Getting home to the UK was her main aim. When we decided to move here, maybe she felt obliged to come with us when she really didn't want to.'

'She can always leave if she doesn't like it,' Elodie said. 'Nobody's forcing her to stay, but I hope she does.'

Gabby's heart rose at Elodie's words, only to fall sharply with her next.

'I have several questions I want answered before she disappears again. I am determined to learn the name of my father, for a start.' Elodie stopped suddenly and grabbed Gabby's arm. 'Do you know who it was? I mean, you've never ever mentioned who it is to me. And I've never really asked you before, not wanting to upset you by mentioning it. Did she tell you?'

Gabby closed her eyes and took a deep breath. The identity of Elodie's father was one of the things that had hurt the most, the way Harriet had refused to talk about who it was, saying he didn't need to know and it was none of her mother's business. She'd so wanted Harriet to confide in her, but Harriet had never ever talked to her about Elodie's father. 'No, I don't know the name of your father. Neither do I know the reason why Harriet refused to tell him about you,' Gabby said as they reached the crossing on the main road and Elodie stabbed the pedestrian button on the traffic light control panel.

Silently, they stood patiently waiting for the traffic to stop and the little green man to indicate it was safe for them to cross the road. Once across, they made for the small lane that went under the arch and ended in the courtyard where the brocante was situated.

'But you can tell me something,' Gabby said quietly as they walked. 'Why are you suddenly determined to find out who your father was? The last time I remember you asking was when you were about five or six and upset about something that had happened at school.'

Elodie took a deep breath. 'It's because now Harriet is back in our lives I have a chance to learn the full story of what happened all those years ago. I want to know the truth about how I came into existence. How long they were a couple – if they were a couple. Were they in love? Do I look like him? Have I inherited any of his talents? Any of his habits? What else does she know about him?'

'Sadly, I don't know the answer to any of those questions, but some-times it's better to leave the past alone,' Gabby said. There was no time to say any more as they stopped in front of the brocante. The bract leaves of the bougainvillea climbing the front of the building itself were starting to show their rich magenta colour. A few more weeks and the wall would be covered in the glorious dominate colour of the plant. The old-fashioned bicycle they'd seen in December propped against the wall of the building was still there. Tumbling scarlet and white geraniums full of buds ready to burst into flower had replaced the hyacinths in the wicker basket.

Looking at the brightly painted bike again, which, when she'd seen it for the first time at Christmas, she'd convinced herself was Colette's old one, Gabby smiled. As small children, she and Colette had been close friends and by the time they were teenagers, inseparable, more like sisters. Standing there daydreaming about those times, a special memory popped into her mind.

The two of them frequently cycled along Cap d'Antibes towards Garoupe Plage, both of them singing at the top of their voices, 'Les Bicyclettes de Belsize', the Mireille Mathieu hit song of the late sixties. They had been convinced then that they would go through life best friends and be in each other's life forever. That their children would be friends just like them. That nothing would change between them. How naive they'd been. Within a couple of years, Gabby's own world had fallen apart and Colette had disappeared off to America and now the family brocante, although still in business, had a stranger at the helm. The fact that it was still going all these years later was good. If only it still belonged to Colette's family, Gabby could maybe get in touch with Colette again but sadly that didn't appear to be an option.

The front door of the shop was held open by a glossy large black and white pottery cat with beady blue eyes. Elodie and Gabby wandered in, answering the bright 'Bonjour' greeting from the young woman sitting by the table that served as a desk, with their own.

Elodie led her grandmother down one of the narrow aisles with cupboards, chairs and tables on either side, before stopping in front of a large dresser. 'What d'you think? We, or rather Harriet, could make something of this. Shabby chic or something.'

'You don't think it's too big for the kitchen?' The thought, would Harriet mind being tasked with the job of updating it flashed into her mind, but Gabby didn't voice it.

Elodie shook her head. 'No. I measured it yesterday. And it would fit on the end wall perfectly alongside the fridge. It would hold a lot of stuff.' She moved a little further up the narrow aisle. 'And look. Here's our perfect table for the terrace.'

The table, a long wooden one, had an eye-catching mosaic top depicting an underwater seascape where dolphins, fish, crabs, coral, wrecks and even a diver bubbling his way through the sea were pictured.

'Isn't it wonderful? We can seat at least ten people round it when we have pool parties.'

Gabby laughed. Elodie's enthusiasm was infectious. 'You're planning pool parties when we've barely arrived and don't know anybody?'

'We know the Vincents. And we've got to have a housewarming party sometime. There's four of them and three of us, which already adds up to seven, so we only need another three people and the table is full.'

'I will happily be the eighth person around this table on an evening,' a quiet voice behind them said. 'Bonjour, Gabriella. *Ca fait longtemps.*'

Elodie watched as Gabby's face froze with shock and her whole body became rigid before she slowly turned to look at the elderly woman who had spoken. 'Colette?' she said, her voice barely above a whisper.

'Oui.'

A bemused Elodie watched as the two women almost fell into each other's arms, both speaking at the same time in rapid French, which Elodie made no attempt to decipher and understand. Both women had tears streaming down their faces that they tried in vain to stem, whilst all the time words of delight poured out from them. Elodie recognised Colette as the woman who had been serving yesterday when she came to look around and who had also been the one who had served her at Christmas.

'Ever since your granddaughter bought the Hôtel Le Provençal ashtray as a birthday present for 'Gabby her grandmother who had worked there years ago', I've been expecting you,' Colette said in English, as she finally stood back and caught hold of Gabby's hands. 'I knew it was for you and hearing that you were planning to return made me so happy. And now here you are.'

'And now here I am,' a dazed Gabby replied. 'I can't believe you're here, running the brocante. The name on the business card you gave Elodie with the hotel ashtray was different. If I'd realised, I would have banged on your door at New Year. I thought your parents had sold the business on. How long have you been back? Are you staying? I have so many questions.'

Colette laughed. 'We have so much to say, to learn about each other. You come tomorrow? We have lunch and tell each other our secrets like we did when we were young. I too have the questions for you.'

Gabby nodded. 'Of course I can come. I'll see you tomorrow.'

8

Once her mother and Elodie had left, Harriet began to finish painting the kitchen. Overnight, the two walls she'd painted yesterday had dried and were looking fresher. This morning, she had the opposite two shorter walls to do – one with the window overlooking the front garden and the other one that separated the kitchen from the hallway.

Harriet hummed to herself as she concentrated on painting around the window frame carefully, relishing the silence that came with being completely alone in the villa, and found her thoughts drifting to Gabby. It had to feel strange being back in her childhood home. A home she hadn't returned to for well over forty years and where the last of those years had been less than happy. Harriet could only hope that new family memories the three of them were sure to make over the next few weeks and months would keep the old horrid ones buried deep in Gabby's subconsciousness.

As she stepped back to check the edge of the window frame, the electric gate intercom buzzed. 'Hi Harriet, it's me, Jessica. Joel is also here.'

Harriet had met Jessica Vincent, wife of Mickaël, at New Year when she'd joined Gabby and Elodie in the apartment they were renting from them. A tentative friendship had sprung up between the two of them and she was looking forward to getting to know Jessica better.

Quickly, Harriet pressed the button for the small pedestrian side door of the electric gates and stood by the open front door to greet the two of them.

Joel introduced himself and went straight through to the garden to begin work on the pool.

Jessica waved a small cardboard box at Harriet. 'I wanted to welcome you to Juan-les-Pins. Coffee? I have cakes. Oh, you're painting? I can smell paint. Can I see?'

'I'm painting the kitchen wall not creating a masterpiece,' Harriet said, laughing. 'Always happy to stop for coffee and cakes,' Harriet said. 'I've nearly finished anyway.'

'Where are the others?'

'Gone to the brocante. Elodie saw a few things there yesterday that she thinks we could do with,' Harriet said, checking the water level in the coffee machine before pressing the button.

They took their coffee and the strawberry tartlets Jessica had brought into the sitting room.

'This is a lovely room,' Jessica said. 'I wish sometimes we'd gone for a villa rather than an apartment.' The owl painting leaning against the wall caught her eye. 'That is a beautiful painting. Is it one of yours?'

Harriet nodded. 'A very early one. I look at it now and can see all the amateur mistakes I made.' She couldn't tell Jessica how touched she'd been to discover that her mother had kept the painting for so many years, or the fact that she now planned to have it hung in pride of place on the chimney breast. Learning that had brought an unexpected lump to Harriet's throat when Gabby had mentioned it.

'Well, I simply see a beautiful picture,' Jessica said, giving the painting another look before turning to face Harriet.

'I've been singing your praises by the way, saying how talented you are, and I know Hugo's keen to see your work as soon as possible.'

'Hugo?' Harriet looked at her puzzled.

'The art gallery friend I told you about at Christmas. The friend who is going to give you an exhibition.'

'I didn't think you were serious,' Harriet admitted. 'I thought the friend you mentioned was called Harry anyway. Is this someone else?'

Jessica sighed. 'Did I say Harry? Blame it on my menopausal brain fog.

There are days when I can barely remember my own name. I do have a friend called Harry who is lovely, perhaps I ought to introduce you to him as well. Anyway, it's Hugo who is really keen to see some of your work, so I hope you've been busy doing some?' Jessica's voice trailed off as Harriet bit her lip. 'You haven't done any, have you? Oh Harriet. Paint pictures not walls.'

'I'm sorry. I just haven't been in the right frame of mind and until we're settled in here properly,' she shrugged. 'I did stumble across a wonderful art gallery in town that sells artist supplies and I have promised myself to go and have a look around the next time I'm in town.'

'Well, that's something, I suppose,' Jessica said. 'Be warned I shall nag you at every opportunity to start sketching and painting. You are so talented.'

Harriet gave her a sheepish smile. 'I really want to try,' she said. 'But I saw some very good paintings in town. There are people a lot more talented than I ever was here.'

'Stuff and nonsense, as my old dad would say,' was Jessica's answer. 'You're as good, if not better, than most.'

Harriet shrugged. Starting to paint again was one thing, showing her efforts to anyone, let alone someone with a professional interest, was quite another thing. She wasn't sure if she was brave enough to take that step. As for an exhibition, no way. It would be a long time before she was ready for that kind of exposure, if ever.

9

The next morning, Gabby paused as she walked under the arch into the brocante courtyard and surveyed the scene before her. This place had been like a home from home to her. Sometimes more. A refuge that she'd been reluctant to leave whenever Tante Marie, Colette's mother, gently suggested it was time for her to go home. The two mothers were friends and, like their daughters, there were no secrets between them. If it hadn't been for guilty thoughts about how her own mother needed her, Gabby would happily have run away to live with Colette many a time.

Alongside the brocante, the cottage with its red-tiled roof and olive-green shutters, oleander bushes either side of the open front door, looked shabbier than Gabby remembered. Perhaps she'd never noticed the cracked paintwork when she was younger. Perhaps it was a sign of the economic times they lived in now.

'Coucou,' Gabby called out as she walked through the open doorway into the cottage.

'Come through. I am in the kitchen,' Colette answered.

The kitchen Gabby remembered had changed. The walls had been tiled with pretty Provençal colours, a light modern fitted kitchen had taken the place of the dark free-standing cupboards and dresser, a La Cornue stove had replaced the old range and a large fridge-freezer stood in one corner. The oak table and chairs standing in the centre of the room were all that remained of the kitchen she'd known years ago.

'This has changed,' Gabby said. 'But I do envy you your stove. I'm hoping to have a similar one but not a fitted kitchen. You must think we're *insensé* trying to recreate a traditional kitchen in Villa de l'Espoir.'

Colette shook her head. 'The kitchen was Maman's choice. To be honest, apart from the modern stove, I miss the old kitchen here, it was comfortable. I wish more people would go for the vintage stuff. These days, people drive along the coast to Ikea at the drop of a hat. They forget we exist.' She shrugged. '*C'est la vie.* Coffee?'

Gabby placed a paper bag on the table. 'I hope palmiers are still your favourite?' She watched as Colette scooped coffee into the stovetop Italian-style espresso coffee maker, screwing the two halves together before placing it on the hotplate, something Gabby had seen Tante Marie do hundreds of time in this kitchen. Both their mothers had traditionally worn the all-enveloping floral overall like the good French housewives they were. Today Colette wore a scarlet plastic apron with a picture of the Eiffel Tower, but the resemblance to her mother was nevertheless absolute. The way she stood, the quick movements of her hands, the smile she gave Gabby as she turned. 'Three minutes and the coffee will be ready.'

Seeing Colette busy with the coffee, Gabby couldn't help wondering, did she resemble her own mother now she was old? When she'd left all those years ago, she'd thought of her mother as old already, but in reality she'd have only been in her mid-forties. It was only as she herself had grown older that she realised how hard life must have been for her mother. Her father had not been an easy man to live with.

Sitting out in the enclosed yard at the back of the cottage with its many pots of geraniums, lavender and a bushy oleander a few minutes later, Gabby glanced at Colette.

'So, how long have you been back here? And why?'

'Fifteen years. No single reason, just life ganging up on me, like it does sometimes. I got married, divorced, became a single mum. I'm guessing my son, Hudson, must be about your daughter's age and my granddaughter, Lianna, is twenty-two, similar to Elodie.' Colette picked up a palmier and took a bite. 'Mmm. And nobody but nobody makes these like us French. Another reason to come home.'

'You met Lianna yesterday. She helps me here. Hudson works in Nice, so isn't around much during the day, but you'll meet him soon.'

'They both came with you?'

Colette nodded. 'They had no reason not to.'

'Your ex in America? Does he not want to see them?'

'*Oui*, but he's not in America. I went all the way to the U S of A and ended up marrying a Frenchman. He's in Marseille and they visit him. He comes here sometimes too. Life after divorce is civilised these days, non?' Colette paused and regarded Gabby thoughtfully. 'You had a happy marriage in the end?'

Gabby nodded. 'I lost the baby that forced me to leave here soon after I arrived in England.' She paused, remembering how hard those early years had been. 'But a couple of years later I met Eric, married and had Harriet. And until he died, life was good. The regrets were still there, obviously,' Gabby paused. 'But in the end you learn to live with them and don't let them define you.'

Colette nodded in agreement. 'About a year before he died, your papa came here to see me a couple of times,' she said quietly. 'By then, he was not physically the man you remember, and he'd changed in other ways too. Especially after your maman died. He could still be difficult, but on the whole he was easier to get on with.'

'What did he want with you?' Gabby gave Colette a curious look.

'On one of the visits he asked me, if I ever saw you again, to tell you that he was sorry. When I told him to tell you himself, he stomped off, muttering that he couldn't see himself going to England now, and besides, it made no difference to him what you inherited once he was dead.'

'How strange,' Gabby said. 'The notaires dealt with everything for me and didn't unearth any problems. Tying up things was pretty straightforward. There was only the villa and a few thousand euros in the bank. A bit more after the house was cleared. Most of the euros went on settling the notaire and tax.' Gabby drained her coffee cup. 'I can't believe after all those years the word sorry passed his lips. Do you think he genuinely was?'

Colette shrugged. 'Something was definitely on his mind, peut-être his guilty conscience?'

'Bit late in the day if it was,' Gabby said sadly.

10

Whilst Gabby was spending time with Colette at the brocante, Harriet and Elodie walked through Juan-les-Pins towards the address Harriet had been given when she'd phoned about the dog. As they walked, Elodie toyed with the idea of trying to somehow get her mother to open up about the past, but Harriet was striding out fast, making talking difficult. Elodie sighed. One day the time would be right.

Avenue Nicolas Aussel with its big Casino supermarket was busy, but they quickly found the villa they were looking for and Elodie rang the bell.

Listening to the volley of barking that instantly filled the air, Harriet laughed. 'She's got a good bark on her.'

A harassed-looking woman opened the door. 'You've come about Lulu? Come in. I'm Shelley.'

Lulu, who had stopped barking, looked at them before cautiously edging forward to sniff the hand Elodie held out.

'I love the name,' she said. 'And she's beautiful. I love her coffee and cream colouring. And her tail curled along her back, so sweet.'

'Why are you looking for a new home for her?' Harriet asked.

'She's my mother's dog and she's going into a retirement home which sadly doesn't allow pets. Mum is desperate for me to find the right forever home for her. A couple of people have said they'll take her, but,' Shelley shrugged, 'they didn't feel like the right people.'

'Can't you take her?' Elodie asked. 'Keep her in the family.'

'I work as a troubleshooter for a travel firm. I can be sent anywhere at a moment's notice. And my husband isn't always around either.'

Harriet and Elodie listened as Shelley explained that as a breed Tibetan terriers liked company, were wary around strangers, but they could be a nuisance with their barking if left alone for too long.

'Once she's got to know you, Lulu is a fantastic little dog. And despite all the hair, which needs regular brushing, she doesn't shed.'

'Well, there's three of us living together, so we can practically guarantee she'll always have a human around for company,' Harriet said, bending down to gently stroke Lulu on the head. 'Such long floppy ears.'

'Please may we have her?' Elodie said. 'We both promise to take really good care of her. Send your mother photos if she would like that.'

'She'd love it.' Shelley watched as Lulu tried to climb on to Elodie's knees as she was bent down. 'She seems to like you, she didn't behave like that with any of the others who came. Okay, she's yours.'

A quarter of an hour later, all the official paperwork, including Lulu's dog passport, had been signed and handed over. Lulu's toys, food and the beanbag she liked to sleep on 'when she's not sleeping on somebody's bed', Shelley had said laughing, had been placed in a large tote bag and Shelley clipped the lead onto Lulu's collar. Before handing the lead to Elodie, Shelley gave Lulu a big hug, 'Be good, sweetie.'

Walking back to the Villa de l'Espoir, Lulu trotted happily alongside Elodie. 'I can't believe we've got a dog,' Elodie said. 'I've wanted one for so long, and Lulu is just so beautiful.'

'Let's hope she settles with us,' Harriet said. 'Thankfully, she's been spayed, so we won't have a problem with any puppies.'

'I think that's a shame. She'd have had beautiful puppies,' Elodie mused.

Back at the villa after her lunch with Colette, Gabby too made a fuss of Lulu and the three of them spent the rest of the day playing with the new addition, brushing her and helping her to explore and settle in to her new home.

Lulu's first night at the villa was spent on Elodie's bed, ignoring her own beanbag on the floor. For a smallish dog she certainly took up a lot of room. Elodie tried once or twice to coax her off the bed onto the beanbag, but Lulu wasn't to be moved. In the end, Elodie gave up and curled her legs around the dog and the two of them stayed like that all night.

11

The days started to settle down into a routine. Once Joel had the pool sparkling and fully functional again, Elodie swam fifty lengths every morning before breakfast under the watchful eyes of Lulu from the terrace. She was determined to counter the hours she spent sitting in front of her computer and get fit. After a shower, Elodie would take Lulu for her first walk of the day to the boulangerie. Lulu wasn't allowed on the beach, but most mornings Elodie and Gazz had a takeaway coffee together on the Promenade du Soleil before Gazz kissed her goodbye and she and Lulu ran home with the breakfast croissants.

Once the furniture they'd bought from the brocante had arrived, Harriet began giving the dresser a makeover. The table with its inlaid mosaic design was washed, its metal legs wire brushed and treated before being placed on the terrace with an eclectic collection of chairs. And the transat loungers were wire brushed and given a coat of teak restorer oil before being placed around the pool to dry.

'They need some cushions now,' Gabby said, 'I think I need a visit to the Carrefour hypermarket outside Nice. I'll ask Philippe if he can take me one afternoon.'

Elodie and Harriet became used to Philippe's presence in the villa. He and Gabby spent most days together, they often walked Lulu in the nearby

woods in the afternoons and he was almost their resident 'little man' who
could change light bulbs, hang pictures, put up shelves, and they were
already very fond of him.

Saturday morning and the three of them were sitting out on the
terrace drinking a mid-morning cup of coffee when they heard the sound
of a van briefly stopping before driving away.

'La Poste,' Elodie said, jumping up to go and fetch it. Opening the
postbox fixed to the electric gate pillar and taking out a large white A4
envelope addressed in her own handwriting, she smiled. The bundle of
forwarded mail from Dartmouth. She took it out to the terrace. 'Look we
have our first forwarded post from the UK.' She opened the envelope and
half a dozen or so smaller envelopes fell out onto the terrace table. She
quickly sorted them out. Five 'good luck in your new home' cards for
Gabby, three similar cards for herself and a large square shaped white
envelope for Harriet.

Harriet sighed. She knew exactly what it was almost before she with-
drew the stiff card embossed with gold lettering out of its envelope.
Secretly she'd been hoping that Lizzie would forget.

'That's looks interesting,' Gabby said.

'It's an invitation to Lizzie's daughter's wedding,' Harriet said. 'She said
she'd send me one. Not that I'm going of course.'

'Why not?' Gabby said. 'You'd be sure to meet up with lots of old
friends. Nice to Bristol is a short flight.'

Harriet shrugged. Meeting up with old friends was the problem. 'I've
been away too long. I'm not likely to have anything in common with any of
them now. We'll all have changed.'

Gabby gave her a thoughtful look but didn't say anything as Harriet
stood up, collecting the coffee cups together, intent on escaping the
conversation.

* * *

Later that morning, Harriet sat at the table on the terrace to write a quick
RSVP to the wedding invitation. She hesitated after she'd written the date.
Was it rude not to put her address at the top? Manners surely dictated she

should? It was something she was reluctant to put in case Lizzie gave it to other people, so-called old friends. In the end, she wrote Antibes Juan-les-Pins, France in the top right-hand corner. In a town of sixty-four thousand people, even if Lizzie were to leap on a plane to seek her out, it was unlikely she'd find her without a lot of effort.

Harriet thanked Lizzie for the invite and apologised for being unable to accept as she had moved away and was now living in France. She wrote a line or two wishing Kelly and Nathan every happiness in the future before signing the letter and popping it into an envelope and addressing it. She'd post it on her way into town to meet up with Jessica.

She dressed carefully before setting off with Lulu. The plan today was for Jessica to finally introduce her to Hugo and his art gallery and she wanted to make the right impression. She didn't want him thinking she was some pathetic middle-aged woman with a grandiose opinion of her talent. But she didn't want to go too far the other way either and present herself as a humble artist grateful for the attention. Not that she could call herself an artist these days. It was literally years since she'd put brush to canvas.

In the end, she settled for her most comfortable jeans, teamed with a short-sleeved Breton top and her new Converse trainers. Her hair, crying out for a cut, she simply screwed into a bun secured with a clip. Oversized Mulberry square-framed sunglasses completed the look and she was ready.

Lulu trotted happily alongside her as she walked through town. Tomorrow would see the start of the long Easter weekend which was late this year, nearly at the end of April, and shop windows were full of chocolates, Easter bunnies and fluffy yellow chicks. The chocolatier's window was especially tempting. On her way home after meeting Hugo, perhaps she'd stop and do something she hadn't done for so long: buy Easter eggs for her mother and daughter.

Jessica was waiting for her outside the art gallery and after fussing and patting Lulu and declaring her to be a really beautiful dog, she led the way inside.

Hugo was a surprise. Harriet had been expecting him to be either a bohemian type or a successful suit-clad businessman. He was sort of in between, she decided, as he walked towards them. Tall, with a shaved head and wearing tailored navy shorts, a white shirt and bare feet, he looked more like a member of the crew from one of the expensive yachts moored in the marina. No, not crew. Skipper. This man had an air about him that commanded not just attention but respect.

Hugo shook her hand firmly. 'At last, Jessica has kept her promise to introduce us,' he said, giving Harriet a smile that lightened his face and years ago would have made her heart race. 'She insists that I need to sign you up to the gallery before I miss out on the opportunity of the decade.'

'As you are friends, you must know how she exaggerates,' Harriet said, shaking her head at Jessica. 'I haven't painted properly in years. I have nothing to show you yet.'

'Yet?' Hugo repeated the word with hope. 'To me that signifies you will have soon.'

'Maybe, but you already have several seriously good artists here,' Harriet gestured around. 'I love this one,' and she moved across to stand in front of a still life oil painting. It was labelled 'Communication. Freya Jackman'.

'Freya's married to my best friend, Marcus. I'll introduce you. You'll like her. It always helps to have a friend on the same wavelength to talk shop with.'

'Thank you.' Harriet hadn't talked shop about painting with anyone for so long, she wasn't sure she'd remember how or be able to.

'I'd love to take you both out for lunch,' Hugo said. 'But sadly I have no staff today. Nobody seems to want to work these days. I don't suppose you have any more friends who would like a permanent part-time job?' he asked, looking at Jessica, who shook her head.

'Sorry, no.'

'I don't want a part-time job, but I could be your emergency staff member,' Harriet said quietly, surprising even herself with her words. 'If that would help. My French is not brilliant, but using it can only improve it. We're more or less straight now in Villa de l'Espoir,' she shrugged. 'Even if I get back into a painting routine – okay, when I do,' she added quickly, seeing the look on Jessica and Hugo's faces, 'half an hour's notice and I can be here. I might have to bring the dog, but she's no problem.'

'If you're serious, give me your number and I'll definitely give you a call the next time I have a staff emergency. Thanks,' and Hugo tapped her number into his phone. 'I'll be in touch soon.'

'You're expecting an emergency?' Harriet said.

Hugo smiled. 'I'm sure there will be an emergency fairly soon, but before that happens I want to take you out for dinner.'

A surprised 'Oh' passed Harriet's lips as she looked at him, but before she could say anything, Hugo gave her another smile.

'Bientôt.' And he turned to greet a patiently waiting client, leaving a bemused Harriet to look at Jessica, who was grinning at her.

'I think Hugo likes you. Come on, let's go for that coffee.'

Harriet followed Jessica out of the door, turning to take a last look at Hugo, who, seeing her turn, smiled and raised a hand in farewell.

Joining Jessica outside, Harriet acknowledged that her heart rate had indeed increased and she felt a little flustered at the thought of being treated to dinner by Hugo.

* * *

Elodie was considering whether to go for a swim early that evening when her mobile buzzed with a text from Gazz.

If you can get here in the next ten minutes we can have that paraglide I promised you!

Elodie tapped,

On my way

And ran downstairs, barely stopping to tell Gabby where she was going.

Gazz and Mickäel were ready and waiting for her when she reached the jetty. 'Papa is going to pilot the boat for us so that I can join you,' Gazz explained as he gave her a quick welcome kiss.

Mickaël greeted her with a hug. 'How are you settling in at Villa de l'Espoir? Philippe, he says everyone is happy to be here.'

'Philippe is right,' Elodie answered, laughing. 'I know I am.'

Gazz handed Elodie a life jacket before putting one on himself. Once they were fastened and checked, they stepped onto the boat and moved to the stern platform. Here they were secured into the double harness, which then had the towing cable attached to the front of it, with the other end of the cable running forward to the winch that would allow them to rise up and eventually be returned to the boat.

Mickaël fired up the engine, untied the mooring rope from the jetty and pushed off before he moved the throttle to 'ahead' and the boat began to motor through the water, heading for the open sea. He pushed the throttle lever further forward and they began to gain speed, the parachute behind them filling with air, but not yet pulling hard enough to raise them from the deck. Faster and they began to rise from the platform. Higher and higher they climbed above the sea, the boat pulling away from them as the cable was let out.

'Wow,' was all Elodie could say as they were pulled up and through the air. 'It's amazing.' Within minutes, she was gazing at the coastline and Gazz was holding her hand as he pointed out landmarks of interest.

'The Provençal is easy to see. If you look right from there and follow along, you'll see the lighthouse on the Cap.'

Mickäel turned the boat so the view below them changed to the island of St Marguerite with its fortress, before slowly altering course and showing them once again the Riviera coastline. Five minutes later, Mickaël slowed the boat and they began to lose height, dropping lower and ever lower until their feet dipped into the sea and soon the water was just below their knees.

'Papa,' Gazz said. 'Enough.'

Mickaël laughed before increasing speed again and winching them back until finally they were once more on the stern platform of the boat.

'That was amazing,' Elodie said. 'I bet your paragliding trips are going to be the hit of the summer. Thank you for taking me up. Can we do it again sometime? I feel the need to do more exciting things in this new wonderful life of mine.'

12

Good Friday morning and Gabby made her way to the brocante, after simply telling Elodie and Harriet she was spending an hour or two with Colette. She'd tell them where they'd been afterwards.

Colette was ready and waiting for her when Gabby arrived and the two of them walked to the nearby florist to collect two bouquets of lilies Gabby had ordered especially for today, before joining the queue for the bus to take them to the cemetery at the top of Antibes.

Gabby knew that Philippe would willingly have driven her on her mission this morning, but this first visit she wanted to go with Colette for one simple but shameful reason. She couldn't remember the layout of the cemetery or the exact location of the Jacques family grave.

The two of them were silent as they walked slowly through the grave-yard. It was Colette who broke the silence as she indicated they needed to take another path.

'Since I've been home, every first of November, Toussaint, I've placed pots of cyclamen on both mine and your family grave,' she told Gabby.

'That's so kind of you,' Gabby said, feeling herself welling up and choking back on a sob.

She remembered Toussaint as being a particularly sad time during those first years in England when she'd missed home so much. Toussaint was always an important family day in the French calendar, when garden centres and florists all over France overflowed with pots of cyclamen or chrysanthemums, and families travelled home from near and far to pay their respects and remember their loved ones.

The first time an English friend had cheerfully handed her a bunch of chrysanthemums, saying 'I brought you these from my garden, aren't they beautiful,' she'd muttered her thanks, hidden how upset she was and put the flowers outside the back door.

Afterwards, Eric had gently explained that in England people loved chrysanthemums and liked to grow them in the garden and have them in the house.

'But they're a flower for graves,' Gabby had protested.

Eric had shaken his head. 'Only in France. Here they are just beautiful flowers.'

Colette's voice brought her back to the present. 'Aunt Theresa was very kind to me. She and my maman were like sisters.' She stopped in front of a simple granite headstone with a mound of earth in front of it. 'Here we are. I'll go and pay my respects to my parents who aren't far away.'

Gabby held out one of the bouquets of lilies. 'Don't forget these. Wrong time of the year for cyclamen or chrysanthemums, otherwise I would have bought them instead.'

Colette took them with a smile. 'Take as long as you want or need, okay?'

Gabby nodded, before bending down and placing her own bunch of lilies by the headstone. Standing there with her head bowed, and eyes closed, she said a heartfelt 'sorry' to her parents. 'I know I let you both down and I can never change that. Saying you were always in my thoughts, Maman, doesn't make up for leaving you when you needed me. That guilt will never go away. I should have stayed for your sake. I loved you then and I love you now.'

Gabby stayed where she was with her eyes closed and tears flowing down her cheeks for several moments, before lifting her head up and opening her eyes as she searched for a handkerchief in her skirt pocket. Once her eyes were dry, she looked around for Colette. Five minutes later and the two of them were making their way out of the cemetery.

* * *

When Gabby got home after having a quick coffee with Colette, Harriet was doing an energetic front crawl in the swimming pool while Lulu watched her from the safety of the edge of the terrace. Gabby sat down on one of the now cushioned transats to wait for Harriet to finish her swim and Lulu instantly got up and walked over to her. She stroked the dog and watched Harriet swim a couple more lengths. As Harriet climbed out of the pool and picked up her towel, her phone rang.

'Hugo, how nice to hear from you.'

There was silence as Harriet listened intently for thirty seconds or so.

'It's not a problem. I'll be there in half an hour.' She turned to Gabby as she ended the call. 'Hugo wants me to help out in the gallery for a couple of hours today and tomorrow. Are you home now to keep Lulu company? Or shall I take her with me?'

'Don't worry about Lulu, I'm not planning on going anywhere else today. I expect Philippe will be here soon and we'll take her for a walk later.'

'Thanks,' and Harriet went to shower and get dressed. Ten minutes later, she called out, 'Bye. See you later.' And she was gone.

13

A couple of customers were browsing in the gallery when Harriet arrived and Hugo flashed her a welcoming smile from behind the desk.

'I can't thank you enough for helping me out,' he said. 'I hope you didn't have to cancel any family plans?' As Harriet shook her head, he added, 'Good. Right let me give you a quick run-down on things before I throw you in at the deep end.'

Harriet had always been a quick learner and soon mastered the till through which everything went and the card machine.

'No card payments over one hundred euros without checking with me,' Hugo explained. 'Been caught out a few times by stolen cards. I know most of my art-buying clients personally, but well-dressed summer tourists aren't always what they seem. Parisian thieves also take *les vacances* in the south of France.'

The gallery sold a wide range of cards, posters, prints of old Antibes, cards, framed prints, all things that Hugo described as 'tourist-funded rent money'. Of course, there were original paintings and limited edition prints, as well as artist supplies, like water colour paints, oils, sketch books, paper, and a 'framing and stretching service' of canvas was offered. But Hugo told Harriet that customers over Easter would be mainly holidaymakers keen to buy souvenir pictures and cards.

At one o'clock, Hugo turned the door sign to 'Closed' and popped next door to the takeaway cafe for two salad baguettes, two raspberry tarts and two cold low-alcohol lagers.

'It's easier to eat here,' Hugq said. 'The town will be heaving this lunchtime. Rather spend an hour here getting to know you. Come on through.' He opened a door at the end of a small utility room that led into a backyard with a wrought-iron table and two chairs that almost filled the space. The yard wall was covered with a pale pink bougainvillea reaching up towards the azure sky and the sun. Muted sounds of people and traffic muffled by the thick walls of buildings in the old town's narrow lanes drifted on the air. 'All the salad baguettes had gone, so chicken or tuna?' he asked, holding the baguettes out. 'Oh, I didn't think to ask – you're not vegetarian or vegan, are you?'

Harriet laughed at the horrified expression on his face. 'No, I'm not. Chicken baguette please,' she said and the two of them sat companionably at the small table to enjoy their lunch.

'I'm so grateful you could help me out today and tomorrow,' Hugo said as they both finished eating. 'I'd honestly planned on taking you out for dinner one evening so we could get to know each other before I asked you to work. That was before my part-time weekend girl sent me a text at seven o'clock this morning saying she'd got a crewing job on one of the floating gin palaces. Sorry to leave me in the lurch on a busy weekend, but it was an opportunity she couldn't say no to. She's currently on her way to Corsica.' Hugo shrugged. 'It's annoying, but I'd probably have done the same thing at her age. In fact, I think I did something similar to get to St Moritz for skiing one winter.'

'You obviously had a different childhood to me,' Harriet said. 'The nearest I got to a ski slope in my childhood was the dry run at Plymouth, but in later years I did get to the Blue Mountains several times.'

'Now that's somewhere I've never been,' Hugo said, breaking off a piece of baguette. 'I'll have to take you to Isola 2000 skiing this winter. Nearest ski resort about an hour from Nice,' he added, seeing her puzzled look. 'Did you find the Blue Mountains and Australia inspirational for painting?'

Harriet looked at him, wondering how much she could share with him about her time in Australia. She liked Hugo and it was important to make sure he knew the truth about her past from the beginning of their friendship.

'I hardly painted the whole time I was there,' she said finally. 'It was difficult. Todd, my husband, didn't think my paintings were good enough to find a market so believed it was a waste of my time to even try.' She unscrewed the cap on her lager and took a drink. 'I realise how pathetic that must sound, but at the time not painting seemed to be the only thing to do. It definitely made life easier.'

'Not pathetic, it's not easy to give up doing something you love,' Hugo said quietly.

Harriet acknowledged his words with a small smile. 'It turns out that it was easier to stop than it is to start again. I've done a few pencil sketches in the last months but no actual painting.' She finished her drink and glanced at Hugo, wanting to move the conversation away from herself. 'What about you? You're an art gallery owner, but are you a frustrated artist too?'

Hugo shook his head. 'No. I do, however, have a passion for art. I also love marketing and business. So I did a degree in Art History with the ultimate aim of combining all those skills and opening a gallery to promote lesser-known artists but also being involved in the bigger world of art. And bingo, here I am.'

'Just like that?' Harriet said quizzically. 'Somehow I doubt it.'

Hugo gave her a rueful smile, 'You're right. It's taken a few years and a lot of upsets along the way, as well as a huge amount of work, but I sincerely love what I do. Not many people can say that.' He pushed his chair back and stood up.

As Harriet went to pick up the empty lager bottles, Hugo put a hand on top of hers, causing an unexpected tingle to seep through her fingers.

'Do you believe that people come into your life for a reason? I feel that about you and I'm really looking forward to us getting to know each other. I think we're going to be good friends.' His eyes shone as he smiled at her and she had no hesitation in returning his smile with a happy one of her own. 'Come on, there's time before we open to introduce you to some of my favourite artists' work.'

Harriet followed him back into the shop, strangely happy at the prospect of getting to know Hugo better.

* * *

Good Friday evening and Elodie was looking forward to spending time with Gazz. The paraglide they'd shared recently had been a wonderfully exciting time and this evening they planned to grab something to eat and drink and to spend at least three hours together. Maybe even hop on Gazz's scooter and go along the coast to Cannes.

Gazz and Mickaël were busy securing everything for the night when she arrived on the beach and Elodie gave them a hand placing the rest of the paddleboards in the storage cage ready to be pulled up the beach.

Gazz snapped the last padlock into place and stood up. 'Merci, Papa. *Tout sécurisé maintenant.*'

'Happy to help,' Mickaël said, before turning to say goodbye to Elodie. 'We look forward to you, Gabby and Harriet coming for lunch on Sunday. Philippe, he insist he cooks the roast lamb for us all. Jessica, she is so happy for him to do it.'

After Mickaël had left, Gazz looked at Elodie. 'I'm a bit of a beach bum this evening, I'm afraid. Not sure I'm tidy enough for any restaurant. I forgot about allowing time to get home and change.'

'You look just fine to me,' Elodie said. 'But if you're bothered, why don't we just buy a takeaway pizza and drinks and stay on the beach?'

'Sounds like a plan,' Gazz said. 'Come on,' and they began to walk slowly along the beach, hand in hand, towards the wood-fired takeaway pizza hut.

Half an hour later, they'd found a sheltered spot and were sitting with their backs against the sea wall, happily munching pizza and watching the Mediterranean lapping the shore with the sun shining on the Iles de Lérins out in the bay.

'How are things between you and Harriet?' Gazz asked.

Elodie shrugged. 'About the same. She knows I want answers to all my questions, but she won't actually sit down and talk to me about the past. I just worry that she's going to up and disappear again. If she does, she does, but Gabby would be absolutely devastated if that happened.'

'It's probably hard for her, remembering the difficult time she had when she became a mother with no partner to help her cope. And then there has to be the very real anguish she surely felt leaving you with Gabby,' Gazz said thoughtfully.

'I get all that, honestly I do. And she's admitted that she made a big mistake leaving me. But if she'd just tell me my father's name, how they met, whether they were in a real relationship, does he know about me? That's basically all I want to know. I'm not going to rush off and try to find him. I don't see much point in doing that.'

'Talk to her, tell her that. Maybe that's what she's afraid of. You connecting with someone she doesn't want back in her life.'

'I suppose that is a possibility. But if she'd only tell me the few facts I want to know, then we could all settle down with no secrets and live together en famille happily, like Gabby wants.'

Gazz placed his arm around her shoulders and pulled her closer. 'I'm sure things will work out in the end, but right now, take a look to your right. The sun is setting over the Esterel mountains.'

Elodie turned her head and rested it against Gazz as she watched in amazement as the setting sun turned the mountains red, while above them the sky became a mixture of streaks of blood red, lavender and magenta. It was like no other sunset she'd ever seen before, even the ones at Christmas hadn't been like this one. Sitting there with Gazz's arm around her shoulders, accepting and returning his gentle kisses, Elodie knew this romantic evening on the beach would be etched into her memory forever.

14

Easter Sunday morning, on her way to the boulangerie, Elodie stopped at the chocolatier and collected the three Easter eggs she'd ordered. One each for Gabby, Harriet and Gazz. Gabby, she knew, would have one for her, but she wasn't expecting one from Harriet or Gazz. At the boulangerie, she bought a brioche loaf with raisins instead of the normal croissants. She'd missed the traditional hot cross buns on Good Friday and hoped brioche slices toasted and spread with the cinnamon butter she'd made would, in their own way, be a belated substitute.

Back at the villa, she put two Easter eggs on the terrace table and took the remaining one into the kitchen while she prepared the brioche. Taking a plate full of the warm toast out to the terrace, she was surprised to see both Gabby and Harriet had added eggs to the table.

'Happy Easter,' Gabby and Harriet said, as Elodie placed the plate on the table.

'And the same to you, thank you for the eggs,' Elodie said. 'Hope you like my substitute for hot cross buns.'

'Different but good,' Gabby said. 'It's funny the things one misses, isn't it? I'd never heard of hot cross buns when I first went to England, they just don't make them in France, but I too missed them this year. Next year maybe I'll try making some – or I'll ask Philippe to make some,' she added with a laugh. 'I'm sure he could easily whip up a dozen hot cross buns.'

'Mmm, it really is delicious,' Harriet said, reaching for a second slice.

After breakfast, the three of them spent a leisurely morning all doing their own thing before getting ready for lunch with the Vincents. Walking through Juan down towards the Promenade du Soleil, the town was quiet, but as they approached the Pinède Gould, there were more people about enjoying the sunshine and making for the restaurants and bars.

'Can we walk a little away along Boulevard Édouard Baudoin before we go up to the Vincents?' Gabby asked. 'I'd like to see how far on the renovations of Hôtel le Provençal have progressed since Christmas. I doubt that we'll be able to see very much.'

The hoarding was still up around the site, deserted today with no one working, but there were definite signs of progress. Everything looked more pristine, with fresh paint around newly inserted windows on several of the floors, and there was a tantalising glimpse of landscaping being started.

'At least the building is being cared for now,' Gabby said. 'It will have a new lease of life rather than being left to rot for another forty years.' She took one last look at the iconic building still shrouded in tarpaulin and covered with scaffolding and pushed away the memory of how imposing it had once looked before it had been left to decay.

'Come on,' Harriet said. 'We're going to be late if we aren't careful. Didn't Jessica say twelve thirty for one – it's almost that now.'

* * *

Both Jessica and Mickaël were waiting for them as the lift doors opened for the penthouse and received the Easter eggs and the wine the three of them had brought as a thank you with delight.

'Philippe's in charge of the kitchen today and assures me everything is on schedule,' Jessica glanced at Elodie. 'Gazz hopes to join us in time for lunch. But first, Mickaël has organised aperitifs out on the balcony.' As Jessica handed Harriet a glass of sparkling crémant wine, she said, 'So how did you enjoy working with the delicious Hugo?'

'It was good,' Harriet said. 'It was busy but not too busy to cope with. He's asked me to become his permanent Saturday girl.'

'Have you agreed?'

'I've told him I'll think about it.' Harriet took a sip of her drink. In truth, she'd done nothing but think about it since he'd suggested it. And still couldn't decide whether to agree. There had been an almost instant rapport between the two of them and she'd enjoyed working with him. They both had a shared interest in art and he would, she sensed, be a good friend. But would he want it to turn into more than friendship as they got to know each other? Something she wasn't sure she was ready for yet. She sipped her wine thoughtfully. Perhaps she was reading too much into the connection that seemed to have sprung up effortlessly between them.

Moments later Philippe in the kitchen called out 'À table' and Jessica ushered them all in to the dining room. Philippe carried the roast lamb in, placing it on the table and starting to carve it just as Gazz arrived.

'Apologies, everyone,' he said as he slipped into the empty seat next to Elodie. 'I eat and then I leave again. Everybody they want to hire a paddleboard today. Désolé.'

The roast lamb was followed by light individual raspberry soufflés, which had everyone murmuring ooh and mmm as they ate, they were so delicious.

Afterwards, everyone raised their glasses in a toast to Philippe and declared it to be the best Easter lunch ever. As Gazz replaced his glass on the table he leant in towards Elodie. 'I'm sorry I have to go. Can you come to the beach as you walk home? I need to talk to you about something.'

Elodie gave him a worried look but was reassured by the smile he gave her and the words, 'Don't worry, it's nothing serious, just something you need to know.'

'Okay. I'll see you on the beach later then,' Elodie promised.

It was late afternoon before the three of them said their goodbyes to the Vincents, thanking them all, especially Philippe, for a wonderful meal and a lovely time. Once they were down on the Promenade du Soleil, Elodie told Gabby and Harriet she'd see them back at the villa later and set off towards the jetty on the beach.

Gazz saw her coming and walked up the beach to greet her with a hug and a kiss. Afterwards Elodie gave him a quizzical look. 'Come on then, talk to me.'

'It's about Fiona,' Gazz said, after taking a deep breath. Elodie felt her heart sink.

'What about her?'

'She was here early this morning inviting me to an Easter party tomorrow evening.'

Elodie stayed silent and waited for Gazz to continue.

'Of course I turned down the invitation and I tell her again about you and me being together now. She ended up storming off. I needed to tell you in case she,' he shrugged. 'You know what she's like.'

'I do,' Elodie nodded. 'Thank you for telling me though.' And she reached up and gave him a kiss, secure in the knowledge that Fiona was not about to come between them.

15

After Easter, life at Villa de l'Espoir settled back into the routine that had
started to establish itself over the previous weeks. The three of them did
their own thing most days but usually met up for lunch or dinner. Elodie,
ever the practical one, had found a beautiful calendar with glorious
photographs of Provence and the Alps Maritime and pinned it up in the
kitchen. With the three of them sharing housekeeping duties, she insisted
it was essential to have some sort of reminder, even a rota, on the wall.
'You know, like, rubbish day, food shopping, bathroom, kitchen, feeding
Lulu, walking her, cooking dinner. And whose turn it is for each particular
chore.'

The kitchen was still a bit of a mishmash, but in pride of place was the
dresser that Harriet had worked her artistic magic on. Now cream, with a
painted garland of green olive leaves running along the top and down the
sides, its shelves were full of crockery and the cupboards at the base were
filled with kitchen paraphernalia. Philippe had brought the heavy Hôtel
du Provençal ashtray that Gabby had left with him for safekeeping in
January, after Elodie had given it to her for her seventieth birthday. It was
in pride of place in the centre of the open work surface of the dresser, now
filled with keys and the gate remotes.

Deciding that she liked the idea of having something to fill her time and give structure to her week, Harriet had agreed to be Hugo's Saturday girl for the summer, as well as his midweek emergency staff member. To her surprise, she found that she actually enjoyed working in the gallery, learning about the paintings that Hugo exhibited and meeting the public. Saturday lunchtimes, when she and Hugo ate together, always surprised Harriet by how quickly they disappeared. The two of them laughed a lot and conversation was never dull. Getting to know each other slowly was fun and Harriet began to value Hugo's friendship. The dinner date still had to happen, but Hugo kept assuring her it would very soon. 'In the meantime, I'm enjoying our lunches together,' he said.

As she returned from walking Lulu one morning in the middle of May, the yellow La Poste van pulled up outside the villa and with a cheery 'Bonjour', the postman handed her a packet of forwarded mail.

Gabby was in the kitchen making a coffee as Harriet walked into the house and held up her cup. 'Join me?'

'Please,' Harriet answered, bending down to unclip Lulu's lead. 'There's more forwarded post.'

'Let's take it out to the terrace. I'll open it while we have our coffee.'

As Harriet sipped her drink, Gabby went through the contents of the envelope.

'It seems to be all for Elodie this time – looks work-related. Oh, there's one for you,' and she handed Harriet a brown envelope with a handwritten address, postmarked Torbay.

Harriet frowned. She didn't recognise the handwriting. It didn't look like Lizzie's. The wedding would be over now. She was the only person from the old days who knew she was back from Australia and living in France. Harriet slid her finger under the flap and tore the envelope open. A photograph slipped out and Harriet saw the signature at the end of the accompanying letter. A letter she quickly pushed back into the envelope. Aware that Gabby was watching her, Harriet held out the photograph. 'Wedding day photo of Lizzie's daughter.'

'Lizzie looks good as the mother of the bride and her daughter was a beautiful bride,' Gabby said, before handing it back. 'That was kind of Lizzie to send you a photo. Aren't you going to read the letter?'

'Later,' Harriet said, putting the photograph back in the envelope with the letter. She wanted to be alone when she read it. 'You're looking very glam this morning by the way. You off out?'

'Philippe is taking me to Cannes. I've finally tracked down a kitchen shop there that sells La Cornue stoves.' And Gabby gave Harriet a happy smile. Telling Colette that the one thing she wanted in the kitchen was a La Cornue range cooker had prompted her to begin the search for one. It would be the perfect stove for the villa's kitchen.

'Where's Elodie this morning?'

'Gone to interview an ex-pat couple for a woman's magazine.' Gabby looked at Harriet. 'Have you got anything planned for today?'

Harriet shook her head. 'Not really.' The vague plan of going for a swim and then seeing if Jessica fancied meeting up for a coffee had been pushed away with the arrival of the post.

'Lovely bright light today. Might be a good day for art,' Gabby said quietly. 'You keep promising you're going to start painting again, but so far I haven't seen any evidence of that.'

'We've barely been here five minutes,' Harriet protested. 'Now we're more settled I will make a proper start soon, I promise. Need to find my confidence before I dive into the oils, though. Start with a few pastels or something,' Harriet shrugged.

'You've got the house to yourself for a few hours so you could sketch away and start to try to find that confidence.' The gate intercom buzzer interrupted Gabby's words. 'Ah, Philippe's arrived. We'll continue this conversation later.'

Harriet stayed out on the terrace after Gabby had left, deep in thought. She knew her mother was right. It was more than time for her to start painting again. Hugo kept teasing her that he was still waiting for her to show him something, but right now a few pencil line drawings seemed to be all she was capable of producing, which, she told herself, was better than doing nothing.

As she reached out to pick up the envelope, her mobile rang. Hugo.

'Are you a mind reader?' she said, laughing. 'I was just thinking about you nagging me to do some painting and up you pop.'

'That wasn't why I'm ringing,' Hugo said. 'But I'm glad you're at least thinking about painting. I was actually ringing to see if you're free for dinner tonight?'

'Yes, I am.' Harriet answered without having to think about it. She liked Hugo and enjoyed his company, dinner with him would be fun.

'Good. I'll pick you up at seven thirty.'

'Thanks, Hugo. See you then.' Harriet pressed the button to end the call before picking up the envelope. She stared at it for several seconds, wishing she could ignore it, throw it away unread, before she slowly pulled the contents out, placing the photograph on the table and unfolding the letter.

Seeing the wedding photograph, Gabby had assumed Lizzie had sent it and Harriet hadn't corrected that assumption, not wanting to have to find answers for the questions that would follow. As she started to read the letter, Harriet struggled to control the panic that threatened to engulf her.

Dear Harriet,

Lizzie gave me your mother's old address in Dartmouth and I hope this letter will be forwarded on to you. Lizzie tells me that you are now living in France with both your mother and daughter.

I was thrilled to hear from Lizzie that you were back in Europe and I had hoped we could catch up in person at Nathan and Kelly's wedding. I am so disappointed that didn't happen.

France is on my list to visit this year, sometime in the next couple of months – maybe we could arrange to meet somewhere convenient for you? If that proves to be impossible, could we at least write the occasional letter to each other, maybe even a Zoom call, get to know one another again and learn about how each other's life has been since we last met?

I look forward to being in touch with you again and to hopefully meeting up in the not too distant future.

Yours in friendship, Jack Ellicott.

Harriet gave a frustrated sigh as she put the letter down on the table and picked up the photograph to study it properly. A family group standing on the steps leading into the church porch, all with happy smiles on their faces. The bride looking radiant; Lizzie, a typical mother of the bride the world over, wearing a large hat; John, her husband, smart in his morning suit, fatter and balder than when Harriet had known him. To the left of the handsome groom stood a tall elegant woman, a neat fascinator pinned at a rakish angle to her head, his mother presumably. And standing alongside her was the man who completed the family group – Jack Ellicott. Still as handsome as ever and clearly a successful family man.

Harriet closed her eyes in an effort to shut out the world, the photograph, the letter, Jack. There was no way she was going to meet up with him here in France. Their friendship was in the past and there was no point in trying to resurrect it in the present. Too much had happened since they'd last seen each other, the common ground between them would have shifted. She wasn't the same person she had been back then and she was damned sure Jack would have little in common left with the man he'd been all those years ago.

It was the future that mattered now. The only part of the past she cared about was trying to heal the rift between her and Elodie. That was the most important thing; the thing she had to concentrate on. Her future did not include renewing her friendship with Jack Ellicott.

Harriet tore both the letter and the photograph into tiny pieces before standing up. No need to keep them. Walking down to the hedge at the bottom of the garden where Joel had installed a metal compost bin, she lifted the lid and sprinkled the pieces on top of the last load of coffee dregs. Jack might know she was living in France, but thankfully he didn't have her address. She'd simply ignore his letter and surely Jack would get the hint and realise that she didn't want to talk to him about how their lives had been after they'd gone their separate ways. In fact, she didn't want to talk to him ever again.

16

It was a slow journey along the bord de mer to Cannes due to the traffic, but neither Gabby or Philippe minded. Gabby especially was more than happy to watch the passing scenery and leave Philippe to concentrate on his driving.

Cannes itself, when Philippe drove into the town, was heaving with both traffic and people, with several roads closed with 'Route Barrée' signs. It wasn't until they passed the Palais des Festivals, they realised why. It was Film Festival week, always held in the middle of May, it was the biggest event in the town's yearly calendar.

'Wonder if we'll see any stars we recognise,' Gabby said. 'Have to confess, I don't know many of the younger modern stars, but I'd love to see Richard Gere or Clint Eastwood. It would make my day,' she added with a cheeky smile at Philippe.

It took them twenty minutes to find a parking space several floors down in one of the underground car parks not too far from the centre of town.

'Do we need a map? Do you know where the shop is?' Gabby asked as they exited the car park into a busy street.

'No need of a map. I know the shop,' Philippe said, and within minutes he was opening the shop door and ushering Gabby in.

'Bonjour Monsieur Vincent. Madame. You are well? It has been a long time since we see you. You enjoy your retirement?' The man greeting them was clearly the owner and shook hands enthusiastically with Philippe as he explained what they were looking for.

Gabby, watching the two of them, realised she should have known that of course Philippe would be familiar with this well-stocked kitchen shop. He'd been a famous chef back in the day in the UK as well as in France, writing books and appearing in TV programmes.

'We have just the one La Cornue stove in stock at the moment,' the man said, turning to Gabby. 'If you like it, we can deliver next week. If you desire another model,' he shrugged, 'there will be a delay.'

And he led them to a room at the back of the shop, where a gleaming cream stove with golden brass trim dominated the space. As Gabby looked at it silently, already visualising it in her kitchen, Philippe was opening oven doors, gesturing at the hotplates and asking question after question about the stove's capabilities.

Finally, he turned to Gabby with a smile. 'If your heart is set on a La Cornue stove, you should buy this one. Perfect for your needs.'

Gabby needed no further encouragement and turned to the shop owner. 'I'd like to buy it.'

As they left the shop after the excitement of buying the stove, Philippe insisted they celebrate by having lunch.

'I know just the place by the old harbour,' he said.

Fifteen minutes later, they were being shown to the last available table with a perfect view of passers-by and the moored boats. Ordering a glass of rosé for Gabby and a non-alcoholic beer for Philippe they looked at the menu before both deciding on the set menu for the day.

Sitting there sipping her wine and people-watching, Gabby gave a contented sigh. If anyone had told her this time last year that she would be living back in France, she'd never have believed them, but here she was. It was too early to call it one of the best decisions she'd ever made, but the last few weeks had seen things definitely falling into place in a good way. It had been the right time to return. Living under the same roof as her daughter and granddaughter was a dream come true, even though there was so often an air of tension between Harriet and Elodie bubbling beneath the surface which would need to be addressed at some point. Elodie asking if she knew the name of her father had proved that she wanted to be told the truth about the past. Who knew how much longer she would wait before tackling Harriet again with the questions that her mother was loath to answer.

Thoughtfully, Gabby took another sip of her wine. Sometimes learning the truth about the past only stirred up trouble and more bad feeling. She could only pray that in this instance common sense would prevail.

'Gabriella,' Philippe's voice broke into her thoughts. 'I heard some news about the old Hôtel le Provençal the other day. There's talk that there is going to be an open day once all the renovations are finished and before the apartments are sold. It's an opportunity for locals to have a look around. There isn't going to be a charge, but one has to register. Would you like to go?'

'I'd love to,' Gabby said instantly, pushing her worries away. 'To see inside the fabric of the old building would be wonderful. It would put to bed a lot of memories for me,' she added quietly.

'As soon as I can, I'll register our names for a viewing,' Philippe said. 'Ah, our lunch is here.'

* * *

Harriet was ready and waiting for Hugo when he arrived that evening. Unsure of where he planned on taking her, she'd pulled on a favourite pale blue vintage-style dress with a scooped neckline and a gently flaring skirt that she knew suited her. It was a dress she felt comfortable wearing for all occasions. Sandals with a wedge heel gave her a bit more height and would be comfy if they went for a stroll before or after dinner.

Hugo was a little early and she took him through to the terrace to introduce him to Gabby and Elodie before they left for the restaurant.

Walking through the sitting room on their way out, Hugo stopped and looked at the owl painting now hanging in pride of place on the chimney breast.

'Is this one of yours?'

Harriet nodded. 'A very early one. Mum loves owls. I did it for her before... before I left.'

'It's beautifully executed. You really should start painting again,' Hugo said, tactfully ignoring her words about the original reason for painting it.

As they left and the electric gates closed behind them, Hugo pressed his key fob and the passenger door of a parked silver Porsche Cayenne opened.

'Wow, some car,' Harriet said, sliding as gracefully as she could manage into the luxurious interior.

'A major indulgence and a guilty pleasure,' Hugo said as he closed the door before walking round to the driver's side. 'I thought we'd go up to Mougins this evening. Have you been before?'

'No.'

'It's one of my favourite places. Full of restaurants and art galleries, so I'm hoping you will like it too.'

As they drove the short distance towards Mougins through the countryside above Cannes, Hugo told her a little about the medieval hilltop village, how it was surrounded by forests, how artists had flocked to it down the years for its light and how these days it was recognised as a centre of gastronomy. Harriet was captivated by her first view of the village as they drove towards it and before Hugo had even parked was feeling excited at exploring.

Walking through the narrow ancient streets, made even narrower with the addition of olive trees in pots and tubs of colourful flowers placed in front of the old houses, she kept pausing to look in windows of closed galleries, with paintings and sculptures displayed. A couple of the galleries were still open on this balmy Mediterranean evening and people were taking advantage of the quieter time to browse and to treat themselves to a painting or a sculpture.

'I'm going to have to come back during the day,' Harriet said. 'Such a lovely place to explore.'

Narrow streets led to flights of stone steps crowded with pots of tumbling red geraniums that led in turn to more narrow streets with nooks and crannies everywhere and finally to the restaurant where Hugo had booked their table.

Tables and chairs had been placed on a large open space in front of the restaurant, more olive trees in pots were dotted around and fairy lights were strung between the tall eucalyptus trees that lined the edge of the eating area. They were shown to a table for two with a wonderful view down over the countryside.

Sitting there sipping a glass of pinot noir after ordering their food – *maigret du canard* for Harriet and *steak au poivre* for Hugo – Harriet looked around at the other diners. A multi-generation family party was clearly happening on the large table set down one side. At the head of the table there were several helium balloons, all with seventy-three written across their surface, tied to the back of the chair occupied by a silver-haired man. Cards and wrapped gifts had been placed on a small table near him, laughter and happy conversation floated in the air over the table.

Harriet felt a familiar ache in her heart. An ache for the large family that she would never have; an ache for the family she'd torn apart. And the realisation, once again, that it was all her own fault.

The waiter arrived with their food at that moment and another glass of red wine for Harriet and a non-alcoholic beer for Hugo.

'The drinks are with the compliments of the birthday table,' he said, smiling. 'They pay for everyone to have a drink with them. In case they make too much noise, they want you to forgive them.'

'Of course,' Hugo said, raising his glass in the direction of the party and Harriet did the same. Together they called out '*Bon anniversaire et merci.*'

'How lovely of them to do that,' Harriet said, putting her glass down and picking up her cutlery. 'This looks delicious.'

As they ate, the two of them chatted about things in general, but by the time dessert arrived they were into a fun argument about who was the better artist, Matisse or Picasso.

Darkness had descended and lights were twinkling in the far countryside and down towards the Mediterranean when Hugo and Harriet left the restaurant, both of them calling out '*Bonne nuit*' to the family party still going strong.

A quarter of an hour later, Hugo drove the car into the impasse parking in front of the villa and Harriet turned to him. She leant across as she undid her seatbelt and gave him a gentle kiss on the cheek. 'Thank you for a wonderful evening. I've had a lovely time and I love Mougins.'

'I hope it will be the first of many evenings,' Hugo said. 'Despite you favouring Matisse over Picasso.'

17

One of the things that Elodie really enjoyed about her new life was getting out and about, discovering the delights of the Riviera and meeting new people. People like the ex-pat couple she'd interviewed yesterday. The couple had seemed so happy in their apartment overlooking the Mediterranean, the only flaw the woman could tell her about their new life was missing the family. 'It's wonderful when they visit, so we're hoping to persuade them to join us permanently,' the woman had said. 'It's not right for families to be separated.'

A day later, those words were still running through Elodie's mind as she made her way homewards along the Promenade du Soleil, having snatched a quick coffee with Gazz between customers, when she bumped into Harriet, walking Lulu. The little dog gave Elodie an enthusiastic welcome and Harriet fell into step alongside her to walk back to the villa.

Elodie, not stopping to think about the timing of what she was about to say, took a deep breath before looking at Harriet and bursting out. 'I need to ask you two questions – questions I've been going to ask you ever since you turned up back in my life. You once told me that you wanted me to know the truth about the past, but all these months later and you still haven't talked to me about anything – I'm beginning to wonder if you'll ever get around to giving me the answer to these two questions: Why isn't my father's name on my birth certificate? Why is there such a big secret over his identity?' Elodie knew she sounded like a spoilt brat and the guilt she felt about that irrationally increased the anger she was feeling.

Harriet briefly closed her eyes. The questions weren't unexpected, but the timing was. She had been delaying talking to Elodie about the past, but if she and Elodie were to build any kind of relationship, she couldn't lie over these most basic of questions. She had no option but to give Elodie the true answer to her first question, but she knew that Elodie wouldn't leave it there, she'd probe behind it. Because the truth wouldn't change anything, she still wouldn't have a name, which is what she wanted.

Harriet took a deep breath.

'You can't register a man as the father of your baby without him being present and I went on my own to the registrar,' Harriet said, waiting for the inevitable next question.

'Why didn't he go with you?'

'Because he didn't know.'

'About the fact you were going to the registrar – or didn't know about me at all?' Elodie said, turning in front of Harriet and stopping to face her.

'Both.' Harriet sidestepped Elodie and carried on walking. This wasn't a conversation she wanted to have right now and certainly not in public.

'Gabby told me once you went off the rails when granddad Eric died. Are you ashamed to name my father because of that? Was he a part of it all?' Elodie's voice was getting louder and Harriet registered the anger as she caught up with her mother. 'It's not as if I want to meet him if that's what you are worried about. I don't. I just want to know his name, how you met, how you felt about him. And I don't understand why you won't tell me about him. I do have the right to know about my father, surely?' Elodie stepped in front of Harriet again, this time blocking the way and forcing her to stop. 'Or is it a big secret because you simply don't know who my father is?'

'Stop shouting at me. I refuse to have this conversation with you in the street,' Harriet said. 'We'll have this discussion another time – when you can keep calm and behave like a grown-up. Here you take Lulu,' and she thrust the lead into Elodie's hand. 'I need to be alone for a bit.'

Elodie cursed under her breath, staring after Harriet as she turned and stormed away. It was her own fault. She'd been an idiot to start asking questions without warning, and Harriet was right. She had acted like a child. Wrong time, wrong place. But Harriet needn't think she was going to stop asking questions. Because what was the point of living 'en famille' if she didn't know the truth of her own personal family history?

* * *

Harriet took several deep breaths as she marched away from Elodie. She was furious with herself for letting Elodie's questions get to her. Questions that she knew wouldn't go away. Questions she knew she had to answer if the two of them were to build a meaningful relationship. But the ferocity in Elodie's voice as she'd suggested that she couldn't tell her about her father because she didn't know who it was had shocked her. Because the truth was, she had gone through an out-of-control period of drinking too much, smoking and, yes, having several casual relationships, until the day Lizzie had taken her to task over her behaviour.

She and Lizzie had been in Lizzie's bedroom getting ready for a Saturday night out in Torquay with friends when Lizzie had turned to her.

'Hattie, promise me tonight you'll behave? No drinking too much, no going outside with anybody and—'

Harriet had given her usual brittle laugh. 'No point in going clubbing then is there? We're going to have fun, fun, fun tonight.'

Lizzie had sighed. 'Hattie, people are talking about you. Calling you names. You've got yourself quite a reputation in the last few months for being easy, being a tart. I hate being the one to tell you this, but your drinking and your behaviour are out of control.' She'd paused. 'You've changed from being the friend I know to being a stranger, who, quite honestly, I'm beginning to think I don't want as a friend, or even to be associated with these days. This is the last Saturday night I'll go out with you if you don't behave this evening.'

Harriet had wanted to shrug her remarks away, instead she'd collapsed in a heap on the bed unable to stop the tears. But Lizzie's words got through and forced her to take a long hard look at herself. Was that how people really thought of her? Her mum would be horrified and upset if she heard what people were saying. Her dad too, would have hated her living such a life and being talked about so crudely.

Harriet had choked back a sob. Deep down, she hated the person she'd turned into, but the spiral of grief over her dad had sucked her down so quickly she'd barely noticed what was happening to her. Lizzie's words, the contempt in her voice, shook her. From that evening, all she wanted was to be the girl she used to be, the one who'd had self-respect, the one who wanted to make her father proud and her mother happy.

It was hard, so hard, but with Lizzie's help, she gradually managed to change things. She gave up smoking, stopped drinking so much, didn't go out on dates, let alone sleep with anyone, and slowly she got her life back on track.

It was several months after the fateful evening when Lizzie had forced her to face the truth about her behaviour that she'd met Jack Ellicott.

Dartington Hall, the beautiful Grade 1 medieval building outside of Totnes, now a renowned cultural centre set in acres of beautiful land-scaped gardens and grounds, had been holding a retrospective exhibition of the artist and book illustrator E. H. Shepard. Harriet had been standing in the Gallery there, drinking in the details of his sketches for *The Wind in the Willows*, before moving on to look at the original Winnie the Pooh drawings, when she had heard an American voice behind her.

'Gee, I loved those books when I was a kid.'

'Me too, but he did so much more. Look at these sketches he did in WWI,' Harriet had said, moving to her left. 'He was so talented. Paintings, cartoons, book illustrations, he did it all. He was a real trailblazer in the middle of the twentieth century. I wish I had half his talent.' She'd turned to see who had spoken and found herself standing next to a tall man about the same age as herself with a disarming smile.

'Hi, I'm Jack.'

Harriet had swallowed and nodded. 'Hi.'

Jack had given her a quizzical look. 'And you are?'

'Me? Oh, I'm Harriet, friends usually call me Hattie.'

'Are you an artist, Hattie? You dress like you are.' Jack had flashed her another disarming smile. 'Very colourful.'

Harriet had glanced down at her tiered dress and her favourite embroidered brocade coat she was wearing over the top of it, before returning his smile. 'I'll take that as the compliment I'm sure you meant it to be. Yes, I am an artist – an amateur one at the moment, but hoping to become a professional. You?'

Jack had shaken his head. 'Nope, couldn't paint a picture to save my life, but I do admire people who can. Tell me more about Mr Shepard here.'

'Well, these days people remember him for "Winnie" and the "Willows" illustrations, but he did so much more. Look at this ink sketch "Scenes of battle and bustle". He did that one when he was nine. Nine.' Harriet had shaken her head. 'He might have been born in the Victorian age, but he led the way for the modern artist.'

For the next ten minutes, Jack had followed her around the exhibition as she gave him a quick rundown on the life of Mr Shepard, as Jack had called him.

As they had arrived back at the entrance, Harriet had looked up at him. 'Sorry, if I've been wittering on.'

Jack had shaken his head. 'When I return home, I shall look at my copies of those books with a different eye. May I buy you a coffee now? I saw a cafe somewhere outside in the grounds.'

'That would be great, thank you.'

The two of them had left the gallery together, found the cafe and talked non-stop for the next hour over coffee and cake. Harriet learnt that Jack was six weeks in to a European tour, courtesy of his father for obtaining a 2.1 degree in Business Management.

'Downside is that once I go home I have to join the family business.'

'Which is?'

'Leather – travel gear, luggage and handbags. We have outlets all over the States.'

Harriet had sensed, from the way Jack talked about his life and family in America, that he came from a well-connected, wealthy family. A world away from her own working-class roots.

She had told Jack about being in her first year of art college, lodging with Lizzie in Torquay, and talked about how much she missed her dad after his unexpected death less than a year ago which had thrown her world upside down. Something she'd never talked about with anyone else. It was because Jack was such a good listener, she decided, and when he asked if they could keep in touch when they parted, she happily agreed.

Over the next couple of weeks, they saw each other as often as they could, growing closer all the time, but neither of them dared to mention the major obstacle that lay between them – the Atlantic Ocean. Harriet longed to introduce Jack to Gabby but dreaded admitting to her how she felt about Jack. If she and Jack were to become a proper couple, she would likely be leaving to live in the USA. Leaving her mother alone was something that Harriet couldn't bring herself to contemplate yet.

One evening as they had walked to the cinema in Torquay, Jack had said he had something he needed to tell her. 'My parents, ever since I was knee-high, have been keen for me to marry the daughter of one of their best friends.' Harriet's heart had plummeted at his words. With a month to go before he returned to the USA was he telling her this to prepare her for the inevitable separation? To think she had finally plucked up the courage to introduce Jack to Gabby.

'Do you still want to come to Dartmouth this weekend and meet my mother?'

'Of course I do,' Jack had said instantly. And his next reassuring words had her heart singing again. He was serious about her.

'I've never had any intention of obeying them and now I've met you, they are going to have to finally accept it's not going to happen.'

But Jack and Gabby had never met. The next day, the urgent phone message calling him home because his father was ill had happened and instead he was gone before Harriet really had time to take it in.

They emailed each other, but the distance and family commitments kept him busy on the other side of the Atlantic Ocean with no chance of them meeting up in the near future.

Jack had been gone about a month when Harriet had realised she was pregnant and her life had once again started to unravel. She obviously knew exactly who the father of her baby was, but telling him was pointless. The chances of Jack returning seemed remote, he was so busy running the family business after his father's heart attack. As much as she wanted to tell him, it would only add to his problems and seemed an unfair burden to place on him. His parents had never been likely to welcome her with open arms when they'd planned for Jack to marry a woman they had chosen. The fact that she was pregnant would probably add to their dislike of her.

It took a week or two, but she finally convinced herself a clean break would be better all round. She'd be a single mum rather than force fatherhood on a man who now lived thousands of miles away with enough insurmountable problems of his own.

With tears running down her face, Harriet had written a 'Dear John' letter, saying she'd met someone else since he'd left and it was over between them. As the letter dropped into the letterbox, she'd turned away and went home to tell her mother that, unexpectedly, she was destined to be a single mother. And that Gabby would be a grandmother soon. And however much Lizzie asked her who the father was, she would not be telling anybody his name, neither did she intend to ever tell the father himself. Not then, not ever.

* * *

Harriet walked unseeingly past the entrance to the impasse deep in thought, still too shaken to go home and face Gabby or Elodie. Twenty-four years later, the secret she'd been determined never to divulge to anyone had been dragged to the forefront of her problems, with Elodie demanding to be told her father's name.

Would learning the name change anything for Elodie though? The name would mean nothing to her, Harriet could simply pluck one out of thin air and Elodie would never know. Answers to the other questions that would follow could be vague. Perhaps that was what Harriet should do? Give a made-up name and be vague with all other details? But deep down Harriet knew she couldn't do that. She'd told Elodie that she would tell her the truth one day. Which she would, despite doing her utmost to put that day off for as long as possible. Nobody knew just how much she regretted her past behaviour. Elodie was right when she'd accused her of being ashamed of herself and the way she'd behaved in those awful months after her dad had died, talking about that time made her feel so grubby, and dragging it all up was so painful. The fact that she'd pulled herself out of the trough she'd sunk into before she met Jack didn't mean that she'd forgotten those times. Telling Elodie the name of her father was one thing, remembering the hard times that had preceded that meeting was something else.

The last few busy weeks, moving to France, settling into the villa, decorating the kitchen, giving the dresser a shabby-chic makeover, helping Lulu to settle in, working for Hugo, everything had conspired to keep both her body and her mind occupied, with little time for thinking about the past. But now that things were settling down, her thoughts were free to delve back to a time when her heart had been broken, a place she had no desire to return to. She needed to find something to do to shut them out.

Art, in the days before she met Todd, had always been her 'go-to' escape from real life. Losing herself in creating an abstract painting, or mixing the exact shade of green for oak leaves in the landscape she was trying to recreate on the canvas, had always calmed and refreshed her in those long-ago days. She missed that. Making excuses to Gabby, Jessica and even to Hugo that she wasn't ready to pick up a paintbrush was no longer strictly true. Because with sudden clarity she realised that what she was ready for, in fact needed desperately, was that elusive feeling of being totally lost in the creation of whatever she was painting. The vague sensation of being not quite there as she came back reluctantly to the everyday world and her problems. Painting wasn't going to solve anything, or make the questions from Elodie go away, but starting to paint again would be a major step forward to finding her old self.

Reaching Avenue Amiral Courbet, Harriet stopped and looked up to watch as a train passed slowly along the line and across the bridge that spanned the road. Art Deco geometric decoration and floral designs on the support columns, Juan-les-Pins written in large letters across the top, gave the bridge a certain individual vibrant, edgy energy all of its own. As the train disappeared along the line, Harriet took a deep breath.

Art Deco had always fascinated her, but she'd never really painted in that style. It could be the challenge she needed, trying to master a different technique. Taking a last look at the bridge decorations, Harriet shivered with excitement before she turned for home.

It might be too late, her talent might have shrivelled and died. But the decision had been made. She was going to start painting again.

18

To Elodie's relief, Gabby was still out with Philippe when she reached home, which meant she didn't have to face her while still reeling from the confrontation with her mother. Releasing Lulu from the lead and hoping a few lengths in the pool would help calm her down, Elodie quickly changed. Fifteen minutes later, after swimming twenty lengths in a vigorous, thrashing, front crawl she climbed out feeling infinitely better.

Showered and dressed back in her room, Elodie tried to push all thoughts of Harriet and her secrets out of her mind and switched on the computer to start writing up her feature about the ex-pat couple. While the computer booted up, Elodie stared out of the window, deep in thought. Demanding answers from her mother had failed to work, that was for sure. Harriet had said she would tell her the truth one day, so Elodie had no choice but to wait for that day to arrive.

Several email pings drew Elodie out of her thoughts and she glanced at the computer screen. One was a rejection, another expressed tentative interest in a feature she'd pitched to one of the nationals and the other, the other made Elodie's heart skip with delight.

Downstairs, the villa door banged. Elodie opened her bedroom door.

'Gabby?'

'Yes, we're back.'

Elodie, running downstairs hoping the 'we' meant Philippe and not Harriet, breathed a sigh of relief when she saw him. 'I've been offered a weekly lifestyle column contract by a national paper for their Sunday magazine – can you believe it? They want to entitle it, "English Girl Abroad".'

'Brilliant news,' Gabby said. 'Well done. And my news is, I've bought a stove which is brilliant too. Being delivered next week. The kitchen will finally be fully functional.'

'I'm going to run down to the beach and tell Gazz,' Elodie said. Taking her denim jacket off the hook in the hall, she turned to Gabby. 'I should probably warn you, I upset Harriet with a couple of questions and she went off in a strop. It might be an idea to stay out of her way when she gets back if I were you. See you later.'

Gabby sighed as the villa door closed behind Elodie. 'Not sure what I'm going to do with those two. Bang their heads together?'

'You have to wait and to have the faith,' Philippe said. 'Time will sort things.'

Gabby was relieved when Harriet did arrive home that she'd got over her strop, as Elodie had described it. In fact, she seemed positively happy, even if she did disappear up to her room almost straight away.

Gabby and Philippe were both in the pool when Harriet reappeared clutching her old easel which had spent the last twenty years in the loft of the Dartmouth house and which Gabby had insisted that 'Yes, of course it's coming to France' when they moved and had been in the corner of Harriet's bedroom gathering dust ever since they'd arrived.

'All right with you if I set my easel up in the corner of the veranda? The light is good there and it's under cover to give me a bit of shade,' Harriet called out to Gabby. 'I'm going to buy some supplies tomorrow at the gallery.'

'Place the easel wherever you like,' Gabby answered. She turned to Philippe and added sotto voce, 'Finally. I was so afraid that she would never paint again. It would have been such a waste.'

* * *

Later that same evening, after Philippe had left and Elodie was still out somewhere with Gazz, Harriet poured herself and Gabby a nightcap of a glass of rosé and they sat out on the terrace companionably watching the rising moon. Harriet sniffed appreciatively, deeply inhaling the perfume of the night scented jasmine growing in the side hedge.

Gabby glanced across at Harriet and paused before speaking. 'I'm sorry Elodie upset you with her questions today. Want to talk about it?'

Harriet hesitated. Did she want to talk to Gabby about it? Maybe ask her advice? Or would talking about it only serve to increase her worries? On the other hand, maybe talking with Gabby would help clear her thoughts.

'She's fixated on her right to know about her father,' Harriet said slowly. 'And today she accused me of not knowing who he was. Which I found unexpectedly hurtful.' Harriet closed her eyes and sighed. 'I've promised I will talk to her soon and she insists she's not going to start searching for him, but what if she changes her mind once she knows his name? And if she succeeds in finding him, what happens then? Is he going to want to play happy families?'

'He might not want to meet her at all after all these years. Did...' Gabby hesitated. 'Did you ever tell him about Elodie?'

'No,' Harriet shook her head. 'I decided he was better off not knowing. I've never told anyone else who Elodie's father is either. I know you were upset that I didn't tell you, but I got it into my head that not telling anyone was the best way to cope. If no-one knew no-one could put any pressure on me or inadvertently on him by letting details slip,' Harriet shrugged. 'And it's worked for twenty-four years.'

Harriet picked up her glass and took a drink before replacing the glass on the table and glancing at her mother.

'There's something else worrying me too. You remember the letter and photograph that you thought was from Lizzie? Well, it wasn't from her.' Harriet took a deep breath. 'It was from an old friend who was at the wedding and they would like to get back in touch with me.'

Gabby gave a thoughtful nod. 'Is it someone you knew well?'

Harriet gave a half shrug. She wasn't ready yet to say Jack's name out loud to anyone.

'It's good to have old friends in one's life as well as new ones,' Gabby said.

'Yes. But that doesn't mean I want to rekindle this particular friendship. Or that I want them back in my life. Living in France is a completely new beginning for me. I'd hoped the past would stay that way – in the past. Oh, why does life have to be so complicated.'

Gabby sipped her drink, sensing that Harriet was not telling her everything and wondering how to answer. She knew now was not the time to quote the old saying, 'What a tangled web we weave, when first we practise to deceive.' Instead, she opted for the more tactful, 'Try not to worry too much, it will all come out in the wash, as my mother used to say. Life has a way of sorting things out.'

Whether or not it would be sorted the way Harriet wanted, only time would tell.

19

Hugo gave Harriet a curious glance as she arrived for work at the gallery the next day.

'Are you all right? There's something different about you today,' he said, giving her his now customary cheek kisses in greeting.

'I'm fine. In fact, I'm more than fine. I came to a decision yesterday. I need to paint. I've set up my easel at the villa and today I need to buy some canvas, paper, brushes, pastels, watercolours and a few oils. Do I get staff discount?' She smiled up at him cheekily.

'Twenty-five per cent,' Hugo said. 'You're finally going to paint again?'

Harriet nodded. 'Try anyway. That's a very generous discount.'

Hugo shrugged and waved the comment away with his hands.

It was close to lunchtime before the gallery was quiet enough for Harriet to start gathering a few things together under the counter ready for Hugo to add it all up and tell her how much she owed.

Harriet went to collect their lunches from the cafe while he did that and the two of them then settled companionably at the table in the court-yard. Hugo's phone pinged with a text message, which he read quickly before picking up his cheese and ham baguette.

'Are you itching to start painting tonight?' he asked.

'Well, it's Saturday night and my social diary is empty to say the least, so why not?'

'That text a moment ago was from an old mate who keeps his boat in Monaco with a last-minute invitation. It's Grand Prix weekend and he's having a party tonight. Should be a lot of fun. Please come with me.' Hugo looked at her expectantly.

Harriet hesitated. She'd done her best to avoid parties for a long time. She didn't do small talk easily and she'd rapidly learnt it was better to stay silent and to watch what she said around her husband if she did speak to anyone. Todd had always complained she killed any enjoyment he might have by being 'so uncommunicative and silent'. Once home everything was dissected and judgement passed on her behaviour, good or bad. For the last few years, it had inevitably been bad, never good. And, of course, he assured her, he only did it for her own good, to help her to improve her social skills, when, in reality, he'd been effectively killing them off, although she hadn't realised that until it was too late.

'I'm not good at small talk,' she said. 'Or meeting a lot of strangers en masse. Todd always maintained I gave out an aura of not being approachable and it put people off. I wouldn't want to spoil the party for you.'

Hugo looked at her in astonishment. 'Harriet Rogers, I have never heard such absolute bullshit.' He shook his head in despair. 'I'm sorry, I rarely swear, but that is absolute tosh. What is it you think you're doing with the customers here? You're making small talk all day.'

'That's different,' Harriet protested. 'Most times, I simply take their money and ring it into the till. Sometimes they talk about how much they love Antibes Juan-les-Pins, or mention how hot it is and I agree. I'm just practicing my French really.' She stopped and looked at Hugo. He was shaking his head from side to side and smiling at her.

'And what pray is that but small talk? I can promise you much more interesting small talk tonight. It's decided. I'll pick you up at 7.30, okay? Wear comfortable shoes, Monaco will be heaving and we're probably going to have to park some way from the harbour.' Hugo put down his half-finished baguette and sighed as he gave Harriet a serious look. 'I'm sorry. I didn't mean to sound like a bully there. I'd really love you to come to the party with me, but if you don't want to, you don't have to.' Hugo gave her an anxious look.

'You didn't sound anything like a bully, and, believe me, I know what one sounds like. I'd love to come to the party with you,' Harriet said quietly. 'I'll be waiting for you at 7.30, comfortable shoes at the ready.'

* * *

When Harriet came downstairs to wait for Hugo, Gabby and Philippe were out by the pool enjoying a glass of wine before going out for dinner later that evening. Watching the two of them for a few seconds before Gabby saw her, Harriet smiled. There was an ease around their body language as they chatted and laughed that showed how close the two of them had become already, like a couple who had known each other for years rather than the comparatively newish friendship it was. Her mother deserved every happiness at this stage of her life.

'I'm not sure how late I'll be,' Harriet said as Gabby looked across and saw her. 'I've no idea how long boat parties in Monaco go on for.'

'I've been to a few and they vary,' Philippe said. 'But parties in Grand Prix week always have a special atmosphere. Don't expect to see many F1 drivers tonight though. Most of them will be up in their motor homes, or hotel suites, psyching themselves up for tomorrow's race.'

The gate intercom buzzed at that moment. 'I'll see you in the morning, Mum. Enjoy your dinner.'

'Have fun,' Gabby called as Harriet left.

Hugo, standing waiting by the car holding the passenger door open for her, smiled and gave her a cheek kiss before she got in.

Within moments, they were on the road approaching the A8 and its first toll booths with queues of traffic in almost every lane. Hugo barely slowed the car as he chose an empty lane on the left and drove towards the barrier, which, to a suddenly apprehensive Harriet, lifted just as she thought they were about to hit it, and they drove through without stopping to pay. She glanced at Hugo, who had a big grin on his face.

'That was scary to say the least. Do you do that with all your passengers?'

'No, especially not with my mother.'

'How does it work anyway?'

Hugo grinned and pointed to a card placed high on the windscreen behind the rear-view mirror. 'The money's probably already out of my account,' he said.

Hugo was a good driver who clearly enjoyed driving and the car ate up the miles. There were several more payages before they reached the exit for Monaco, and Hugo went through them all in the same way, a big grin on his face. Harriet, now that she knew, shook her head at him each time. 'You're a big kid. I keep expecting the gendarmes to give chase.'

Once in Monaco, it was twenty minutes or so before Hugo found a place in one of the car parks up near the casino. Walking back down to the port, Harriet had her first proper view of the harbour crammed with luxury yachts, the numerous temporary F1 team garages with all their technical paraphernalia along the pit lane and the starting grid marked out on the main road. As they walked, Hugo explained about the barriers that were everywhere. How it took over a month to get Monaco ready for the Grand Prix every year just in terms of the street furniture that needed to be put in place. Being a road race, it was crucial to ensure not only the drivers were safe but also the watching public.

They passed several big TV screens, one at St Devote, the first corner in the race close to the starting grid that in some years in the rain had seen several drivers come to grief. And there was Grand Prix regalia everywhere. Scarlet Ferrari flags were out in force. Charles Le Clerc, a born-and-bred Monegasque driving for Ferrari, smiled out from posters pinned up in windows and from the T-shirts that teenage girls were wearing. Restaurants were heaving, people were wandering around nonchalantly in designer clothes and priceless jewellery, enjoying the unique party atmosphere that the Monaco Grand Prix generated.

Absorbing the high-octane atmosphere all around her, Harriet knew that tonight the small principality of Monaco was truly living up to its reputation as the most glamorously opulent place on the Riviera. The harbour area was noisy. The sound of music, laughter, chatter, champagne corks popping drifted around all the boats moored there.

'Ah, here's *My Folly*,' Hugo said, stopping by the gangplank leading onto one of the boats.

My Folly, a highly polished, beamy motorsailer, was moored between two other equally shiny yachts, also in party mode. A group of people were sitting around on the yacht's aft deck and a man jumped up as he saw them.

Hugo caught hold of Harriet's hand as they stood by the gangplank. 'Don't forget you are here to enjoy yourself. And my friends don't bite or judge.'

'Hugo. You made it. Come on board,' and the man lowered the 'No Entry' sign on its chain across the gangplank for them to step aboard and kick their shoes off.

Hugo quickly introduced Harriet to Justin and his wife, Ginny. Justin pressed a glass of champagne into her hand as he went round the group reeling off their names. Harriet, knowing she didn't have a hope of remembering who was who, smiled and nodded as she said hello to everyone.

It was a lovely evening, balmy and clear. Harriet, sitting on the aft deck of *My Folly* sipping her champagne, gave herself a none-too-gentle pinch as darkness fell and the principality behind her and around the coast lit up. She was on a yacht in Monaco mixing with people who were clearly what Todd had always described as 'A-listers'. The type of people he'd always wanted to cultivate. The type of people he didn't like her meeting because she was sure to let him down. Crossly, she pushed the thought of Todd away. Hugo, it seemed, had no such fears and was more than happy to sit with her and make sure she was enjoying herself.

She discovered she was quite good at small talk after all, although this small talk was different. Hugo's friends were interested in her, wanting to engage her in conversation. Everyone was friendly and conversations in a mixture of French and English flowed. A couple of people had visited Australia, and they talked about places they both knew. The only moment she felt the tiniest bit tongue-tied and shy was when Mark Webber, the retired Australian former F1 driver, came on board for a drink. She'd watched him racing so often on TV and now here she was, meeting him in the flesh.

The yacht moved gently with the swell as various boats entered and left the harbour, its navy fenders gently squeaking when rubbing the hulls of the boats on either side. A yacht moored two boats away had a party of exuberant Americans on board and as the evening went on the noise from there increased.

It was gone midnight when Hugo suggested they had better think about leaving and they said their goodbyes to Justin and Ginny. To Harriet's surprise, both Justin and Ginny hugged her goodbye.

'Hugo is going to bring you to dinner one evening soon,' Ginny said. 'We can get to know each other better without this rabble.'

Making their way along the harbour, Hugo stopped briefly to greet a friend on the American party boat, before they continued their walk back to the car.

Hugo took the Lower Corniche road for the return journey to Antibes. 'I have to drive slower on this road, which means I get your company for a little while longer as I don't want the evening to end,' he said, glancing at Harriet. 'I hope you enjoyed tonight as much as I have?'

Harriet nodded. 'I did, although I have to confess it was all a bit surreal at times. The yachts, the people, the lights, everything.'

When Hugo eventually parked outside the villa, he went round to open the passenger door for her. 'Come on, I'll see you safely inside the gates,' and he took her hand.

Harriet pressed the remote for the side gate to open and turned to thank Hugo before stepping through.

'Harriet, I'd really like to kiss you goodnight, may I?'

'I'd like that.' She smiled and tilted her face up slightly towards his.

Hugo's kiss was short but good. Harriet sensed he was holding back, not wanting to rush anything, which she was grateful for.

She answered Hugo's quiet 'Goodnight' when he moved away with an equally quiet 'Goodnight.'

20

Harriet was late getting up the next morning and was still bleary-eyed when she joined the others for coffee by the pool mid-morning. She was grateful that Elodie seemed to be relaxed and not about to reignite their last conversation and start to ask questions again.

'No croissants left, but as a Sunday treat we've got a couple of pain au raisin,' Elodie said, pushing the plate towards her. 'Good party last night?'

'I've never been to anything like it,' Harriet confessed. 'Monaco is something else too.' She drank some coffee and felt her lethargy drain away before she picked up one of the patisseries and took a bite.

'Talking of parties,' Elodie said. 'We haven't done anything yet about organising a house-warming party. We must do it soon.'

'Do we need to have one?' Gabby asked.

'Definitely,' Elodie said. 'We must celebrate moving here.'

'Do we know enough people to invite?' Harriet asked.

'You'll be surprised,' and Elodie began counting them off on her fingers. 'The four Vincents, Colette and Lianna, Joel and Carla, his partner, Hugo – did you meet anyone else last night you'd like to invite?' she said, turning to Harriet, who shook her head.

'Not really.'

'Midsummer's day is only about three weeks away, we could hold it then. Give us time to meet a few more people and organise things.'

'As long as you don't turn it into a fancy-dress party,' Gabby said.

'Now, there's an idea.' Elodie laughed and pulled out her phone to check the calendar. 'Midsummer day is in the middle of the week this year, so how about the Saturday the week before. Gives us two weeks to organise things. Plenty of time.'

Harriet got as far as saying 'No' to the idea of fancy dress, when the rest of her words were drowned out by lots of car horns blaring non-stop. 'What on earth?'

'Sounds like a wedding,' Gabby said. 'They'll all be on their way to the reception.'

'Ooh, exciting. I love weddings,' Elodie said, jumping up. 'I'm going to have a look.' And she ran through the house and out to the front gates.

A white vintage convertible car was leading a slow parade of cars around the grass roundabout. The bride and groom were smiling and waving happily as a couple of people threw rose petals over them. In the car behind, three teenage bridesmaids were laughing and giggling together. And all the time, drivers of the following cars were sounding their horns. It was all over in less than five minutes as the cars left the impasse and made for the main road.

Elodie went back into the villa and re-joined Gabby and Harriet out on the terrace.

'The bride looked so happy,' she said, flopping down onto a chair. 'The bridesmaids too. I'd have loved to have been a bridesmaid when I was little, but nobody ever asked me.' She was quiet for a moment, remembering how she and her school friends, Carole and Beth, had promised to be each other's bridesmaids when needed. Carole had got engaged at Christmas, but would she remember the promise the three of them had made now that Elodie lived in France?

'That's not true. You have been a bridesmaid,' Harriet said.

Elodie glanced at her. 'No, I haven't. I would have remembered. Anyway, how can you possibly know. You haven't been around for years. Oh sorry,' she said. 'Gabby would probably have written and told you, I expect, but I wasn't.'

'No, she didn't write to tell me,' Harriet said. 'Because I was the bride. You were my bridesmaid when I married Todd.'

The intense sudden silence that enveloped all of them at Harriet's words exploded in Elodie's head, like a bad migraine, as she stared at her mother. The silence hung in the air for half a minute before Elodie spoke. 'I was your bridesmaid? So why did you and Todd not take me to Australia with you?'

Harriet closed her eyes. Why, oh why, had she entered into a conversation about bridesmaids? This was no easier to answer than any of the other questions Elodie had voiced.

'Because he didn't want to bring up another man's child,' she said quietly. 'And he didn't really like children, never wanted any of his own.'

Gabby stood up. 'Harriet, I need you to help me fetch something from the garage. Elodie, please wait here.'

Elodie gave a shrug. 'Whatever.' Her brain was positively buzzing with Harriet's words as she tried to drag up a memory that she was sure didn't exist. She knew she'd been four years old when Harriet had left, other people had memories from that young age. Why didn't she? Harriet had no place in her childhood memories at all. All her early memories had Gabby in them, not her mother. Gabby, who waited patiently at the side of the slide in the park as Elodie climbed up again and again. Gabby, who hugged her when she fell over and scraped her knees. Gabby, who cuddled her on her lap and read stories. Gabby, who promised never to leave her.

She must have been about six years old when she saw a bridal group outside St Saviour's church posing for photographs. The bride was wearing a white dress with lots of layers and to Elodie she looked like Cinderella going to the ball. Two children, about Elodie's own age, were standing in front of the bride. The boy had a proper grown-up suit on, but the girl, oh, the girl's dress made Elodie gasp. It was a pale pink miniature version of the bride's dress with a few less layers. It was in that moment the desire to be a bridesmaid had been born in Elodie. She wanted to wear a dress just like that. Only blue, she didn't much like pink. She remembered that moment quite clearly.

But it now appeared that she had been a bridesmaid two years earlier, to her own mother. An event she had no recollection of at all. Not even of wearing a fancy dress, which she must have surely? Fancy dresses were a prerequisite of being a bridesmaid.

Elodie wrapped her arms around her chest and closed her eyes. If she had been at the marriage of her mother to Todd, how could she have forgotten such an important event? One that was to have such an impact on her own life. There must be some sort of memory lodged somewhere in her brain.

Elodie opened her eyes as Harriet and Gabby returned. Harriet was carrying the unopened box from the garage and she placed it on the ground by Gabby's chair.

'I think it's about time we unpacked this box,' Gabby said.

'Why? What's in it?' Elodie said truculently, unfolding her arms.

'Lots of memories.' Gabby's voice was quiet as she bent down and pulled open the flaps on the box. 'Memories we need to talk about.'

She began to take things out of the box and lay them on the table. Folders, sketchbooks, loose photographs, misshaped pottery pots, a photograph album, old birthday cards with childish handwriting on, Beatrix Potter books, a copy of *Pride and Prejudice* and some Enid Blyton books that had belonged to Harriet and which Gabby had read to Elodie.

Harriet reached out and picked up a folder with her name on it. 'You kept my school reports,' she said, flicking through the papers.

'Of course. Elodie's are in here too, somewhere. Ah, here's what I was looking for.' Gabby lifted a white drawstring cotton bag from the bottom of the box and pulled it open. Elodie and Harriet watched in silence as she carefully took something flat wrapped in tissue paper out of the bag. She gently unfolded the tissue to reveal a child's summer dress. Pink with daisies scattered over it.

Elodie gasped. 'I remember that dress. Why on earth did you keep it? Can I see it properly?'

Gabby didn't answer the question but nodded and handed the dress to Elodie before reaching for the photo album that was on the table.

Elodie sat there touching and staring at the dress while her head started to pound again as a memory emerged from the fog of her brain. She vaguely remembered Gabby buying it for some occasion, telling her the day she wore it she had to be a really good girl for mummy's sake. Why, why was it such a special day? The answer refused to come. The more she tried, the more her head hurt.

Gabby's voice broke into her thoughts. 'We've never been much of a family for photographs, not like people today, but there are some in here the two of you need to look at.' She looked up from the album. 'Elodie, you have first look. The important photo is one of the last ones.' She held out the album to Elodie, open at the double page she wanted her to look at.

Still clutching the dress, hoping it would encourage more memories, Elodie stared wordlessly at the photos. At first, she didn't recognise what or whom she was looking at. The photos, like the clothes being worn, were quite formal, poised shots, the body language was stiff, as if the people standing there couldn't wait for this to be over. The little girl holding the woman's hand in one of the photographs gave off an air of wanting to break free, her hand held firmly by the woman.

Elodie smothered another gasp and stared at the photo again. 'Is this me? Wearing this dress?'

'Yes. Being my bridesmaid when I married Todd,' Harriet said in a matter-of-fact voice.

'These are your wedding photographs?' Elodie looked at her mother, shocked. 'You didn't get married in St Saviour's? You don't look like you. You don't even look like a bride – and I definitely don't look like a proper bridesmaid.'

'We got married in Totnes Registry Office, Todd didn't want a church wedding. Or a big fuss.'

'You did though, didn't you,' Gabby said quietly.

Harriet nodded and sighed. 'I'd always dreamt of being married in St Saviour's with Dad walking me down the aisle. That was no longer possible and was the main reason I agreed to a low-key civil wedding. The date was booked and we had a month to organise things, didn't we, Mum?'

Gabby nodded. 'It was such a small wedding that there wasn't much to arrange. Reception for fifteen guests, a few buttonholes and a bouquet, I made a cake and agreed to take the few photographs. We went shopping in Torquay for your outfit and a dress for Elodie.' She gave Harriet a sad smile. 'You knew my heart wasn't really in it as I had a gut feeling you were marrying the wrong man.'

'I should have listened to you,' Harriet admitted. 'But I thought I was doing the right thing. That you would give Elodie the happy, secure childhood that I didn't think I could provide.' She glanced at her mother. 'Todd had promised me a new beginning in Australia and that I could come back regularly to see both of you. It was a year before I realised he had no intention of keeping that promise. I would never have left if I'd known that was his plan.'

'Six hours after these photographs were taken you were catching the train to London that took you out of our lives.' Gabby bit her bottom lip. 'I had no way of knowing then that you would be unable to visit regularly.' She sighed. 'Recriminations at this late date are useless, but I wish with all my heart that you'd never married Todd. *C'est la vie*. It's in the past and needs to be buried. It's the future that matters now for the three of us.'

'I don't remember the occasion at all,' Elodie said, shaking her head. 'It wasn't the Cinderella dress that I longed for later. Maybe if it had been, I'd have remembered it.' Elodie gave an involuntary shiver as a memory finally fell in to her brain.

Suddenly she did remember wearing the dress. It was the day her mother had given her a big cuddle, squeezing her so hard she could barely breathe, and said she loved her and that she was to be a good girl for Gabby. Harriet had been crying so much, her tears had soaked the top of the dress before Todd had almost dragged her away. Elodie remembered too, with sudden clarity, taking the dress off that evening, throwing it across the room and shouting at Gabby.

'I hate Mummy. I'm never ever wearing that dress again.'

Elodie closed the photo album and handed it back to Gabby, glancing at her mother as she did so. 'I'm sorry your marriage didn't turn out to be a happy one, but seeing those photographs changes nothing. I remember the dress now, but I still don't remember being your bridesmaid.' She pushed back her chair and jumped up. 'Right, I'm going to take Lulu for a walk.' No need to explain that she needed some time apart from Harriet to try and process this forgotten information about her childhood.

* * *

Sunday evening, the box was still out on the terrace and Gabby suggested while it was there the three of them should sort through it and throw anything away that wasn't worth keeping. Harriet, initially reluctant in case the contents of the box caused another scene with Elodie, helped Gabby to carefully empty the contents of the box onto the table and spread them out.

Harriet smiled as she picked up a wonky pottery pot that she faintly remembered making in primary school. She'd loved the feel of the clay in her hands and had spent ages trying to get the shape exactly right. 'Obviously I was not destined to be a potter,' she laughed. 'But I can't throw it away so back in the box with it.'

Elodie leant across and picked up two or three exercise books held together with a rubber band. 'I remember these. I was about ten. After I read *Tom's Midnight Garden*, I had dreams of being the next Philippa Pearce.' She placed the books to one side with a sigh. 'Still haven't got around to writing a novel, though.'

'But you are writing,' Harriet said. 'You've still got time.'

Gabby gently pulled out a cardboard folder tied with red ribbon that had wedged itself to the very bottom of the box and handed it to Harriet. 'A few of your sketches, I think.'

Harriet's fingers were trembling as she untied the ribbon and laid the folder flat. This was part of a college project – the one that never got handed in because she gave up long before she ever finished it. The task had been to 'choose a painter from the twentieth century, write an essay on why you admired him or her and to do some original work in that style'. It was the reason she'd been at Dartington Hall the day she'd met Jack.

Looking at the top pen-and-ink sketch of a female fox with her two cubs was enough. Too many memories were stirring.

Before she could reach out to retie the folder, Elodie had picked up the fox sketch. 'Oh, this is lovely. Reminds me of the paintings in *The Wind in the Willows*.'

'Yes, that was my inspiration,' Harriet said, holding her hand out for the sketch and returning it to the folder. Quickly tying the ribbon again, she hesitated before placing the folder to one side rather than on the pile to go back into the box.

Twenty minutes later, there were two distinct stacks on the table – one for throwing away and one for returning to the box to keep. Harriet's folder of sketches was to one side on its own.

Elodie picked up the child's dress that had upset her earlier in the day. 'We can throw this, can't we? It's got nothing but bad memories for everyone,' and she placed it firmly in the bottom of a black rubbish bag she'd got from the kitchen before starting to throw the rest of the unwanted pile on top of it. Harriet and Gabby watched her silently but neither protested.

Gabby and Harriet repacked the box and Harriet went to close it.

'You are keeping your sketches out?' Gabby said.

'Yes, they might inspire me again someday,' Harriet answered quietly as she picked them up.

21

The next two weeks passed quickly. Gabby had a frustrating phone call from the kitchen shop. They apologised profusely, but there was going to be a ten-day delay with delivering the stove. There was no technician available until then to come and install it. Gabby was cross but realised there was nothing she could do about it.

Elodie and Gazz were both busy working during the day, Gazz with the holidaymakers and Elodie writing features and pitching ideas to as many magazines and newspapers as she could. The two of them slipped into a routine of evening dates and the occasional lunchtime pizza together. Not ideal but Elodie knew that once the busy summer season was over both of them would have more free time.

Harriet spent most of her time either walking Lulu or out on the veranda painting. Although she was definitely out of practice and rusty, with no-one standing over her criticising her work she began to enjoy herself. Techniques she'd learnt years ago in college began to bubble back into her mind and out onto the canvas and once again she frequently found herself so absorbed in her work that she forgot the time. She'd also volunteered to do the big weekly Friday shop on the basis that Elodie was working and Gabby would find the bags too heavy. And Saturdays, of course, she worked for Hugo – something she was enjoying more and more. When Hugo asked her if she felt like having a go at changing the window dressing, she gave an enthusiastic yes and thoroughly enjoyed herself.

Joining forces to organise the house-warming party for the seventeenth of June – a date that seemed to come round much quicker than anticipated – created a fragile truce between Elodie and Harriet. On the surface, their relationship appeared to be mending, but they both realised that it wouldn't take a lot for it to be torn apart again.

The three of them decided on a menu of finger food from the supermarché and the boulangerie rather than try to organise things themselves in the still unfinished kitchen. The day before the party the three of them went to the supermarché and bought everything they could think of. Lots of cheeses, crackers, crisps, olives, pâtés and some stuffies – tomatoes and round courgettes filled with rice, herbs, fried mushrooms and onions. There was just space left for the small jar of crème fraîche to accompany bite-sized meringues to slide into the fridge.

The shelves of the small under-the-counter fridge that Elodie had found in the brocante and insisted they needed for cold drinks were also full with bottles of rosé, white wine and champagne. And now the day had finally arrived.

'What time did we say we'd collect the rest of the food from the boulangerie?' Gabby asked at breakfast. As a backup, there were baguettes and three dozen each of small savoury pastries, miniature strawberry tartlets and individual tarte tatins.

'Twelve o'clock,' Elodie said. 'What is left on the list to do ready for this evening?'

'Nothing really. The garden and the pool are both looking good. Joel and Philippe have strung the lights and hung the candles ready. We can put plates and glasses out on the table late afternoon,' Gabby said. 'But the food will have to be done at the last minute.'

'I'm sorry I'm at the gallery today,' Harriet said. 'But I can do the table and last-minute stuff with the food when I get back. Hugo has promised I can leave early.'

'I just hope we have enough food and haven't forgotten anything,' Gabby said.

Harriet gave her mother an amused smile. 'I think we have more than enough even if all the neighbours turn up, which I doubt they will.'

Gabby had decided that in a gesture of friendship they should invite the neighbours and earlier in the week had dropped written invitations into all the postboxes in the impasse. She suspected that most of the villas had changed hands several times in the last forty years, but there might be new generations of the families she'd known living in the houses. She had paused as she'd dropped an invite into the letterbox at number three. That was definitely a familiar name – Rochefort. She'd been friends with Amelia Rochefort, who'd lived there with her brother and parents. The two of them had walked to school together, giggled over silly things. Never as close as she and Colette had been, but a good friend. She'd definitely enjoy catching up with Amelia if she did come this evening.

At ten to eight, the three of them met down by the pool and Elodie popped open a bottle of champagne and poured three glasses.

'Santé. We're ready to party!'

'Where's Lulu?' Gabby asked anxiously.

'Where she spends most of her time – on my bed,' Elodie said. 'I've closed the door and she'll be fine for a couple of hours.'

'People are starting to arrive,' Harriet said, hearing the gate buzzer. 'I'll go and be gatekeeper and let them in.'

Jessica, Mickaël and Philippe were the first to arrive, clutching three bottles of champagne – one for each of them, Jessica laughingly explained. 'The three of you are hosts, so you each get a thank you.'

The neighbours from number three were the next to arrive and Gabby was delighted to remake the acquaintance of Amelia's brother, Richard, and his wife, as well as Amelia herself who apologised for tagging along when she no longer lived in the impasse. 'I just wanted to make contact with you again after all these years,' she said.

'Please don't apologise. I'm so glad you came.' Gabby smiled at Amelia. 'We have lots to catch up with.'

Colette and Lianna arrived next and gave the three of them a beautifully decorated wooden name plaque for Villa de l'Espoir that Lianna had made. When Hugo arrived, Harriet took him through to introduce him to Colette before going back to let more guests in – this time the neighbours from next door. Harriet welcomed them and sent them through to the garden before turning to greet Joel and his partner, Carla.

Gazz was the last to arrive and half an hour later, the party was in full swing as Harriet closed the gates and walked down the side of the villa to the garden, intent on joining the party and finding Hugo. She paused at the corner of the villa and looked at the scene in front of her. As well as the fairy lights Joel and Philippe had strung around the garden, looping them up and down the trees and shrubs, a dozen or so solar candle lights had been pushed into the flower beds around the garden over a week ago to charge up and were now little beacons of light as the sun sank. The pool too, with its floating candles that Elodie had insisted they purchased in the absence of underwater lights, was adding a certain something to the ambience. It wasn't midsummer's day, but the garden definitely had a fairy-tale air about it this evening.

Harriet found Hugo talking to Gabby and Philippe and they'd been joined by the man who'd arrived as part of the group from next door. As Harriet reached Hugo's side, the man held out his hand to Gabby.

'I just want you to know that my offer still stands should you change your mind. If you do, my granddaughter will always give me a message. *Bonne nuit.*'

Gabby ignored his outstretched hand. '*Bonne nuit.* Harriet will see you out,' and she turned pointedly to speak to Philippe.

Harriet, surprised by the order, caught hold of Hugo's hand as she went to follow whoever the man was, wanting him to accompany her. She opened the gate and politely said. '*Bonne nuit, monsieur?*'

'Moulin, Jean-Frances.'

Harriet took a step back and quickly closed the gate once he'd left.

'What a cheek. If I'd realised who he was, I would have refused him entry, friend of the neighbours or not,' she said.

'More than friends of the neighbours, he's related to them. Your mother was pretty upset when she saw him. What was this offer he made her?' Hugo asked her.

'He wanted to buy the villa and the field that comes with it, knock the house down and build a small estate. He'd even gone as far as seeking outline planning permission, even though he didn't own anything. Gabby

told him no way when we were down here at the beginning of the year.'
She shook her head. 'Come on, I'd better get back and make sure Gabby is
okay, although Philippe is with her, so I'm sure she is.'

As they wandered back down to the terrace, music began to drift on
the air. Harriet guessed that Elodie had pressed the Spotify button on the
laptop she'd set up earlier. Gabby and Philippe were down by the back
hedge now, talking to Colette and they'd clearly been discussing the
unwelcome visitor.

'It's a little unsettling that his granddaughter lives next door,' Gabby
was saying. 'I hope he doesn't visit very often.'

There was a short silence as Colette gave Gabby a curious look.

'Standing here in the garden with everything looking so good, and
with a lovely party atmosphere tonight, has brought up memories of the
past for me when it was so different. Your maman did her best, but Hervé
was never very sociable, was he?' Colette laughed. 'Although I do
remember the occasional fourteenth of July fireworks party.' Colette
turned to Gabby.

'Have you been in the cave at the villa since your return?' she asked.

Surprised, Gabby shook her head. 'No, I haven't. I've been in the
garage, but I'd forgotten all about the existence of the cave. Houses in
England rarely come with a cellar these days, so I'm out of the habit of
having one. Why?'

'Talking about Hervé reminded me about something he muttered after
one of his unexpected visits to me. As he left, he said something like "tell
her to be certain to check the villa's cave herself" under his breath. It was
as if he had something hidden down there,' Colette answered. 'Something
that he wanted to make sure you knew about.'

'The notaire dealt with everything, so he would have checked the
cave and he never mentioned anything unusual,' Gabby said, even as
she wondered whether the notaire had known about the cave. Its
concealed entry was hard to find even when you knew where it was.
Thinking about the house clearance itinerary from the notaire listing
the contents of the villa room by room, she couldn't recall anything
about any items found in the cave on its various pages. If she had
forgotten about the cave, why should a stranger even suspect there was

one? Especially when there was no outward sign anywhere of its existence.

'Did you know how to get in?' Colette said.

Gabby nodded. 'Yes, I know and I can remember how to open the door. And now it's on my list to check it out. I dread to think what I'm going to find down there.'

Philippe placed a comforting arm around her shoulders. 'If you want me to, *ma cherie*, I'll come with you when you're ready to take a look.'

'That would be good, thank you,' Gabby said, smiling at him.

'For now, put it out of your mind and we dance, yes?' And taking her by the hand, he led her up to the terrace, where Gazz and Elodie were already making the most of the opportunity to snuggle together in each other's arms.

Hugo pulled Harriet towards him. 'I warn you, I am the world's worst dancer, but I can certainly stand still with you in my arms and pretend to move my feet.'

'I can't dance either,' Harriet said softly. 'But I can do that too.'

* * *

It was nearly midnight before people started to leave. Hugo was the last to go and Harriet went outside with him to say goodbye. 'Thanks for a lovely evening. I think your mother is wonderful. Reminded me of my grand-mother in a way. Will you have dinner with me on Monday evening?'

'That would be lovely, thank you,' Harriet replied.

'I'll pick you up about seven.'

As Hugo took her in his arms to kiss her goodnight, Harriet tensed. She was sure she caught a movement in the shadows of the green and turned quickly, but it was too dark to see anyone. Had someone been watching them?

Hugo opened his car door. 'I'll wait until you're in the drive and the gates are closed.'

Harriet looked at him, had he sensed someone hanging round too? No, it was something he did whenever he dropped her off even in broad daylight, he made sure she was safely home behind the locked gates before he left. Harriet quickly did as she was told and closed the gate. She was being silly. If there was someone there, it was probably a neighbour out for a late dog walk.

Indoors, she ran upstairs to let Lulu out before going back out to the terrace to share a last drink with Gabby and Elodie. The remains of a bottle of rosé was poured between their three glasses and they congratulated themselves on the success of the party.

'I'm really pleased that so many of the neighbours came,' Gabby said. 'It's often said that Juan is like a village to the locals and tonight proved that. I heard about people I went to school with from their next-generation relatives. Not sure about Jean-Frances Moulin's granddaughter being such a close neighbour, although I do find the fact that they live next door in number six interesting.' She took a sip of her wine and sighed happily.

'I'm so happy we moved over,' Elodie said. 'I love living here, I no longer write advertising copy, I feel like a proper writer now with regular features in magazines and newspapers, even the occasional e-zine.' She gave a contented sigh. 'And I have a lovely boyfriend.'

'How about you, Harriet?' Gabby asked quietly. 'We know you expected to live in England when you left Australia, how are you finding life in France?'

'Surprisingly good, and happy that it's all working out for the best,' Harriet admitted. If she was honest, she was happier than she'd been for years. Life here for her was good. She and Elodie hadn't yet fully relaxed with each other but were at least being civil. She'd always known that becoming close would take time. Working in the art gallery was fun and she was painting again. And then there was Hugo. Starting a new relationship had never been on her radar, but she knew she was becoming very fond of him. Whether it would ever turn into something serious, only time would tell.

'I think our new life deserves a toast,' Elodie said. 'We are all agreed that moving here has been the right thing to do, so here's to living our best life in France.' The three of them clinked glasses in a toast for a final time that evening, happily looking forward together to the future. 'To the good life in France.'

22

Breakfast on the terrace the following morning was a more subdued affair than normal, only Gabby appeared to be her usual self. Elodie made a plateful of toast rather than do the usual boulangerie run, while Harriet organised large coffees and slowly they both woke up.

'I think the party was a great success. Everyone seemed to enjoy themselves,' Gabby said.

'I think the number of empty wine bottles in the kitchen could be something to do with that,' Elodie commented. 'The food was delicious too.'

'I'll walk Lulu after breakfast and then probably do some painting,' Harriet said. 'What are you two planning?'

'Philippe is taking me for a drive out to Théoule-sur-Mer, followed by lunch at a beach restaurant. He knows the best restaurants everywhere,' and Gabby gave a happy smile.

'I'm meeting Gazz on the beach hoping that he's got time to stop for something to eat, Sundays are generally busy though,' Elodie said.

Harriet stood up. 'Come on, Lulu, let's get walking. Did anyone check the postbox yesterday? No? I'll do that as I go out.'

No post in the box, just a folded piece of notepaper. Harriet took it out, expecting it to be a thank you note from one of the neighbours who'd been at the party. Glimpsing the signature as she unfolded it, her heart rate jumped several notches before she shoved the paper into her pocket and walked quickly away from the villa.

She was sitting on a bench on the Promenade du Soleil before she took the note out of her pocket to read.

Dear Harriet,

I am here in Juan-les-Pins and would love to meet for a catch-up. I'll hang around down by the jazz pavement in Pinède Gould at eleven o'clock, Monday morning in the hope that you will come. Together we'll find somewhere for coffee. I do hope you can make it – we have lots of catching up to do – twenty-four years' worth.

Jack

Harriet screwed the note up and sat staring out to sea. Why was he here? How long was he here for? How the hell had he found her? And what exactly was he implying with that last sentence? Had someone said something? Told him the truth. That he had a daughter. Could Lizzie have mentioned Elodie at the wedding? Not that she knew the connection between the two of them.

Harriet closed her eyes and shook her head. There was no way that Jack knew about Elodie. She'd stuck to her resolve to never tell anyone who Elodie's father was. The only person who had any right to that information was Jack and she'd taken the decision before Elodie was born not to burden him with the news. He was too far away to help and had enough family problems of his own. But now he was here and wanted to talk.

Without warning, the guilt she'd felt consumed by at the time and for years afterwards was back. Sweeping through her mind, swamping her thoughts with how brutally cruel she had been, She was going to have to tell Jack the truth, admit that she'd been totally in the wrong acting, the way she had. Harriet brushed her wet cheeks with the back of her hand.

Perhaps Jack did just want to get back in touch, talk about their shared past, unaware that her daughter was also his. But how would he react to that news? Two immediate responses sprang into Harriet's mind: he was likely to be angry with her for withholding the information and secondly,

he would surely want to meet Elodie. Which led straight to a new problem. If Elodie had expressed the desire to meet her father then things
would have been easier to organise but she'd repeatedly said she simply
wanted to know about him, not meet him face to face. How would she
react to the news that her father wanted to meet her?

Lulu, sitting at her feet, whimpered and placed a paw on Harriet's
knee. Absently, Harriet stroked the dog. 'Sorry, Lulu. Not much of a walk
for you sitting here, is it? Come on, let's go to the lighthouse.' A long walk
which would serve a dual purpose – exercise and thinking time.

* * *

After both Harriet and Elodie had left, Gabby made herself another coffee
and sat out on the terrace to enjoy it and admire the garden in the
morning sunshine. Over the past few weeks, she and Philippe had worked
hard out here, pulling weeds, trimming shrubs and replanting the borders
with daisies and cosmos for some summer colour.

Sitting there alone, her thoughts drifted to thinking about how well
last night's party had gone. The only potential hiccup had been the
unwanted appearance of Jean-Frances Moulin, but thankfully he'd left
peacefully without creating a scene. Hearing Harriet this morning repeat
openly that she was happy to be living here in France, had been a huge
relief. There was still tension between her and Elodie, but things were
slowly improving between them and hopefully could only get better given
time.

And then Colette's remembered message from Hervé sprang into her
thoughts and her mind went into overdrive.

She'd told Colette the truth when she'd said she'd completely
forgotten about the cave's existence. Hervé had rarely allowed either her
or her mother down there. But on the occasions she had been down, she
couldn't recall anything out of the ordinary being there. To her, it was just
an extra storage place under the villa filled with her father's uninteresting
junk. Something, though, told her that there had to be a reason for her
father taking the trouble to seek out Colette and give her the message
about wanting Gabby to check the cave herself.

When she opened the old concealed door and went down, was it going to be full of stuff Hervé had obtained by dubious means? Had he left her a final, unexpected problem to deal with? Gabby sighed.

Briefly, she toyed with the idea of going down into the cave right now - and discovering how bad it was. But it had been locked up for over ten years, there was no real rush, and Philippe had offered to come with her. Finishing her coffee, Gabby came to a decision. Rather than go down by herself she'd wait until the three of them could go down together with Philippe. She might ask Colette to join them too.

* * *

Back at the villa a couple of hours later, Harriet unclipped Lulu's lead and the little dog made straight for her drinking bowl before curling up in her basket. Harriet opened the fridge and assembled a plate of party leftovers for her lunch before pouring herself a glass of rosé and sitting out on the terrace.

On her walk, all sorts of things had gone through her mind, including running away for a few weeks and not telling anyone where she was, and hoping by the time she returned Jack Ellicott would have disappeared. The only flaw in that plan was that he knew where she lived, so could easily just knock on the door and introduce himself to Elodie and Gabby. He'd only have to take one look at Elodie and he'd know instantly that she was his daughter from the colour of her eyes.

Thoughtfully eating the last piece of her savoury tart, Harriet knew the only thing she could do was to stick to the decision she'd made on the walk. Tomorrow morning at eleven o'clock she would meet Jack Ellicott down by the Pinède Gould and take it from there.

* * *

Elodie had been right when she'd said Sundays on the beach were usually busy, this one, the day after the party, proved to be no exception. Gazz and Olivier, the man he'd recently taken on for the summer realising he needed proper help as well as teenage Enzo, were all busy with customers when she arrived at midday. She stayed out of the way, enjoying the panorama of the beach scene in front of her: golden sand, blue sky, the whiff of ozone in the air mingling with the smell of cooking from a nearby beach restaurant, lovers side by side holding hands on beach towels, happy families laughing and playing together. Elodie, looking at the idyllic scene with the Iles de Lérins shimmering in the distance under a heat haze, thought about Gabby and Harriet, and how the three of them had toasted their new lives in France after the party.

Harriet saying she was happy living in France must have reassured Gabby that she wouldn't disappear again, but Elodie knew that she, personally, was treading a difficult line in her relationship with her mother by pushing for answers to certain questions. Perhaps she should stop antagonising Harriet by demanding to know about her father. She'd lived all this time without knowing his name and it wasn't as if she was desperate to go searching for him. Seeing the dress and the photographs of Harriet's wedding, the sudden memory of how wet the dress had been from her mother's tears, on what should have been a happy day, had definitely made her think a bit more about the way Harriet's life hadn't turned out as she'd once expected it to.

Maybe if she backed off and the two of them were able to get closer, Harriet would eventually tell her the truth voluntarily. If not, she'd have to learn to live with it.

Elodie gave Gazz a wave as she saw him look in her direction and came to a decision. It was time to stop asking questions and try to get closer to her mother. She'd stop pushing so hard and forget about learning the name of her father because, really, what was the point of knowing it when he'd never been in her life and was never going to be?

23

Monday morning and Harriet was on edge as she got dressed ready to walk into Juan and meet up with Jack. She wanted to look good but didn't want to overdo it, so she pulled on what she'd come to regard as her go-to smart 'gallery uniform'. Skinny white jeans and a pink T-shirt with a denim waistcoat slipped over the top. Her oversized sunglasses completed her look. Elodie was working in her room and Gabby was having a leisurely swim when Harriet clipped on Lulu's lead, called out a cheery. 'See you both later,' and left before either of them had the chance to ask where she was going.

It was a perfect south of France summer day – deep blue sky with the occasional wispy cloud visible and the sun shining brightly. Holiday-makers were thronging the pavements and the shops. Walking through to the Pinède Gould, Harriet had to step off the pavement several times to avoid meandering pedestrians.

She saw Jack studying the hand imprints of famous jazz legends embedded in the pavement. There was no mistaking the man she knew was actually the love of her life and her heart missed a beat as she watched him, just like it had back in the day when she couldn't wait to be with him. Guilt rose like bile in her throat – what had she thrown away so carelessly all those years ago?

Quickly she stepped behind a plane tree to catch her breath and to get a dispassionate look at him before he noticed her. The slim figure and the crewcut hair were the same, although the hair was more grey than blonde now, and there was an aura of sophistication about this older man that the younger man she'd known and loved had lacked.

As she moved out from behind the tree and walked slowly towards him, Jack glanced up and saw her. His face immediately lit up as he gave her such a well-remembered smile that her heart skipped several beats. Yes, Elodie had definitely inherited her father's eyes. The blue of a deep ocean with a crystal-clear gaze that could see right through to her soul.

'Hello, Jack.'

'Harriet.'

For a second, Harriet thought he was about to swoop in and hug her and she moved back a little but he simply stood looking at her.

'And who's this?' Jack bent down to stroke Lulu, who was doing her usual trick of wrapping herself around Harriet's legs in the presence of people she wasn't sure of.

'This is Lulu.'

'Hello, Lulu,' Jack said, crouching down to fondle her ears, before straightening up to look at Harriet again. 'It's good to see you. You're looking good.'

'You too,' Harriet said, unable to deny that it was good to see him or the fact that he still had a disturbing effect on her. Not that she was about to let him see that. 'How did you find me?' Harriet could hear the tremble in her voice and stared at him. 'And why now, Jack, after all this time?'

'I have to admit it was difficult to know where to begin, but then I had a little bit of a lucky break, thanks to your boss, Hugo. As for the why,' he shrugged. 'Look, let's get a coffee and we can talk properly and I will tell you why I'm here.'

Wordlessly, Harriet turned away and made for the nearest cafe with empty tables and chairs on the pavement. How the hell did Hugo fit into this?

Once they were seated and ordered their coffees, she fixed Jack with a look. 'So, this lucky break?'

'Lizzie told me that you'd moved to France. The only address she could give me was the old Dartmouth one or simply Antibes Juan-les-Pins. Did you get my forwarded letter by the way?'

Harriet made a non-committal movement with her mouth. No way would she admit to having received it and throwing it in the compost bin.

'You went to a party in Monaco the Saturday of Grand Prix weekend,' Jack said, his voice matter-of-fact.

'How do you know that?'

'Because I was there. On a boat moored two away from the yacht you were on.'

Harriet nodded. That would be the extremely noisy American one. She remembered Hugo stopping to speak to a friend on board that yacht as they passed after they had left the party. 'I didn't see you on there.'

'There was quite a crowd on board that night.' Jack shrugged. 'I recognised you. Couldn't take my eyes off you. Wanted to say hello then and there, but I wasn't sure how you would react if I suddenly appeared in front of you, and you were with someone, so I stayed quiet. After you'd left, I asked about the man you were with. Hugo. Art gallery owner, your boss and, I was told, currently your boyfriend. Once I had his name and the address of the art gallery, the rest was easy. I loitered outside the gallery every day of the next week, waiting for you to turn up for work. I followed you home the next Saturday.'

'You stalked me? That's a criminal offence.' Harriet replied lightly. The fact that she'd been so easy to find was unsettling.

'I wouldn't call it stalking – there was no evil intention, I assure you. I just wanted to get everything clear in my head before I contacted you. Which I planned to do Saturday evening, but you were busy with a party, hence the note.'

'If there hadn't been a party, what had you planned to do?'

'Ring the bell and say hi to whoever opened the gate and tell them I was an old friend of yours.' He flashed her a smile.

Harriet shook her head. 'I'm glad that part of your plan failed. You weren't in the impasse late that night, were you?'

Jack shook his head. 'No. I did hang around for a bit, but I left after about an hour and walked back to my hotel.'

'Why were you looking for me anyway after all this time?'

Jack gave a deep sigh. 'It was something that Lizzie said at the wedding. Initially I put it down to her having drunk too much champagne, but then I started to wonder. Ah, coffee.'

The waiter placed the two coffees on the table and they both muttered their thanks.

Jack picked up the sachet of sugar from his saucer and carefully tore off the corner and poured the sugar into his cup. 'Never give you enough sugar in French cafes, I find.' He looked at the sachet in Harriet's saucer. 'Do you take sugar these days? You never used to.'

'And you always took too much,' Harriet said, pushing her unused sachet across the table towards him, wishing he'd hurry up and get to the point.

'That Dear John letter you sent,' Jack said. 'Almost broke me, thinking of you with someone else. I thought we had something special. I'd known the future was going to be difficult, but I truly believed we'd overcome our problems and the little matter of the Atlantic Ocean being between us and be together.' His voice took on a hard edge. 'I wanted to jump on the next plane, find you, confront you, make you see you were making the wrong choice, but everything conspired against me doing that.'

'My first wrong choice of many,' Harriet said in a sotto voce.

'My father died, my mother needed me – oh, so many things.' Jack shook his head and took a deep breath.

'I'm sorry about your father.'

'I got over it, over you, got married and life carried on.'

'So what do you want now?' Harriet asked quietly, looking at him.

'The truth from you. I think you might have something to tell me. Lizzie said you had a baby girl, Elodie, six months after I left. That little gem got me thinking. Most pregnancies last for nine months, don't they? She also said...' Jack stirred his coffee thoughtfully before glancing up at her. 'That no one knew who the father was. You hadn't even confided in her, your best friend.' Jack's eyes narrowed as he stared at Harriet. 'So either your daughter was very premature or you were pregnant when I left and you chose not to tell anyone, including me. Something tells me that it was the latter.'

Harriet closed her eyes in defeat, in relief almost, that after all these years it was finally happening, her secret was out in the open. The one person she'd longed to tell finally knew he had a daughter. There was no point in denying it.

'It would never have worked. We were from different worlds, different cultures. You were an all-American preppy boy,' Harriet said defiantly, fiddling with her coffee cup. 'And I was...' She shrugged. 'I was a working-class English girl who wanted to paint. I lived in a totally alien world to the one you knew.'

'Rubbish. I knew you and the world you lived in. A world I felt perfectly at home in. You didn't even know mine.'

'But I knew you came from a family with money, and I didn't.'

Jack stared at her. 'There's more to it than that.'

Harriet took a deep breath, trying to calm herself down before she spoke. 'Remember, you'd also told me that there was a girl back home whom your parents expected you to marry. I guessed they wouldn't react too kindly to me upsetting their plans. And once you'd left, I sort of accepted that you would find it difficult to return. Family ties would bind tighter and tighter to keep you over there.' She paused and fiddled with her silver bracelet.

'Sure, there was that arrangement both sets of parents wanted, but like I told you, I'd never agreed to it. It was one of the reasons I was in Europe that year. I'd hoped making myself absent for a few months would give everyone a chance to realise that I was serious when I refused to accept their plan.'

Harriet looked at him and despondently shook her head. 'I also didn't realise I was pregnant until after you'd left. If we'd still been together, of course I would have told you, but you were miles away with family problems in another country.' Harriet looked at Jack, her eyes glistening, the guilt as strong as ever. 'Telling you would have added to your problems and I didn't want to do that. I didn't want you to feel trapped into marrying me. But you have to believe me, not telling you and writing that Dear John letter was one of the hardest decisions to make, and follow through, of my life.'

'It was the biggest mistake of your life – for both— all of us.'

Harriet bit her lip and blinked rapidly as she heard the sad unhappy tone in Jack's voice.

He shook his head and gave her a despairing look. 'I loved you, Harriet. I would have moved heaven and earth for you both if you had chosen to tell me the truth. At least you are not denying that Elodie is mine.' Jack drained his coffee cup before he spoke. 'But Lizzie also told me you left her behind with your mother when you married and went off to Australia. Why didn't you contact me then? I would gladly have offered to have her. Given her at least one parent in her life.'

'I regret leaving Elodie more than you or anybody will ever know, but you have to know how wonderful my mother has been for all these years,' Harriet said quietly. 'Gabby has been a tremendous mother stroke grand-mother to her, a real rock in Elodie's life. Probably a better mother than I would ever have been. Elodie adores her. How would your wife – I suspect you were married by then – have taken to having your illegitimate toddler thrust into her life to look after? And you're still married judging by the wedding photo – how's she going to react to learning the news now?'

'There won't be a problem. Sabrina and I divorced five years ago,' Jack answered flatly. 'We met up for Nathan's wedding like civilised adults. When can I meet Elodie?'

Harriet bit her lip and shrugged in despair. The question she'd been dreading. 'I don't know. She doesn't know anything about you, not even your name. Just recently she has been asking questions about who you were, how long we were together, but at the same time insisting that she doesn't need to meet you. She just wants to know who she is. I'm going to need time to tell her if you want to meet her.'

'There is no if about it. I want to meet her – and I'm going to meet her.' Jack pushed a business card across the table. 'My cell phone number is there. Please ring me when you've spoken to Elodie and tell me when I can meet her.'

'Even after I've told her about you, I suspect it's not going to be that easy to arrange a meeting,' Harriet said.

'You've had twenty-four years to tell her about me,' Jack said. 'And in all honesty you can't expect me to wait another twenty-four years or even twenty-four days to meet my daughter. I'd prefer to think in terms of twenty-four hours, but I guess that's not going to happen. Today is Monday and I hope very much to have met my daughter by the end of the week at the latest. If not, well, I'm not going away without meeting her, so I guess I'll just turn up at Villa de l'Espoir and introduce myself to her. With or without you there.' He paused and gave her a serious look. 'But I want my first meeting with my daughter to be conflict free and I hope that it will include you as well.'

24

Harriet walked back to Villa de l'Espoir trying to get her thoughts into some sort of order, whilst admitting to herself she didn't have the faintest idea of how to handle the situation. It was admittedly something that had always been at the back of her mind as a possibility but one she'd never truly expected to happen. Seeing Jack after all these years had aroused a mix of unexpected feelings too. Feelings of regret, fury with both the way he'd stalked her and demanded to meet Elodie, but she also couldn't deny there had been a certain pleasure, a recognition of feelings she'd thought were buried forever. Learning he was divorced had given her a jolt. Would the two of them have made a go of being married, if she'd been brave enough all those years ago and told him about Elodie? Or would they too have ended up divorced? The thought popped into her head, *Well you're both single again now, maybe...*

Thrusting that particular unsettling thought aside, she realised she'd been pushed into a corner by Jack. She was going to have to tell Elodie who her father was and break the news that he was in town and wanted to meet her. Would she agree? Or would she refuse? If that happened, Harriet knew she'd have no chance of stopping Jack taking matters into his own hands. He would turn up at the villa and either baldly announce, 'Hi, I'm your father,' or more likely, as he didn't want any conflict, he'd approach it sensitively: 'Hello Elodie. I'm Jack and I understand I'm your long-lost father.'

Harriet could see the genuinely happy smile that would light up his face as he spoke those words. If he chose to introduce himself that way, then Elodie would surely respond positively. Jack had always exuded a certain charisma that made people warm to him, especially women.

Pressing the remote to open the side gate into the Villa, Harriet knew there was only one thing she could do. Tell Elodie the truth and then wait for Elodie's reaction. Now she just had to find the right moment to tell her – and to brace herself for the inevitable questions she knew would follow.

* * *

Jack ordered another coffee and stayed where he was after Harriet had left. She hadn't exactly stormed off after he'd made the comment about meeting Elodie by the end of the week, but she'd clearly been cross and upset. A definite reminder of the feisty woman he'd been deeply in love with all those years ago. And the signs had all been there back then, assuring him she felt the same way about him.

Only it turned out she didn't. Hell, he'd even begged her to go with him back to the States when his father's heart attack made it imperative he returned. But it was impossible for her to leave her recently widowed mother alone. They were all the family they both had, she'd said. Four years later, though, it seemed that she hadn't thought twice about leaving her, and their daughter, to go to Australia of all places. Lizzie hadn't been able to tell him anything about the man Harriet had married, only that she was now back in Europe, a widow.

Jack's thoughts switched to Elodie, his daughter. He'd always wanted a daughter, but after Nathan's birth, Sabrina had dashed any hopes he'd been secretly harbouring about having more children, at least one, if not more, by flatly refusing to have another baby. Which was probably just as well – Sabrina's mothering instincts were, to put it politely, not close to the surface.

He had so much to learn about this new grown-up daughter of his. Jack didn't believe for a moment that she wasn't interested in meeting him.

If she was interested enough to ask questions about him, then meeting up was the next logical step. Hopefully the meeting would happen soon. If Harriet was trying to delay things, she could only do that for so long before he'd take matters into his own hands. He'd leave it for a few days now and then he'd contact her again, insist he'd waited long enough. As Elodie's father, he had every right to meet his daughter and he was determined to do so. There was no way he was leaving France now, not until he and his daughter had become acquainted. Hell, he'd change his visa and extend his stay here if that proved to be necessary.

Getting to know Elodie was the priority now. Learning about her; telling her about her American family. Making up for all the lost years. And it could be fun getting to know Harriet again too in the process. Those long-ago loving feelings that he'd buried deep down, maybe they hadn't died away completely. There was no denying that jolt of attraction for Harriet he'd felt as they'd come face to face for the first time in years. Attraction definitely; it couldn't be more than that after all this time, could it?

Jack drank his coffee thoughtfully. He was single. She was single. Although maybe the relationship with this Hugo was serious. Perhaps he'd flirt a little with Harriet, see if she responded. They were both older and wiser now, not the naive youngsters they'd been back then. Maybe he'd suggest the three of them took some 'family outings' together. He smiled at the thought. Was it possible that this time around their relationship could work out?

Jack glanced at his watch. Time to meet up with the other woman in his life for lunch. How she would react to his news was any one's guess. Maybe he'd keep quiet about it for a little while longer.

25

'Slight change of plan,' Hugo said as he picked Harriet up that evening. 'I hope you don't mind. I'd forgotten that several restaurants close on Monday evenings, among them my favourite. So if it's okay with you, I thought we'd have a wander around the marina and then have supper in my apartment. There's a painting there you might like to see.'

The thought crossed Harriet's mind, was this a 'come up and see my etchings' line? It was a thought she promptly dismissed. Hugo simply wasn't that kind of man. Besides, if he'd asked if she would like to see his apartment she would have said yes immediately.

'A walk around the marina sounds good and I'm more than happy to eat in the apartment tonight rather than go to a restaurant,' she said. With so many eateries around, the chances of bumping into Jack were slim but she'd been on tenterhooks ever since their meeting. Eating in would at least eliminate that risk.

Wandering around Port Vauban Marina, Harriet was amazed by the number of pontoons and the luxury boats moored alongside them. 'The really expensive yachts are over there,' Hugo said, pointing across the harbour. 'Billionaires Quay. Security now keeps both the locals and the tourists away from that area of the marina. Look,' and he gestured towards a hovering helicopter. 'Someone's arriving.' They watched as the helicopter dropped lower and lower until it landed on the landing pad of a large yacht at the far end of the quay and the whine of the turbine decreased as the blades slowly stopped rotating. 'Come on,' Hugo said. 'Time for supper.'

Hugo's apartment, on the sixth floor of an apartment block not far from the marina, had a panoramic view of the harbour from the balcony.

'Thankfully, the delicatessen was open this afternoon,' he said. 'So I haven't had to do any actual cooking.'

'Can I help with anything?' Harriet asked.

Hugo shook his head. 'I'm all organised, thanks. Have a look around while I do the last-minute preparation. The painting I think you will really like is in the sitting room.'

Harriet made her way through to the sitting room with its leather Chesterfield settee and three matching armchairs, a coffee table and a bookcase with glass doors. For a large room, it was quite minimalistic. Harriet's eyes were drawn to the seascape on one of the walls. She stood looking at it for several moments, drinking it in.

Painted in oils with a lightness of hand Harriet envied, it showed an old woman wearing a black swimming costume, evidently fresh from a swim, battling with a breeze that was preventing her from wrapping a towel around herself. It was poignant, evocative and a perfectly executed portrait of a woman totally at ease with herself and her surroundings.

'This is amazing,' she called out. 'Is it a local artist?'

'The artist was my grandmother,' Hugo said quietly, coming to stand at her side. 'She never realised just how good she was. Her life was lived around her family, painting was never more than a hobby done at odd moments.' He handed Harriet one of the two glasses of white wine he was holding. 'Shall we take this out on to the balcony?' and Hugo slid one of the glass doors open.

Standing there near the safety rail looking out at the traffic down below, the yachts in the marina across the way and, in the far distance again, the white horse waves of the Mediterranean dancing in the evening sun, Harriet felt herself relaxing for the first time since the meeting with Jack that morning.

'You inferred earlier that tonight you were glad not to be eating in a restaurant,' Hugo asked quietly. 'Any particular reason for that?'

Harriet breathed out. Time to come clean with Hugo. 'Yes. Elodie's father is in town and wants to meet her. I would have spent the evening expecting to bump into him.'

A buzzer in the kitchen buzzed. 'The frites are ready. We'll talk as we eat.'

A quiche and a bowl of salad were already on the table in the kitchen diner and Hugo quickly tipped the frites into a warmed bowl and placed it on the table. 'Bon appétit,' he said, as he joined her sitting at the table. 'Sorry it's more supper than the gourmet dinner that I planned to treat you to.'

'This quiche is delicious, as are the frites,' Harriet assured him after a few mouthfuls.

'Is Elodie's father likely to be a problem?' Hugo asked, once both their appetites had been sated.

'No... yes, I don't know,' Harriet said, shaking her head in despair. 'It's Elodie who is likely to cause problems, to be honest – I've never told her who her father is. Just recently, she's been asking for his name. She says she doesn't want to go looking for him or anything, just wants to know his name. Whether that will change once I've told her he's here in Juan...' Harriet shrugged. 'If she refuses to meet him, I know Jack will force the issue. I need to find the right moment to talk to her. I can't baldly announce the fact, *oh by the way your unknown father is in town and wants to meet you.*'

'Why can't you say it like it is?'

'Because...' Harriet stopped. Hugo had a point. Why couldn't she do just that? She had to stop making assumptions and taking decisions that weren't hers alone to make. Deep down, she knew it was her guilty conscience for abandoning Elodie and deceiving Jack in the first place that made her intent on trying to put things right, in her own way. Now her secret was known to the one person who had every right to know the truth, it was down to her to put things right between them all. Both she and Jack had been absent parents to Elodie, but her own absence had been a personal choice, one that she'd regretted for the past twenty years.

Whereas Jack, Jack had never had the opportunity to be a father to Elodie. Guilty feelings flooded into Harriet's mind. Why couldn't she simply tell Elodie the truth?

'She's a grown woman, she's not a child, so she can make the decision to see or not to see him. Nobody is going to force her or take her to court,' Hugo said gently.

'I'm not so sure about that,' Harriet said. 'Jack is hell-bent on meeting her. I met him this morning at his request and I've already had a text this afternoon asking if I've talked to her yet. I've ignored it for now.' Harriet fell silent for a few seconds. 'I know he'll take matters into his own hands if she refuses to see him – turn up at the villa, or waylay Elodie in town. Jack is not someone who is going to take no for an answer.'

'Perhaps Elodie will change her mind when she learns he's actually here in Juan?'

'She might eventually, but I doubt Jack would be willing to wait for that moment.' Harriet rubbed her eyes. 'Sorry, I didn't mean to unburden myself on you. Life has become so complicated and overwhelming that I'm beginning to wish I'd stayed in Australia out of everyone's way.'

'But then you and I wouldn't have met,' Hugo said, pushing his chair back and standing up. 'My advice, for what it's worth, is to tell Elodie as soon as possible that Jack is in town and wants to meet. Once you have a reaction from her, you can make a plan on how...' he paused. 'On how we all move forward.' He began to clear the table as Harriet thought about his words. 'Now, I can offer you a cheese course or, if you prefer, there are two lavender crème brûlées in the fridge.'

'Crème brûlée please.' Harriet smiled up at him.

He was right, of course. She had to talk to Elodie, as well as Gabby, soon, but this evening she would try to put Jack Ellicott's appearance back in her life out of her mind. It was time to change the subject.

'Tell me more about your talented grandmother,' she said, as her spoon cracked through the hard sugary top of her dessert.

26

Harriet spent most of Tuesday morning painting and was surveying her work with a critical eye when Gabby brought her a cup of coffee. She smiled when she saw what Harriet was painting. Lulu.

'You've not lost your touch,' she said. 'You've captured her eye expression brilliantly. Come and have your coffee with me.'

Moving across to join her mother by the table, Harriet realised that now was the perfect opportunity to talk to Gabby about Jack being in town. Talking to a non-judgemental Hugo last night had helped, and she instinctively knew Gabby would be equally as helpful, probably more as she was closer to the problem. Besides, it truly was time for her to ask Gabby's forgiveness.

'Where's Elodie this morning?' Harriet didn't want to risk starting a conversation about Jack if there was the possibility that Elodie would walk in on them.

'Gone to the post office and to take some photographs of the children's playground for an article.'

Harriet took a couple of sips of her coffee, followed by a deep breath.

'I need to tell you something. Elodie's father is in town.'

Gabby gave her a startled look and waited for her to continue.

'At his son's wedding, Lizzie mentioned to him that I'd had a baby a mere six months after he returned to America.'

Gabby absorbed the fact that Elodie's father had been an American and waited.

'He did the maths and began to wonder whether it was his baby, decided to track me down and find out the truth. Apparently he's always wanted a daughter,' Harriet said. 'And now he knows he has one, he wants to meet her. Be involved in her life too, I think. He hasn't said that in so many words, but that seems to be the tacit message behind his words.'

'Well, that's only natural,' Gabby said. 'I know Elodie has become curious lately about who she is, so maybe she'll be glad to know he's here and wants to meet her.'

'Elodie has said repeatedly that she just wants to know his name, whether we were in a relationship and what Jack – that's his name – was like. She's told me, and you I think, she's not interested in meeting her father face to face.' Harriet paused. 'And I know Jack isn't going to settle for anything less.'

'Once Elodie knows he wants to meet her, she'll probably change her mind.'

'You know her better than anyone, do you think she will react like that?'

Gabby shrugged. 'I think the chances are quite high that she will be sufficiently curious when she learns he is actually here in Juan-les-Pins, that she'll agree, even want, to meet him.'

Harriet drank some of her coffee.

'Can I ask you something?' Gabby said quietly.

'Of course.'

'Were you in a proper relationship with this Jack? You do know for sure that he is the father? You never brought him home to meet me.'

'We were in love.' Harriet gave a wry smile. 'Really in love. I was scared to admit it to you because I knew he wanted me to move to America and I didn't know how you would react to that. The weekend he had to leave unexpectedly, we'd planned for him to come over to Dartmouth to meet you. Instead he was on his way to Heathrow.'

'I'm relieved to hear that Elodie was conceived with love,' Gabby said.

'I wish you'd talked to me about it, though. Maybe we could have found a way for the two of you to be together.'

'I'm sorry I didn't talk to you, but back then I was a bit lost, overwhelmed really with everything. You were still grieving Dad too. I didn't want to add my troubles onto you. Being a single mum from the offset seemed like the best option at the time.'

'You were wonderful with Elodie when she was little,' Gabby said. 'You've missed out on so much of her life,' and Gabby shook her head, her voice full of compassion.

'I loved her from the moment she was born. Truly, I must have been out of my tiny mind marrying Todd. When he refused to raise another man's child, insisting it would be better all round to leave Elodie with you, I should have realised the sort of man he was and walked away. Like you wanted me to.' Harriet's eyes glistened. 'My only consolation was that I knew you'd love and look after her.' Harriet looked at her mother. 'Which you did.' She fell silent for a moment. 'I'll always be eternally grateful to you for taking her, but I realise now how selfish I was, expecting you to bring her up alone. It put your own life on hold. Until I left Elodie with you, you had no ties, no responsibilities. You were a free woman. You could have done anything you wanted. Travelled. Seen the world.'

Gabby shook her head. 'No, I wouldn't. Your dad had been dead for a few years when you left, but I still hadn't grown used to him not being there. You leaving Elodie with me finally brought me out of the depression I sank into when Eric died. I had to focus on doing, being, the best for her. She was something for me to love unconditionally. And apart from anything else, she helped me get over the loss of you in my life.' Gabby reached out to take hold of Harriet's hand and a silence fell between them as they both sat with their own thoughts. 'Would it help if I'm with you when you talk to Elodie?'

Harriet shook her head. 'Thanks, but this is something I need to do myself, to try to explain it all. But maybe you could talk to her afterwards?'

'Of course. How long is Jack in France for?' Gabby asked.

'I didn't ask. From the way he was talking though, I suspect it's open-ended.'

'I hope there's time for me to get to meet him too.' Gabby hesitated. 'How did you feel meeting him again?'

Harriet knew what her mother was really asking – did she still have feelings for Jack.

'It was weird really. At first, I was more concerned with finding out what he actually wanted from me. But then there was undoubtedly a frisson of something between us.' Harriet sighed. 'I think I need to concentrate on sorting things out between him and Elodie. Treat him like an old friend if I can.'

Gabby glanced at her watch. 'Talking of old friends. Colette is coming for lunch with Philippe and me – but before that we're going to brave the cave. I've put it off far too long. They'll both be here soon. Do you want to join us?'

'Oh, yes please. I was down in the garage the other day and for the life of me I couldn't see a secret cave entrance,' Harriet said. 'Are you sure it hasn't been blocked up?'

Gabby shook her head. 'It's still there. I just hope and pray if there is anything down there that it is not something horrible – or even something I have to report to the authorities.'

* * *

Half an hour later, the four of them made their way into the garage. All the cardboard from moving had been taken to the recycling and apart from a few cleaning things that Gabby had placed on the shelves, a bucket and mop in the corner, the garage was empty.

'How do we get into this cave?' Colette asked, looking around. 'Where is the door?'

'Did you bring the piece of stiff wire I wanted?' Gabby asked Philippe. He nodded and took a short length of wire out of his pocket and handed it to her.

'D'accord,' Gabby said, moving towards the shelves. 'I watched my father open this hidden door several times but he only ever allowed me to open it once, so I hope I can find the exact location to lift the latch inside.'

The other three were quiet as Gabby concentrated on the wooden trimming running down the left-hand side of the shelves.

'Two inches inward between the fourth and third shelves from the top,' she muttered, fingering the pyrography decoration of flowers and leaves on stalks that had been burnt into the trimming around the shelf unit, as her eyes searched for and finally found what she was looking for. Gabby gave a small smile and pushed the wire she was holding into the burnt centre of one of the flowers. A flower with an almost invisible hole in the centre, that nobody would guess covered the secret opening to the cave entrance. Feeling the latch on the other side give, she reached out to grip the side of the shelf unit. As she pulled it towards her, the shelving unit appeared to split into two parts with the left-hand side opening like a door and revealing a flight of steps down into the cave.

'Never seen a door opened like that before,' Colette said, watching in astonishment as Gabby folded the door back safely. 'Secret door to end all secret doors. Trust Hervé to dream up something like that.'

Gabby took the wire out of the hole and put it on the top shelf. If the door was to close when they were all down in the cave, there was a handle to work the latch from inside.

'Mon Dieu, such a brilliant simple design,' Philippe said, shaking his head as he looked closely at the unit. 'Uncomplicated and unobtrusive. Even the hinges were undetectable when the shelf unit was in position.'

Gabby stood at the top of the stairs and reached for the light switch she remembered being on the wall and an overhead light sprang into life. 'Come on then, let's take a look and see what we find,' and Gabby led the way down the steps.

They all stood on the earth floor of the cave looking around in amazement. Floor-to-ceiling wine racks filled with dusty bottles lined three walls, open boxes filled with a variety of goods from ornaments and books to puzzles and toys were on the floor everywhere. There was a table with several old-fashioned suitcases underneath it and on top a solitary blue and white dust-covered pot with a Chinese look about it, an old-fashioned jewellery box and a sealed envelope with 'Gabriella' scrawled across it in faded writing.

Philippe was the first to move. He carefully inspected a couple of bottles in the wine rack, pulling them out to read the labels. 'You've got some good wine here. Several bottles of champagne too.'

Harriet started to look in a couple of the nearest boxes, while Colette joined Gabby, who was standing by the table staring at the three items there.

'I remember that pot being in the sitting room filled with spoons for some strange reason. Family legend always said it belonged to my great-great-great grandfather who sailed on the clipper boats and brought it back from China. And that's my mother's jewellery box,' Gabby said slowly. 'She loved her jewellery, not that she had much, but what she did have was lovely. I remember wondering why there was no mention of it when the house was officially cleared. I assumed that after Maman died, he'd got rid of it.'

'He's left you a letter too. And Gabby...' Colette paused. 'As the proprié-taire of a brocante, I think that pot is more than it seems at first. Hervé, he actually showed it to me on his last visit. He wanted to know what I thought in confidence. I told him it looked like what is called a brush pot, possibly seventeenth century, but he needed to have it checked by an expert.'

'Do you think he took your advice?'

'Seeing it here, set aside, waiting for you to find, I think he probably did.'

Gabby glanced at her. 'How unusual is it?' she asked as Philippe and Harriet joined them by the table.

Colette pulled a face. 'You need a real expert, like I told Hervé, but I think it's quite a rare valuable piece.'

Gabby reached out and picked up the jewellery box and the letter. 'I'll take these upstairs, the pot can stay down here. I've seen enough for now. Let's have lunch.' She turned to Philippe. 'Maybe bring one of those bottles of wine? I think we could all do with an aperitif before lunch.'

27

Lunch was a noisy affair. Elodie had arrived home to find Gabby, Colette and Harriet enjoying an aperitif on the terrace, while Philippe prepared a lunch of croque-monsieur and salads, insisting that the women left him to it. Gabby handed Elodie a glass of wine.

'Are we celebrating something?' Elodie asked, before taking a sip of her wine. 'Oooh, this is nice.'

'Lot's more where that came from in the secret cave,' Harriet said mischievously.

'Secret cave? Have I missed something exciting?'

'There's a secret door in the garage down to a cave under the house that great-granddad Hervé used as a wine cellar and as a storage space for special things,' Harriet explained.

Elodie turned to look at her grandmother, wide-eyed. 'How did you find out about that? When can I see it?'

Gabby shrugged. 'I've always known about the cave, I'd simply forgotten it existed. It certainly didn't have wine or anything special in it when I was living here before.'

* * *

Colette left soon after lunch, saying she'd promised Lianna the afternoon off. 'I can give you the name of an antique expert when you are ready,' she said quietly as Gabby opened the electric gate and saw her out.

'Thank you. I'll come and talk to you soon,' Gabby said. She walked back into the villa, where Harriet and Elodie were clearing the table and Philippe was cleaning the kitchen surfaces and loading the dishwasher. Gabby looked at the envelope with her name on it that she'd placed in the Hotel du Provençal dish on the dresser before lunch.

'Are you going to open it now?' Philippe asked.

'Not just yet. Later.' She needed to get her head around the fact that her father had left her a letter to find after his death. She couldn't think what he could possibly have to say to her after their estrangement for so many years.

'Would you like me to leave you while you read it in private?' Philippe said gently.

'No, please stay,' she caught hold of his hand. 'I'd rather you were with me when I read it than anybody else.'

Philippe gave her a hug. 'Whatever is in the letter, remember it's all in the past. He was the person responsible for his actions, not you.' He placed a gentle kiss on her forehead. 'I promise, whatever life throws at you, either in the letter or in the future, we'll face it together, so stop worrying about the contents of both the cave and that letter.'

Gabby gave a grateful smile. Before she could respond Harriet walked into the kitchen, Lulu following close on her heels.

'Elodie and I are going to walk Lulu and talk,' Harriet said, looking at her mother. 'We'll see you in a bit.'

'Good luck,' Gabby said quietly.

Philippe raised his eyebrows at her as the villa door closed behind them and Gabby held up crossed fingers, before telling him about her conversation with Harriet that morning.

* * *

Elodie had been surprised when Harriet had asked, as they were clearing the lunch things, if she was busy that afternoon.

'Nothing madly urgent that I can't put off. Why?'

'I thought we could walk Lulu together and talk.'

'Talk?'

'Yes. Talk. Properly.'

'I'd like that. I want to talk to you too. A walk in the woods? It will be cooler there.'

For the first five or ten minutes of their walk, conversation was stilted and mundane, about nothing in particular. It wasn't until they'd walked through the suburban streets of Juan-les-Pins, busy with locals and holidaymakers, and were on the edge of Cap D'Antibes woods that Elodie said, 'Does wanting to talk to me properly mean you've decided to answer my questions? To tell me the truth?'

Harriet nodded. 'Yes.'

As they entered the shade of the woods, Elodie bent down and unclipped Lulu so she could wander off the path and explore, and Harriet took a deep breath.

'Your father's name is Jack Ellicott, he is American and I never told him about you because he'd unexpectedly returned to America before I realised I was pregnant. Before you ask, I was in love with him and it broke my heart that it didn't work out.'

Elodie stopped, turning to place her hand on Harriet's arm. 'My father is American?'

Harriet nodded. 'Yes.'

'Why did he return unexpectedly? Didn't he plan on going back?'

'His father was gravely ill. He had another month on his visa before he was due to return.'

'Did you stay in contact?'

'We did keep in touch initially, until I found out I was pregnant when I decided he had enough problems to deal with, so a clean break would be the best thing for everyone.'

As well as struggling to get her head around how different her life might have been if Harriet had told Jack Ellicott about her, Elodie had even more questions she needed to ask now she knew her father's name. 'Did you have a plan to stay together when his visa ended? Would you have gone to America to be with him? Or would he have tried to stay in England?'

'I have no idea what would have happened. We hadn't really talked about it,' Harriet said slowly. 'We loved being together and naively thought everything would work out. But he did tell me that his parents hoped he'd marry a friend's daughter.' She glanced at Elodie. 'So I knew he'd have that to sort out when he arrived back in the US. Jack did ask me to go with him when he left. I didn't feel I could leave Gabby at that time.'

Elodie was silent as they walked further into the woods, Lulu never out of sight. 'This is so ironic.'

'Why?'

'Because I'd decided to stop asking you about my father. I felt I was being unkind in badgering you for answers about a part of your life that was obviously not happy.' Elodie was silent for a few seconds. 'I'm curious though – what made you change your mind about telling me?'

'That's part of the reason I want to talk to you.' Harriet took a deep breath. 'Jack is in Juan and he wants to meet you.'

Elodie stopped dead and looked at her. 'My father is here?'

Harriet nodded. 'Yes. It seems he came here specifically to confront me about you – and to meet you.'

'How did you feel when you met him again? Do you still like him?'

Harriet shrugged. 'I was surprised. I'd never expected to see him again, but I was more worried about protecting you and how you'd react to meeting him, than assessing my own feelings.'

'He's forced your hand, hasn't he? You still wouldn't have told me otherwise would you?' Elodie stared at Harriet.

'That's not true. I was planning to answer all your questions soon, but yes, Jack turning up has rather brought things to a head.'

Seeing another dog walker approaching them along the path, Elodie called Lulu and clipped her lead on. She waited until the woman and the dog had passed them before turning to Harriet.

'I've lived for twenty-four years without knowing anything about my father. Not really wanting to. I'd accepted the lack of both mother and father figures in my life. It was only when you came back that I realised I didn't know the full details of me. How I came into existence.' She paused.

'Basically, I think I needed reassurance really that I was wanted. That I wasn't the result of a one-night stand... or something horrible.'

Harriet gave her a shocked look. 'No.'

'I'm so pleased that you were in a happy relationship with him. I thought that once you'd told me his name, you'd talk to me about him and I'd learn enough about him from you. I honestly thought that would be enough, that I didn't need to start looking for him.' Elodie gave a deep sigh. 'Now I don't know what to do. It wasn't his fault he didn't get the opportunity to be a father. Telling me he's here in town looking to meet me changes things – and meeting him will change everything even more. I don't know how I feel any more.'

'Jack has done nothing wrong. I was the one at fault in all this for not telling him about you. Now he knows, he is determined to right the wrong that I did – even if it is years late.' Harriet glanced at Elodie. 'Jack is one of the good guys. You need to meet him.'

28

Gabby and Philippe sat out on the terrace after Harriet and Elodie left to walk Lulu, the jewellery box and the sealed envelope on the table in front of them. The jewellery box would simply contain her mother's wedding and engagement rings and the few pieces of costume jewellery that Gabby remembered her possessing. The letter, on the other hand...

Gabby stared at her name on the envelope, feeling more unsettled than she had for a long time.

'I think this is the first letter I've ever had from him,' she said. 'I could just throw it away unopened, I suppose. He'll never know whether I've read it or not.'

'Then you would be left forever wondering what he'd wanted to say to you,' Philippe said quietly.

'I know, but what if not knowing was the better alternative to reading the contents?' Gabby looked at him. 'I had his voice in my head for so long, telling me I'd let the family down, I was worthless, I meant nothing to him. It took years for me to silence that. I might be seventy years old, but I'm scared the contents of the letter might cause his voice in my head to start up again. Open old wounds.'

'*Ma cherie*, you have me at your side if it should happen. I promise I will not allow the voice to take up residence in your head again. I know the person you are. You are kindness itself, never letting anyone down, you are not worthless – and you mean everything to me. *D'accord?'*

Gabby nodded and gave Philippe a grateful smile – she was so lucky to have him in her life – before reaching out for the envelope. It opened easily, the sealing glue having deteriorated over the years it had lain in the cave. Carefully, Gabby took out three pieces of paper, two of which were covered in handwriting she recognised even though it was shakier than the last time she had seen it. She placed those on the table and looked at the other piece of paper, delaying for as long as possible the reading of the letter.

This first piece was a typed letter from a firm of auctioneers in Paris, dated eleven years ago. Reading it, Gabby realised it was detailing their thoughts on the provenance of the brush pot in the cave and giving a suggested reserve price if it were to be auctioned. Her eyes widened as she saw the figure. Silently, she handed the piece of paper to Philippe before reaching out and picking up the two pages of the letter and beginning to read it.

By the time she reached the end of the second page, she was biting her bottom lip and blinking hard.

Philippe regarded her with concern. 'Gabriella, *ma cherie, tu vas bien?'*

'I'm okay,' she sniffed. 'Thankfully, it's not as horrible as I had been anticipating. He says my maman never forgave him for driving me away and he regretted his actions that caused her such pain and drove me out of their lives. But then blames me for getting mixed up with Christophe Lampeter and becoming pregnant in the first place. Here, you can read it,' and she held the pages out to Philippe. 'The things in the cellar are apparently his way of trying to make amends. I just wish he hadn't waited until he knew he was dying to write his regrets down. I wish too he could have brought himself to say them to me face to face, but I guess that was a step too far.'

Carefully, Philippe pushed the jewellery box towards her. 'Perhaps seeing and holding your maman's jewellery would bring back some happier memories.'

Opening the box and seeing the pieces her mother had treasured which were now hers was a bittersweet moment for Gabby. There were a couple of pieces that Gabby didn't recognise – two gold brooches and an eternity ring set with what looked like rubies and diamonds.

'These stones are too big to be real, surely,' she said, holding it out for Philippe to take a look. 'The diamonds at least have to be zircons, don't you think?'

'They look real enough. The setting is good.' Philippe shrugged. 'I don't know. There's a piece of folded paper underneath,' he said, moving the jewellery to one side and lifting the paper out.

'What is it? Please, not another letter.' Gabby looked at him anxiously.

'It's the provenance for the ring. It's a genuine 1920s eternity ring.'

Gabby looked at him in disbelief. 'Where on earth did my father get the money to buy something like that? I mean, the wine in the cellar is one thing and the brush pot has been in the family for generations, but that ring...' she gestured helplessly at Philippe. 'I need to go and talk to Colette soon.'

* * *

After Elodie and Harriet had parted, leaving Elodie reeling after learning the bombshell news about Jack being in Juan, Elodie had returned to the villa and gone straight up to her room. She had a tight deadline for one of her features and she'd spent the rest of the afternoon and most of the evening upstairs working. It was nearly ten o'clock when she pressed send on the email and leant back against her chair with a sigh of relief.

Concentrating had been hard with her thoughts constantly switching away from the words in front of her to thoughts of Jack and what she should do. She longed to talk to Gazz, tell him the news, ask his advice, but he and Mickaêl had gone to Monaco for the evening to support the local football team in a fundraising event.

Pushing her chair back and standing, Elodie stretched her arms up and rolled her shoulders. Time for a swim.

One of the things she adored about having a pool in the garden was the fact that she could jump in and swim whenever she felt like it. Since moving in, swimming under the light of the moon had become an occasional delightful treat. Not the thrashing front crawl she did during the daytime, but a leisurely breaststroke for a few lengths, before turning onto her back and floating. It never failed to relax her and tonight she needed that calming effect to help get her thoughts in order.

There was no sign of either Harriet or Gabby as she dropped her towel on the terrace and walked down the steps into the shallow end of the pool. She swam three lengths slowly, deliberately, before turning onto her back and floating. She looked at the moon high in the sky, noticed the lack of visible stars because of the light pollution, heard the faint hum of distant traffic and the noise of the pool pump gently moving the water against the sides of the pool.

Elodie closed her eyes briefly, bliss. No thoughts of Jack Ellicott pushing their way into her consciousness.

'Elodie.'

She opened her eyes to find Gabby standing on the terrace watching her. 'Hi.'

'I'm making a hot chocolate. Care to join me when you're ready?'

'Thanks, that would be great. A couple more lengths and I'll get out.'

Five minutes later, wrapped in her towel, Gabby handed her a mug of hot chocolate and Elodie took a sip. 'Delicious. Thank you for this.'

Gabby gave a nonchalant shrug. 'You're welcome.' She took a sip of her own drink.

'Gabby?' Elodie hesitated. 'Has Harriet told you what she told me this afternoon about my father?'

'Yes, a little. His name and the fact that he is American and that...'

'And that he wants to meet me,' Elodie interrupted.

Gabby nodded. 'How do you feel about that?' she asked quietly.

'Nervous for all sorts of reasons. Life has already changed so much in the last year – first with Harriet showing up and then us all moving here and now a father I never truly expected to meet arrives on the scene. I'm not sure how I'll cope with suddenly having two parents, having had none for so long. Will he like me? Will I like him? Does he plan on staying around? Will he and Harriet get together again? Does he want to play a belated game of happy families?' Elodie gave a huge sigh. 'A large part of me wants desperately to meet him, to complete the missing piece of me and to know where I came from, but I just think it's going to cause a massive disruption to all our lives. Unless of course he just says hi and disappears back to America, never to be heard from again. He could simply want to meet me, acknowledge my presence with some sort of conciliatory gesture and leave again, having absolved his guilty conscience over getting Harriet pregnant. And he's the only one who would benefit from behaving like that. If that's what he plans, there's no real point to meeting him.'

Gabby drank some hot chocolate and sat quietly for a moment. 'What I'm about to say are just my thoughts as I haven't met Jack either. I think he probably does feel guilty, but not for the reason you suggest. The guilt comes from unintentionally letting you, his daughter, down. The way he went about finding and contacting Harriet once he heard that she'd had a daughter soon after he returned to America speaks volumes to me about the man and his integrity. He wants to put things right by acknowledging that you are his daughter and being in your life.'

'You honestly think that?'

Gabby nodded. 'I do. Of course things will change, but I think they will be good changes.'

'So basically you think I should meet him?' Elodie said quietly.

'I think it would be the grown-up thing for you to do, yes, but it's your decision.'

29

The next day, Gabby walked down to the brocante to see Colette. Both Colette and Lianna were at the desk when she arrived and were pleased to see her.

'Can you take a break? I could really do with talking to you,' Gabby said.

Within minutes, the two of them were in Colette's kitchen, the coffee was brewing and Colette looked at Gabby expectantly.

'I took a look in Maman's jewellery box and I found this.' She held out her right hand with the eternity ring on her fourth finger.

'Wow, that's a beauty,' Colette said.

'There was a provenance with it authenticating it as genuine 1920s.' Gabby looked at Colette. 'You told me about Hervé visiting you, do you have any idea of how he could afford something like this? I mean, this isn't something he could pick up at a *vide-grenier* boot sale, is it?'

Colette poured them both a coffee and sat down. 'I honestly don't know the truth, but I can hazard a guess. You know he was always buying and selling things. Not just at vide-greniers but antique fairs and the like. He gained quite a reputation for knowing what was good and what was worth buying. He enjoyed tracking things down too. The last time I saw him, though, he wanted to know whether I'd sell or buy his boat from him.'

'Boat? How long had he had a boat? I never knew him to be remotely interested in owning one or wanting to go fishing – I'm presuming that's what he used it for?'

'Amongst other things,' Colette said. 'Of course I had to say no about the boat, just not my thing. It was a semi-rigid inflatable – a RIB – quite sturdy and speedy. People hired him to take them out to the Iles des Lérins rather than take the regular ferry boats. A more exciting journey, bouncing across the waves.' Colette smiled as she noticed Gabby's wide-eyed stare.

'People actually entrusted their lives to him?'

Colette nodded. 'He did obtain the right licence and the necessary life jackets and things.' She paused. 'The other thing he used the RIB for was taking one or two divers out to dive the wrecks around the coast.'

Gabby looked at Colette and waited. She knew there were several wrecks out in the bay, a couple dating from the eighteenth century, as well as a nineteenth-century steamship. Something in Colette's voice warned her she wouldn't like what she was about to hear.

'Day and night-time dives. I heard that the gendarmes questioned him several times about the divers he took out at night. Evidently, they suggested he stopped taking them out as apparently they were known to be looters of underwater sites. The gendarmes warned him that when the divers were arrested, which they would be, he could be charged with being an accomplice.'

'Did he stop?'

Colette nodded. 'Yes. Told the gendarmes he ran a legitimate business. He then told the divers they had to find someone else for all their diving trips, day and night. Which they did. About a month later, they were arrested returning from a night trip. And they did have several ancient artefacts, pottery and suchlike, on board.'

'Was Hervé ever charged?'

'Not as far as I know. He got rid of the boat, sold it to someone in Golfe Juan. I think he knew he was dying by then. He certainly didn't look well.'

Gabby sighed and fiddled with the ring on her finger. 'So, do you believe him about the divers not bringing looted stuff on board his boat?'

'You know, I think I do,' Colette said. 'When I came back, he'd changed a lot and after your maman died, he seemed to shrink. He kept himself more and more to himself. I think he realised in the past he'd had a few suspect dealings and he didn't intend to be caught up in anyone else's dubious activities.' She reached out and looked at the ring on Gabby's finger again. 'I think this was probably one of his better "deals" with one of the antique dealers, especially as there is a provenance. Wear it and enjoy it.'

30

The days dragged on with no decision from Elodie about meeting her father. Harriet became more and more stressed and uptight wondering what, and when, Elodie was going to decide about Jack. Elodie was clearly avoiding her and Jack had begun sending text messages every day demanding to know if she'd talked to Elodie yet and when could they meet. Harriet answered one with a terse, 'I've talked to her. I'll text you when I have news' and ignored the others.

For the last two nights, she'd barely slept and was up before the sun. She didn't need the concerned look Gabby gave her Wednesday morning at breakfast, knowing that she had bags under her eyes and her skin was pale. When Hugo rang asking her to work that day, she agreed quickly, relieved to have something to do to take her mind off things.

The morning in the gallery was busy and before she realised it the two of them were sitting outside eating their lunch.

'I'm looking forward to introducing you to my friends tonight. I plan on picking you up at eight o'clock,' Hugo said. 'Is that okay with you?'

Harriet looked at him blankly.

'Supper party with Marcus and Freya. I asked you last week.'

Harriet rubbed her face in dismay. 'It had totally slipped my mind that it was tonight. I'm not sure I'm going to be much company, but yes, I'm looking forward to it too.' If nothing else, meeting new people would take her mind off her problems.

'Good. I'm sure you and Freya will have a lot to talk about. Any news on the Jack and Elodie situation?'

'Elodie is avoiding me and Jack keeps texting for news when there isn't any. Elodie hasn't said yes or no to meeting him.' Harriet sighed. 'I know it's only been two days and it will all sort itself eventually, but it's really stressing me at the moment.'

Hugo reached out and took hold of her hand. 'It must be incredibly hard for you at the moment but things will settle down eventually. In the meantime we'll enjoy this evening, okay?'

Harriet blinked away the tears that were threatening to fall. 'Thank you.'

* * *

Elodie and Gazz were sitting on the end of the jetty, their legs dangling in the water, enjoying their lunch. Elodie had got into the habit of bringing a picnic down to the beach most days, saying they were both so busy they'd never see each other otherwise. Today she'd brought salad baguettes and a couple of bottles of orange juice and after they'd eaten, she was hoping there would be time for her to talk to Gazz about her father.

They'd both finished their baguettes when Gazz put his arm around Elodie. 'I want to ask you something. I'm hoping I'll have enough money at the end of the season to rent a place of my own. It's been hard moving back in with my parents after having my own place in Paris. I am obviously extremely grateful to them, but I'm too old to be living at home.'

'I can understand that,' Elodie said. 'I've never actually lived on my own, it's always been Gabby and me. Now there are three of us, it is different and I think Harriet found it difficult too when we first arrived here.'

'I can't imagine not having you in my life now, so I was thinking about us living together,' Gazz said, looking at her anxiously. 'We would be a proper couple, no more snatched moments, no more saying goodnight and going home to separate beds. No pressure,' he added quietly. 'But I'd love that, if you would.'

The unexpected suggestion made Elodie catch her breath. It was something she'd secretly dreamed about happening whenever she and Gazz went their separate ways at the end of any time they spent with each other. Living together would tell the world (and Fiona!) that they were a proper couple, she thought happily. Smiling at Gazz she leant in and kissed him. 'I would love it too. Gabby has Philippe as well as Harriet in her life now, so I wouldn't feel guilty moving out of the villa. What sort of place do you want?'

Gazz waved his hand expansively in the direction of the Provençal. 'I hadn't really given it much thought, but an apartment there would be good.'

Elodie laughed. 'Maybe when you're running the largest beach enterprise on the coast. In the meantime?'

'A two-bedroom apartment in one of the nicer blocks on the seafront. I don't mind really, so long as you're there with me.' Gazz pulled her into his arms to give her a lingering kiss.

As they drew apart, Elodie said, 'Let's do it. But there is something I need to talk to you about today too.' She took a deep breath. 'My father is in town and wants to meet me.'

'Seriously?' Gazz stared at her. 'Your unknown father knows about you and has contacted you?'

'Not me directly, but Harriet.' Elodie paused. 'His name is Jack Ellicott and he's American. I don't know what to do. Harriet says he's a good guy and I need to meet him and Gabby says the same. But now I have the opportunity to do that, I'm not sure I want to.'

'Why not?'

'What if I don't like him? What if he doesn't like me? What if we meet once and that is it? He returns to the States and I never see him again? What if...?'

'What about if you do like him? What about if he does like you? What if he wants to be in your life on a permanent basis?'

Elodie sighed. 'Gabby has been my only family for so long, I never ever expected to have Harriet in my life, let alone my father, but suddenly both my parents have shown up.'

Gazz put his arm around her and held her tight. 'What has Harriet told you about him?'

'That he was the love of her life, that she didn't tell him about me because he had family problems and he was expected to marry a girl his parents had virtually chosen for him. She didn't want to land a baby on him in addition to all those problems.'

'I think you need to meet him,' Gazz said. 'Not only for your own sake but also for your mum's. The two of you meeting will help heal the hurt she undoubtedly caused your father when she failed to tell him he had a daughter.'

'I'll think about it a bit more, but I guess you're right,' Elodie replied. 'But I have to say I find the thought of my mother introducing me to my father absolutely bizarre.'

Before Gazz could reply, there was a shout from his assistant, Olivier.

'Lunchtime is over. I'll see you later hopefully?'

They shared another lingering kiss before Gazz reluctantly left.

Elodie screwed up the paper bags and picking up the empty bottles made her way slowly up the jetty and the beach towards the rubbish bins. She'd think about it a bit more, but she would probably tell Harriet that yes she would meet Jack Ellicott. Right now, though, she wanted to tell Gabby her own exciting news.

Gabby and Philippe were in the kitchen clearing away their lunch things when Elodie ran into the villa.

'Hi, guess what? Gazz is going to get his own place at the end of the season and he wants me to move in with him. Isn't that great? You don't mind do you, Gabby? I won't be leaving you alone. You've got Harriet and Philippe. And I'll still be somewhere in Juan.' She gave them both a beaming smile as she left the kitchen. 'I'm so happy.'

Gabby looked at Philippe in stunned silence.

'I didn't expect that news,' she said. 'I shall have to talk to her – and Harriet. The Villa is Elodie's home more than she realises.'

* * *

That evening, after Hugo had collected Harriet from the villa and driven them the short distance to, and parked in, Antibes itself, the two of them walked down through the market and onto the ramparts.

'I love this part of Antibes,' Harriet said as they stood for a few moments looking down over the rocks and breathing in the sea air. 'It's beautiful.'

'You'll love the view from the rooftop terrace of the Jackmans' town house even more,' Hugo said. 'Marcus bought the house as a project when he and Freya divorced. And then, a few years later, when they got back together, she moved in and they got remarried. A true happy-ever-after ending.'

'I didn't think those existed outside of books,' Harriet said quietly.

Hugo pressed the intercom button. 'Hi Marcus, it's Hugo and Harriet.'

'Come on up.'

The door lock clicked and Hugo pushed the door open.

'I warn you there are lots of stairs, but it is worth it.'

A few moments later, Harriet, standing on the roof terrace, caught her breath, not just from a slight breathlessness after three flights of stairs, but also because the terrace itself was amazing and the panoramic view out across the Mediterranean was truly spectacular.

Hugo introduced her to Freya as Marcus pressed a glass of champagne into her hand before taking Hugo off to ask his advice about a problem they were having with their internet connection.

'Hugo is a computer genius,' Freya said. 'We'd be lost without him. Sorts out all our IT problems.'

'Really? I didn't realise that,' Harriet said. 'I don't know him that well yet.' She took a sip of her champagne. 'I love the picture of yours he has in the gallery – "Communication"?'

'Thank you. Hugo has been talking about your work. Thinks we'd do well together in an exhibition, if you are up for it?'

'I've only managed to paint five paintings since I've started again and I'm not sure they're really up to a good enough standard. In theory, I've got all the time in the world to paint now...' Harriet sighed. 'But real life, it seems, has other ideas and distractions to keep me occupied at the moment. If you'll pardon the cliché, a curveball has thrown everything up in the air, stopping my concentration in its tracks.'

'Had a few of those – they're vicious beasts,' Freya laughed. 'If you want to talk...?'

Harriet smiled, not sure how much to confide in Freya, or how much Hugo might have told her about what was going on. Freya was so easy to talk to, but Harriet barely knew her, so perhaps she'd not tell her too much tonight.

'An ex-boyfriend has shown up in my life without warning.'

'Not a welcome appearance then?'

'Actually, under different circumstances it would have been good to have him back in my life,' Harriet said slowly as she realised that truth behind her words. 'But I think it's far too late.'

Freya gave her a questioning look. 'Sometimes one should grab a second chance at happiness with both hands,' she said. 'Not everyone gets them. Trust me on that.'

'It's not only my happiness, though, that is at stake. It's my daughter's as well.'

'And don't forget Hugo in all this will you?' Freya said quietly. 'I can see he's fond of you, try not to hurt him, won't you?'

Harriet nodded. 'I promise. I don't want to hurt him either.'

Freya went to say something else but at that moment Marcus and Hugo came back out onto the terrace.

'This man's a blooming genius with computers,' Marcus declared. 'Solved our problems within minutes. Right, let's eat.' And the conversation between Freya and Harriet was over, although Harriet found Freya's words were lingering in her mind.

31

Thursday evening, as Harriet was preparing to take Lulu for her evening walk, a text pinged in on her mobile. Jack. She glanced at it and froze as she read the words.

I'm outside

Grabbing her jacket and Lulu's lead she rushed out of the house.

Opening the villa gate she saw Jack standing on the opposite side of the road, once she was on the pavement Harriet quickly pressed the remote and the gate closed behind her as Jack strolled across.

'Hi, Harriet. You all right? You don't look too good.'

'What are you doing here?'

'I've come to see you. It's been days since we talked, you don't reply to my messages, I just want to know what's happening, maybe get things moving in the right direction.'

Harriet's heart sank. She was not in the mood for a confrontation with Jack.

'The right direction for you, maybe.'

Lulu barked and pulled on her lead.

'I have to walk the dog,' Harriet said.

'Fine. I'll walk with you. Maybe we can stop for a drink, even have a pizza, and we could talk.'

'I'm coming straight home once I've walked Lulu.'

'Okay, no drink, although you look as if you could do with one. I'll walk with you and we can talk.'

Harriet stopped at a crossing and pressed the pedestrian button.

'I had hoped you'd have been in touch by now with a date for a meet-up,' Jack said quietly. 'Learning about Elodie has blown my world apart. I just want to talk about my daughter – surely you can see that?'

The green light flashed and Harriet started to cross the road before she answered him.

'I haven't answered your messages because there is nothing more to tell you. I have told Elodie about you and that you are in town wanting to meet her, which came as a massive shock to her. She's currently thinking about what she wants to do. I do know she's worried about how our family dynamics will change. Having two parents in her life is not something she's ever had before.' Harriet held up her hand as Jack went to speak. 'Before you say anything, I know that is totally my fault and not yours.'

'The only thing she needs to do is meet me,' Jack said. 'Can you two not go out for a coffee together and I'll just happen to saunter past all innocent? Would it not be easier to do it that way?'

'No. I'm not doing that.' Harriet shook her head. 'It's going to take time. Elodie has every right to decide for herself whether she wants to meet you or not.'

'Or I could just turn up at the villa,' Jack said. 'Like I did this evening. Introduce myself.'

'Are you even listening to me, Jack Ellicott?' Harriet asked, barely managing to keep her temper. 'You can't force her to meet you, any more than you can force her to like you if or when she does meet you.'

Exasperated, Jack thumped his left hand with his right fist several times. Harriet remembered him doing that in the past when he got stressed. 'All I want is to meet her. To learn what she's like. Get to know her. Tell her about her American roots. Is that so wrong?'

'No.' Harriet sighed. She was starting to feel sorry for him, but there was no way she was going to tell Elodie to hurry up and decide. Jack had probably thought it would all be straightforward once he knew the truth about Elodie. Elodie would want to meet up and... and what? Once they'd met what would happen? Had he made plans for the future? 'If you don't pile on the pressure, I think Elodie will agree to meet you soon but...' she hesitated. Jack was probably going to accuse her of putting up obstacles when she asked the next question, which she truly wasn't, but things were bound to change after the meeting had happened. Life wouldn't be the same ever again for any of them. Family dynamics would definitely have shifted. 'What happens afterwards? You meet up and you go back to America and that's it? Long-distance father-daughter relationship? That wouldn't be fair on her if that's what you're planning on doing.'

'I haven't made any plans,' Jack said. 'I don't intend to until Elodie and I have met. Then we can all sit down and talk the possibilities through as a family.' He turned to look at Harriet. 'I really don't want to fight anyone over this, but I can't not meet my daughter now I know about her.'

Harriet heard the anguished despair in his voice. She remembered the hurt she'd felt deep down last year when Elodie had been so reluctant to meet her. Her hurt, though, had been different. She was guilty of letting her daughter down, whereas Jack had nothing to be guilty over. Once again she was the guilty party.

'Discovering that I have another child is a huge and wonderful thing to me. I wish I had been able to play a bigger part in her life.' Jack ran his fingers through his hair. 'I know you said no earlier to a drink or something to eat tonight but have dinner with me tomorrow night and talk to me about Elodie?'

Harriet shook her head, the word 'No' automatically forming in her head but still unspoken when she stopped. Deep down, she knew the true reason she wanted to refuse to have dinner with Jack was nothing to do with anything she was saying, it was all to do with her own buried feelings about him. Meeting him again had shown her exactly what she had thrown away all those years ago. She was afraid of those feelings showing up and giving her away to Jack.

Which meant that the last thing she wanted to do was to spend an evening with Jack, but if she did, she could tell him some of the things he wanted to know about Elodie. Maybe he'd back off a little then. Wait with a bit more patience.

She looked at him. 'I'm not sure it's a good idea, but okay, I'll have supper with you tomorrow night to talk about Elodie and I'll tell you as much as I can about her. Book an early table somewhere and text me the details. I'll meet you there.'

32

_____

Friday evening and Jack was waiting for her when Harriet arrived at the beach restaurant he had chosen, an ice bucket with an open bottle of rosé already on the table. He stood up to greet her, leaning in before she could step back to kiss her cheek.

'When in France,' he said, smiling at her discomfort before pouring two glasses of wine and handing one to her. 'Santé.'

The waiter appeared and placed the customary basket of bread on the table, handing them both a menu before leaving them to choose their food.

Jack gave his menu a quick perusal before looking at Harriet.

'They don't appear to have our favourites – scampi and chips for you and spaghetti bolognese for me. Shall we leave?'

Harriet laughed, strangely cheered by the way he'd remembered their favourite pub meals from way back when. 'How remiss of them. I guess I'll have to settle for the crab salad with frites please. You?'

'I think in the absence of spag bog, it will have to be the peppered steak and frites for me, boring, but I'm sure it will be good,' Jack said.

Harriet was still giggling when Jack asked, 'Do you remember that time you took me walking on Dartmoor and we got lost?'

'Yes,' Harriet said. 'We ended up in a pub that had a funny name, didn't we?'

'The Mucky Duck. I have never forgotten it. It was a wonderful day.' Jack laughed before giving Harriet a serious look. 'I've never forgotten you either. I see you still wear the silver bracelet I bought you,' Jack said quietly. 'I noticed you had it on the other day too.'

Harriet sighed. 'It's a favourite.' There was no point in telling him she never took it off.

'Jack, please don't, there's no point in going over what might have been. Let's keep our happy memories intact and move on.'

The waiter returned at that moment, ready to take their order. He'd moved on to the next table when Jack returned to their conversation.

'There's more than happy memories though, isn't there? There's the physical proof of our daughter. Tell me, who does she take after – in looks and temperament?'

'She's quite stubborn, which she clearly gets from you,' Harriet said teasingly. 'She's also blonde like you were. Wait a minute,' and she opened her phone and scrolled through until she found what she was looking for and she handed her phone to Jack. 'I took this of her and Gabby last New Year when we went to a party. Elodie turned her head at the last moment, so it's a bit blurred.'

Harriet waited quietly while Jack studied the photo carefully for several long seconds. He was subdued and his eyes suspiciously bright when he handed the phone back to her.

'She may have my colouring, but she's the image of you at her age. She's beautiful.'

'Thank you.'

'Is she an artist like you?'

'No, she is creative, though. She's a journalist and is writing a novel. She's doing really well at the moment. Moving to France has been good for her.'

Jack topped up their wine glasses. 'Does she have a boyfriend? And if she does, is he good enough for her?'

Harriet laughed. 'Jack, you can't play the heavy-handed father any more than I have the right to be an interfering mother, we've both been out of her life too long. Yes, she does have a boyfriend, Gazz, and he's great. He runs his own beach business – jet skis, paddleboats and paragliding trips.' She took a sip of her wine. 'Can I ask you a question?'

Jack nodded.

'Did you marry the girl your parents expected you to, or someone else?'

Jack gave a heavy sigh. 'Yes, more fool me, I married Sabrina, the girl my parents liked. For better. For worse. It turned out to be a little bit of better overshadowed by everything else. How about your marriage?'

Harriet breathed a sigh of relief as the arrival of their meals at that moment saved her from answering and they both fell silent as the waiter placed their plates in front of them. 'Merci,' they murmured simultaneously.

They started to eat and it was several minutes before Jack looked at her, his eyes narrowed. 'You going to answer my question about your marriage?'

'Let's say I was a fool too and leave it at that,' Harriet replied. 'How's your steak?'

'Good. How long have you been a widow?'

'A year.'

'This Hugo you work for...?'

'What about him?' Harriet eyed Jack warily.

'Is he more than your boss?'

'He's a very good friend.'

'How good a friend?'

Harriet put her knife and fork down and gave Jack a hard stare. She didn't want to discuss Hugo with Jack. 'Actually, it's none of your business how good a friend he is to me. We're here to talk about Elodie, not me.'

Jack shrugged. 'Sorry. Just wondering. It's a weird feeling being with you again after so long. A nice weird though.' The happy smile he flashed at her was reminiscent of the ones that years ago she'd grown to love.

Harriet started to eat again. No way was she going to admit how bizarre she was finding the evening. Laughing and sharing memories of the way they were was surreal. Almost as if they'd never parted. She needed to get the conversation back on an even, less personal keel, with safer subjects. But first she needed to find out how long Jack intended to be around.

'When I bumped into Lizzie in Dartmouth, she said you were back in Europe. Are you here permanently?'

Jack shook his head. 'Planning on splitting my time between the States and Europe – six months at a time. Depends on visas, of course. Although now I know about Elodie, I'll probably make my base in France rather than the UK. I'm thinking of looking for an apartment. I really like the hotel I'm staying in at the moment, but I can't stay there forever.'

'Which hotel?'

'The Belles Rives. Incidentally, I'm looking forward to introducing Elodie to her half-brother at some point in the future.'

Harriet's heart sank. Jack clearly had every intention of not only himself being in Elodie's life but also the rest of his family. 'You don't think you're rushing things a bit? You haven't met Elodie yet.' His next words confirmed her fears.

'I've got twenty-four missed years to make up for, of course I'm rushing things. I can't make up for lost time, but I sure as hell can do my best to try to ensure the future is different.'

* * *

At the end of the evening, Jack ignored her protests and insisted on walking Harriet home. As Harriet pressed the remote and the gate opened Jack gently turned her to face him and looked at her seriously. 'Thank you for this evening. It was like old times and I really enjoyed it. I don't suppose you're going to invite me in for coffee to finish it off?'

'In a word, no. Thank you for supper and goodnight, Jack.' And she was through the gate as it was closing, shutting him out.

'Once Elodie and I have met, maybe the three of us can have a family dinner? Goodnight, Harriet. I'll be in touch,' he called.

Harriet sighed. She knew that it was a given he'd be in touch. She also knew that she too was going to have to come to terms with the fact that once Jack was in Elodie's life he would inevitably be back in her own.

She wandered down through the garden on the side path and sank down onto a transat by the edge of the pool. Supper with Jack had been interesting. Reminiscing about their shared past had been fun and Jack had surprised her with how much he'd actually remembered. He'd almost been daring her to remember the good times and he'd jogged her memory with forgotten anecdotes. Several times she'd got the feeling that he was teasing her, flirting with her even, in the hope that she'd respond.

But she couldn't. Wouldn't. Things with Elodie needed to be sorted first. Only then could she begin to think about what it would be like to welcome Jack back into her own life.

33

Elodie was in her room, with the intention of starting to write the first of her 'English Girl Abroad' columns for the Sunday magazine, which was scheduled to begin at the end of the month. For days now, her head had been swirling with thoughts of Jack Ellicott, her actual father, pushing all work-related subjects to the back of her mind.

An hour later, having written less than two hundred words, she gave up and decided to go to the beach and wait for Gazz to finish. They'd already arranged to meet up later that evening, but she couldn't wait that long. Business did quieten down after six o'clock as people went home, so hopefully he'd be free soon.

As she passed the large hotel on Boulevard Édouard Baudoin, where only last Christmas her mother had stayed, Elodie remembered how upset she'd been when Gabby had told her back then that Harriet was in town. And now her unknown father was here. What was that film where a day repeated itself time and time again? *Groundhog Day*, that was it. This was becoming her own personal groundhog day. Only this time it was her father, instead of her mother, wanting to be back in her life. And the burning question was – how could she not meet him now that the opportunity had arisen?

Telling Harriet that she merely wanted to know a few details about her father and she didn't plan on rushing to go looking for him had been a lie. Well, half a lie. She'd merely intended to do a little bit of investigative journalism once she knew his name, see if she could trace him. But now Jack had turned up, there was nothing to stop her from meeting him. So why was she hesitating?

Elodie sighed. Deep down she knew she was afraid. Agreeing to see Jack Ellicott would be an irrevocable step that would be sure to turn her world upside down and she wasn't sure how she'd cope with both her parents in her life after not having either of them until Harriet had shown up. Parents who'd never had joint responsibility for the child they had created. Did they plan on becoming friends, or even lovers again. Or would she have to see them separately, keep them in individual compartments of her life?

Elodie glanced back at the hotel as she made her way down onto the beach. Was he staying in that hotel too? Could Jack be standing in his room looking out at the scenery, not knowing his daughter was part of the view?

Families were making their way off the beach, either to go home or back to hotels and holiday Airbnbs, with fractious toddlers and bored teenagers kicking at the sand. Child-free couples were out enjoying an aperitif or an early-evening meal at one or other of the beach restaurants. Walking down towards the jetty Gazz ran his business from, Elodie found herself looking at every middle-aged man she passed, asking herself: Could you be him?

Gazz was standing on his own in the water down by the end of the jetty, securing a paddleboat, and she increased her pace, wanting to reach him quickly. Although surprised to see her, he waded out onto the sand, smiling happily, and gave her a quick kiss as she ran into his arms.

'Have you got five minutes to spare?' Elodie asked. 'Only I really need to talk to you. And to ask you something.'

Gazz glanced back to where Olivier and Enzo were dealing with a couple of women who had just returned from a paragliding trip and were laughing and chatting with them.

'What's up?'

'I've decided to meet my father – but will you please come with me?'

'Yes, of course, I'll come with you, but I'll need a bit of notice to make sure both Olivier and Enzo are working on that day to cover my absence. If you decide to have lunch with him, I'll probably have to bow out to get back for the boys.'

'Thanks. I don't expect to have lunch with him, not the first time I meet him. You tell me which day you can manage and I'll get Harriet to text the details to... to him. I can't believe what I'm about to do.'

Gazz gave her a hug. 'I happen to believe that you're doing the right thing.'

* * *

Harriet was in her room getting ready for bed that evening when there was a gentle knock on the door. She glanced at her watch, eleven o'clock, as she heard Elodie ask, 'Can I come in and talk to you for a few moments, please?'

'Of course. Come on in. Is something wrong?'

'No, nothing is wrong, but I decided tonight that I will meet my father.'

Harriet smothered a sigh of relief, finally, before giving Elodie a smile. 'He'll be pleased to hear that.'

'I was thinking ten thirty the day after tomorrow by the bandstand in Place Nationale or is that too short notice, do you think?'

'If you rang him up now and told him to meet you there in five minutes, he'd be there. He's really desperate to meet you, get to know you.' Harriet picked her phone up from the dressing table. 'I'll text him right away and tell him where we'll be waiting the day after tomorrow.'

'Um no...'

Harriet looked up from her phone as her fingers hovered over the keypad.

'Please text him the time and place, but I don't want you to come with me.'

Harriet gave Elodie a puzzled look. 'Why not? Surely it would make things easier than going on your own? Smooth the way.'

'I'm not going alone. Gazz is coming with me.'

'Okay,' Harriet said slowly. 'I'm sure he'll be supportive, but I know Jack, I can help.'

'That's the point,' Elodie interrupted. 'You do know Jack. Gazz and I will meet him as a stranger we happened to bump into, if you like. No prior knowledge of what he's really like and Jack has no real knowledge of what I'm like either. We can learn about each other, see how we get on, without the pressure of your, or his, emotional baggage with each other, getting in the way.' Elodie looked at her, a slight smile on her lips. 'You'd be there as an anxious mother, hovering. Trying to influence him, me, to say nice things. Do you understand what I mean?'

Harriet gave a short thoughtful nod. Elodie was her own woman and this important life changing meeting would be done on her terms 'Yes, I think I do.'

'I'm trying to meet him without any preconceived ideas of what he's like. No expectations. Just because he's my father doesn't necessarily mean we're going to like each other or even get on.' Elodie gave a sigh of relief. 'Glad that's sorted. Right, I'm off to bed. Oh, and when you text him, please don't mention Gazz. I want to surprise him. Night,' and Elodie was gone.

Harriet sat on the bed and quickly sent a text message to Jack with the details, finishing it with:

Don't be late

An instant reply pinged in:

I won't. See you there and thank you

She smiled. He was in for a surprise. He'd assumed she would be accompanying Elodie. The day after tomorrow, Sunday, he would meet his daughter with her boyfriend and life for all of them would never be the same again.

34

'Mom, you remember when Dad was first taken ill and I had to dash back from Europe twenty years ago?'

'What a ridiculous question, Jack. As if I could ever forget those terrible days.'

Jack cursed inwardly. As an opening gambit that had clearly not been the right thing to say. After his meeting with Harriet last evening, he'd arrived back at the hotel determined to talk to his mother at breakfast the next morning. He'd never told her what was really behind this trip to France and he needed to do that before things came to a head. He thought he knew how she would react but you never could tell.

Jack watched as she spread a generous spoonful of apricot jam on her croissant and smiled.

'What about it anyway?' Martha Ellicott said.

'Something happened to me during my time in Europe then that I've never told you about,' Jack said, taking a deep breath. 'I was in love with an English girl called Harriet whom I was planning to marry when I had to leave to come home.'

'I'm guessing that would be the girl who wrote to you for several weeks after you came home before the letters suddenly stopped,' Martha said, giving him a look that in his younger days would have quelled him into silence. Today, though, he pushed on.

'Yes. Harriet never told me, but she was pregnant when I left. She had a baby girl. My daughter. Elodie.'

Martha put her croissant down and stared at her son. 'Are you telling me I have an English grown-up granddaughter called Elodie?'

Jack nodded.

'Nice name. When did you meet her? And when can I meet her?'

'I haven't met her yet.'

'If you haven't met her, are you sure she is—'

Jack interrupted his mother. 'One hundred per cent certain it is my daughter, yes.'

'Have you at least got a photograph?'

Jack shook his head. 'Sorry.'

Martha sighed. 'So, I suppose the next thing is we're flying to England to meet up, right?'

'No. Harriet is actually living here in Juan-les-Pins with her French mother and Elodie. I had supper with Harriet last night.'

'Why not Elodie?'

'Me turning up in her life is a big shock, but I'm meeting her tomorrow morning. When that has happened, I would like her to meet her American grandmother too. And of course Nathan sometime soon.'

'Ah, Nathan. How do you think he is likely to react to having a half-sister? We both know how Sabrina is likely to react to the news,' Martha said, pulling a face at the thought.

Jack sighed. 'I am not remotely interested in how Sabrina is likely to react. We are divorced, end of story. Nathan, on the other hand, will, I hope, be pleased to have a sibling. He's often said he wished he wasn't an only child. Well, now he's got a big sister.'

'And when our holiday here is over, what do you think is going to happen?'

'What I want to happen before the end of the holiday will hopefully lead naturally into a whole new relationship with my daughter. Both here in Europe and the States.'

Martha nodded thoughtfully. 'And where does her mother fit into this scenario? What do you hope to happen with her? The woman who neglected to tell you about your daughter.'

'Mom, you ask the most impossible questions. I don't currently have an answer to that one.' Jack was silent for several seconds. 'Every time I see her, this huge wave of joy engulfs me. I enjoyed spending last evening with Harriet, it was like old times. We reminisced, we laughed. It was as if I was finally back with the one person who mattered.' He held up his hand. 'I know it's impossible to turn back the clock, but I would like to get close to Harriet again, if she wants to, of course. But right now I intend to concentrate on meeting my daughter and establishing a father-daughter relationship with her. And then,' he shrugged, 'we'll have to see what happens.'

* * *

Gabby sat out on the terrace after her swim enjoying the morning sunshine, while Philippe stayed in the pool for a little while longer. There was a book open in front of her, but her thoughts were all over the place and within minutes she gave a sigh and set the book aside.

This whole thing with Jack Ellicott turning up unexpectedly wanting to meet his daughter was stressing everyone out and she still hadn't found the time or the opportunity to talk to Elodie about her plan to move in with Gazz. Two major things she had no control over. Thinking about the problems that were outside of her control was so frustrating, she'd be better concentrating on her own immediate problems. Like what to do about the brush pot that was still in the cave. Should she sell it or keep it in the family? Was keeping it in the villa now she knew its value feasible though? The house insurance would be sure to go through the roof. Was the fact that it had been in the family for so long enough for her to keep it? After all, she hadn't seen it for forty years. The chances of it surviving for another forty years without being chipped or accidentally damaged were probably quite low. Besides, if the auctioneers who had suggested the possible price it would fetch were right all those years ago, the money could be better employed.

Gabby sighed. She'd take a couple of photographs later and ask Colette to contact the expert she knew. It was always possible the original auctioneer had made a mistake. It was safe enough for now down in the cave, out of sight, out of mind. If the second valuation came back at a similar figure, she'd decide then what to do.

'Gabriella, *ma cherie*, you look very serious,' Philippe said as he climbed out of the pool and began to towel himself dry.

'I'm frustrated at not being able to sort things out,' Gabby said. 'This whole Jack business is dragging on. It's not only Elodie who wants to meet him, I do too. I can't decide whether I'm going to like or hate him for making my daughter pregnant and not being around afterwards.'

'Which wasn't his fault,' Philippe said softly. 'I think now he does know he wants to try to make amends.'

'And that could bring a whole host of new problems.' Gabby sighed. 'Sorry. I'm being pessimistic, which isn't normally like me.'

Philippe finished drying himself and came over to sit next to her. 'I've news that may cheer you up. We've received our invitation to the viewing of the show apartment in Hotel Provençal. Two o'clock the last Thursday in July.'

'Really? I look forward to that. I wandered down there with Colette the other day, but we couldn't see anything about a viewing day. I was going to ask if Colette could come with us, but I guess it's too late now if you've received the invitation. There is still not a lot to see, even though some of the hoarding has come down, and there is clearly still a lot to do, but the top half of the building certainly looks very pristine.'

'Maybe Colette can go another time,' Philippe said. 'This viewing is definitely just for you and me. And rest assured there will be plenty for us to see. It's not just the outside of the building that is looking pristine, the inside too is looking spectacular I am told.'

35

Harriet was on the veranda at midday on Saturday trying to concentrate on painting a picture of the Antibes ramparts, her thoughts dominated by Elodie and Jack, when Hugo rang. Julia, his main assistant, had gone home with a bad migraine. 'Any chance of you working this afternoon?' he asked.

'Yes, of course. I'm your emergency girl,' Harriet replied. It would be good to be busy. Serving customers would be a distraction, taking her thoughts away from everything else that was going on.

'Thanks. See you later.'

* * *

There was already a queue waiting as Hugo opened up after lunch when Harriet arrived. Within minutes, they were both busy serving customers and it was an hour or two before it calmed down.

'Is it always as busy as this on a Saturday?' Harriet asked as she went through to the utility room to make them both a drink. Coffee for Hugo, green tea for her.

'Yes, I've never worked out why but it's probably something to do with changeover day in the gites and hotels. But it should be quieter from now on until closing time. Or maybe not,' he added as two more women entered the gallery. 'You make the drinks. I'll deal with the customers.' And Hugo wished the women a jovial '*Bon après-midi, mesdames.*' When Harriet appeared a few moments later with their drinks, he was busy wrapping up their purchases and taking their money.

The next customer, an elegant woman, entered alone and Harriet gave her a welcoming smile and a quiet 'Bonjour' and received a smile in return. The woman wandered around for some time, picking up several cards, a notebook and two framed prints before approaching the cash desk. Harriet rang the items into the cash register.

'That comes to ninety-five euros please,' and the women handed her a credit card. 'I'll run the payment through the machine and then I'll wrap everything up for you.'

'Thank you, honey,' the woman said in a soft American accent.

Harriet turned the card over to place it in the machine, barely glancing at the name on it as she did so. The machine passed the transaction and Harriet handed the card back to the woman.

Five minutes later her, purchases were wrapped up and she said her goodbyes. It wasn't until she watched the woman step out through the open doorway into the street that the name she'd subconsciously registered on the card sprang into her mind. Martha Ellicott.

Mentally, Harriet gave a shrug. Ellicott, for all she knew, was probably a really common name in the US. It didn't mean that she was anything to do with Jack. Even if she was related to him in some way, she couldn't have known who Harriet was because surely she would have made herself known to her. Wouldn't she?

Despite Hugo saying the gallery should be quieter in the late afternoon it was busy until seven o'clock when Hugo turned the sign around and locked the door and they both heaved a sigh of relief. Whilst Hugo cashed up, Harriet moved around tidying the displays, straightening pictures, wiping the counter down and finally running the vacuum cleaner over the carpet.

'Do you have to dash off? Only I think we both deserve a glass of wine.'

'That would be good,' Harriet said.

Once Hugo had put the money in the safe, he locked up and they made their way out. It was a relief to sit down at a table in one of the market bars.

'How are things with Elodie?' Hugo asked, as the town hall clock struck, almost drowning out his words.

'Better than they were. She has finally agreed to meet her father.. I actually had supper with Jack the other evening. He wanted me to tell him what I could about Elodie.'

'Was that difficult for you?'

Harriet shook her head. 'No. It was very civilised, quite enjoyable really. He kept reminding me of the funny things that we'd done together.'

'Maybe it's not just Elodie he wants to meet, maybe he wants you back in his life too,' Hugo said quietly. 'How would you feel if that was the case?'

Harriet was quiet for several seconds. 'I think he does maybe still have feelings for me, but they're probably wrapped up in the fact that I'm the mother of his unknown daughter.' She didn't tell Hugo about how Jack had stopped short at outright flirting with her, or how she'd found herself starting to respond.

'And you? What about your feelings?' Hugo asked quietly.

'Still being tossed around in a sea of bewilderment,' Harriet answered. 'I think it's something to do with the fact that we have a shared history – and Elodie, of course. Even after all these years, it's not easy to sweep that kind of relationship aside.'

Hugo nodded and gave her a sad look. 'And you don't truly want to, do you?'

Harriet bit her lip and gave an almost imperceptible shake of her head. She truly didn't want to hurt Hugo but she had to be truthful with him, even though she and Jack were unlikely to rekindle their earlier relationship. 'I think it's going to be impossible,' she said, returning his sad look with her own.

* * *

Saturday evening, Elodie made her way down to the beach as usual to spend a couple of hours with Gazz. They were going to nip along the coast on Gazz's scooter to their favourite pizza restaurant in Cannes. Tonight, though, Elodie was on edge, the nerves over the meeting tomorrow with Jack were already bubbling away inside her, as much as she tried to banish them.

Olivier and Enzo were securing everything for the night and Elodie walked over to help the two of them while Gazz talked to a tall man about booking a paragliding trip for his son and daughter-in-law when they arrived later in the year. Elodie smiled at the two of them as she approached. She didn't recognise the man, but there was something strangely familiar about him.

'Just twenty-four hours' notice is all that is necessary for a weekday trip, weekends are busier,' Gazz was saying as she drew level with them. 'Now, if you'll excuse me, I have to help finish securing everything. I look forward to meeting you again,' and Gazz turned away. 'Hi Elodie. Give me five minutes and we can go.'

'Thanks for your help, Gazz. I'll make sure to book a place in time.'

Elodie froze at the sound of the man's American accent before slowly turning to stare at him, only to find herself under scrutiny by a pair of piercing blue eyes. The sound of the ordinary world around her, waves lapping the beach, shrieks of the seagulls, laughter from diners in the nearby beach restaurant, everything became lost in the intense pounding inside her ears and head.

As she managed to croak out the words, 'Jack Ellicott?' he smiled at her.

'Yes – and you have to be Elodie, my daughter.'

36

It was almost midnight when Gazz walked Elodie home. Stopping outside
the villa's gates, he took her in his arms to kiss her goodnight. 'Eh bien!
What an evening,' he said. 'I like your papa. And I think you do too?'

'Yes. Harriet was right. He is a good man. I only have good men in my
life,' Elodie said, reaching up to return his kiss. 'Thanks for walking me
home. See you tomorrow.'

Gazz waited until the gate had closed behind Elodie before calling out,
'*Je t'aime. A bientôt,*' and moving away.

'*Moi aussi,*' Elodie called softly.

Indoors, Elodie crept up the stairs and into her room, where Lulu was
already asleep on her bed. Part of her wanted to wake Harriet up and talk
to her about the evening, but another part of her wanted to relive it by
herself first.

Once Elodie had recovered from her shock, Jack had apologised if he
was ruining their plans for the evening but please would they both join
him for dinner at one of the beach restaurants. Gazz had offered to leave
the two of them alone to get to know each other, but both Jack and Elodie
had insisted he stayed.

When they'd agreed to have dinner with him, Jack had made straight
for a restaurant and reserved a table for the three of them.

'Your mom and I had dinner here the other evening, so I know the food is good,' he'd said. As soon as the waiter had poured their aperitifs, he'd raised his glass in a toast. 'To fathers and daughters'.

'I love the way you say mom,' Elodie had said. 'Mum didn't tell me she'd met up with you for dinner.'

'We had a great time, reminiscing and...' he'd hesitated. 'Re-establishing contact, I hope.'

Elodie had given him a sharp look. 'Is reconnecting with Mum one of the reasons you're here.'

Jack shook his head. 'No. The main reason was following a hunch that I had an unknown daughter, which, when it proved to be true, wanting to meet you and the two of us getting to know each other. Everything else fades into insignificance compared to that. Please believe me when I tell you that I've never forgotten Harriet and...' Jack had hesitated. 'And if I'm to be in your life – which I hope you will allow me to be – I'd like to be back in her life too again, so long as she is willing to let me. I do find it hard to forgive, but I know she had her own reasons for failing to tell me about you.'

Elodie had given him a thoughtful nod.

'I have so many questions to ask you,' Jack had said. 'I hardly know where to start. I'm going to jump straight in with a serious, make-or-break question: do you like peanut butter and jelly sandwiches?'

Both Gazz and Elodie had stared at him before bursting out laughing.

'Is that some sort of trick question?' Elodie had asked.

Jack had looked affronted. 'To an American, it's important to know. Well, do you?'

'Never ever had one,' Elodie had said. 'I like peanut butter, but not sure about having jelly with it. How about you – do you like marmite on your cheese?'

Gazz had looked at them both in amazement. 'Weird food you both like, but I bet you each pull a face at the thought of eating the French favourite, steak tartare with or without the raw egg yolk.'

'Ugh, raw beef,' Elodie had shuddered.

The waiter had arrived with their food then and the talking had paused for a few moments.

Now, as she sat on her bed cuddling Lulu and remembering the laughter around Jack's so-called serious question, Elodie realised it had been the moment they'd all relaxed and which had set the friendly tone of the rest of the evening. Even the truly serious exchanges between them that had followed had been treated with gentleness and kindness. Like when Jack had said he'd always wanted a daughter and she'd instantly replied without thinking, 'I've never missed the dad I never had.'

'That makes me feel terribly sad for what we've both missed out on,' Jack had said. 'We have a lot of catching up to do.'

'How long are you staying in France for?' Gazz had asked.

'I have another four months on my visa, which hopefully I can extend if I need to. My mother, who is here with me, has the same but will probably want to go home rather than extend the holiday.'

'Hang on,' Elodie had interrupted. 'I've got an American grandmother? Have you told her about me? Are there any uncles and aunts I should know about?'

'I'm an only child, so no uncles or aunts. But, yes, you have an American grandmother who is looking forward to meeting you. You also have a half-brother, Nathan. He's hopefully coming here for a holiday soon, so you'll get to meet him then. Oh, I forgot. You do have a great-uncle, Cooper, my mother's twin brother. He's a bit of a recluse these days, so we don't see him often.'

Jack had handed his mobile phone to Gazz. 'Would you take a photo of us please? If I return to the hotel without evidence of this meeting, my mother will not be happy.'

Gazz had taken the requested photo and then a selfie on his own phone of the three of them for Elodie.

'Whereabouts do you live in America?' Gazz had asked.

'On the east coast up near New York. I can't wait for you both to visit.'

As the evening had worn on, Elodie remembered sitting back, watching the sun set over the Esterel mountains, sipping her wine and listening to Gazz and her father, a father she couldn't yet fully relate to but whom she was already feeling drawn to, genially discussing the state of world tennis. Gazz was a keen follower and bought tickets for the Monte Carlo Masters every year. Apparently her father had played in some

amateur competitions when younger. Elodie had smiled at that. She'd
loved playing in the Dartmouth Regatta Tennis Annual Championship,
had even won the cup one year. Had she unknowingly inherited her love
of the sport from him?

They were still sitting there when the moon was high in the sky and
the beach was emptying. With more than a degree of reluctance, they had
all stood up to leave and Jack, who had barely glanced at the bill in the
small dish, placed several euro notes in it and handed it to the waiter with
a 'Merci. Tout compris.'

As the three of them had made their way along the Promenade du
Soleil, Elodie sandwiched between the two men, Jack had said quietly,
'Your mom has told me her marriage, like mine, was a mistake. Has she
told you anything about that time?'

Elodie had sighed. 'A little. To be honest, selfishly, I've never asked her
outright. I hated Todd for taking her away and I didn't want to know
anything about him. The one thing I do know, though, is that he was very
controlling. You'll have to ask her to tell you the details if you want to
know.'

'I want to know and I intend to ask her,' Jack had said. 'Now, did we
decide on a time for lunch for everyone tomorrow? I think we said twelve
o'clock for twelve thirty in the bar at the Belles Rives.' He had shaken
Gazz's hand. 'It was good to meet you and I trust we're going to be good
friends. I hope you can make lunch tomorrow, but there will be lots of
lunches in the future if you can't.' He'd turned to Elodie. 'May I give you a
goodnight hug?'

Wordlessly, Elodie had moved into his arms and he'd pulled her close.

'It's wonderful to finally meet you. We've made a lovely first memory
this evening. And I promise to be the best father you never knew you
wanted. See you tomorrow.'

Elodie pulled the duvet back with a happy sigh and climbed into bed.
Spending the evening so spontaneously with Jack had been great, and
now there was the family lunch to look forward to tomorrow.

37

Elodie did the breakfast croissant run with Lulu early the next morning and rewarded herself with a quick swim before the others appeared for breakfast. Harriet placed the coffee on the table and watched Elodie dry herself.

'You and Gazz have a good evening last night? I heard you come home.'

'Sorry, I didn't mean to wake you, I thought I was quite quiet,' Elodie said.

'You didn't wake me. I was reading.'

'Morning,' Gabby said as she arrived and pulled out a chair. 'Did you and Gazz get to Cannes?'

'No. We had supper at one of the Juan beach restaurants instead.' Elodie took a bite of her croissant, chewing and swallowing before she said casually. 'By the way, the meeting this morning with Jack is cancelled.'

Elodie immediately felt bad when Harriet reacted with an exasperated, 'Oh for heaven's sake. Why?'

Elodie said, 'It's just a change of plan. The reason we didn't get to Cannes last night was because Jack was on the beach talking to Gazz when I arrived and we both realised who we were.'

Gabby and Harriet stared at her.

'Which is how we ended up at the beach having supper with Jack.' Elodie turned to her mother. 'The same restaurant he took you to.'

'I didn't know you'd had dinner with Jack,' Gabby said, looking at Harriet, who shrugged.

'He was getting frustrated at Elodie not agreeing to meet him so I thought I'd try to calm him down. So what happens now?'

'He's staying around for a few more months,' Elodie said. 'He really wants to get to know me, us. I really like him. Like you said, he's a good man. Anyway, today we're all invited for lunch at the Belles Rives. Philippe too, Gabby. My American grandmother is going to be there also. I'm actually looking forward to it.' She finished her croissant, drained her coffee cup and stood up. 'Twelve o'clock for twelve-thirty in the bar at Belles Rives. We can all walk down together at about twelve fifteen. I need to do some work now, see you later.'

As Elodie left, Harriet gave a strangled laugh as she looked at her mother and they both shook their heads in rueful acceptance.

'Well, at least they appear to have got on,' Gabby said. 'We just wait and see now what happens. I must say I'm looking forward to finally meeting your Jack and his mother too. And lunch at the Belles Rives is sure to be delicious.'

'He's not "my" Jack,' Harriet protested. 'He just happens to be someone I knew a long time ago and is the father of my now grown-up child.' She pushed the thought 'he was most definitely my Jack then' away. Too many years had passed, too many mistakes had been made; it was too late to have regrets for what might have been.

Gabby regarded her shrewdly. 'He's also someone who has gone to a lot of trouble to track you both down. I haven't even met him yet, but I think you may find he would like to be your Jack again. And, for what it's worth, I also think you still have feelings for him.' Gabby stood up. 'I'm looking forward to seeing the two of you together.' She gave Harriet a mischievous smile. 'I'm going to phone Philippe and tell him about our luncheon date and then I'm going to make myself presentable for meeting my American counterpart. Some older American women take their appearance very seriously, I'm told, and I don't want to let the side down.'

Harriet stayed where she was for a few moments. Jack and Elodie meeting, she knew, was the beginning of massive changes in all their lives. Some of those changes were sure to be more welcome than others. And Gabby was right. She did still have feelings for Jack as much as she might try to deny them. Feelings that had never ever gone completely away. But she wasn't about to admit them to anyone.

* * *

'You both look great,' Elodie said, a couple of hours later as she joined her grandmother and mother out on the terrace prior to setting off for the Belles Rives. 'Where's Philippe?'

'He's going to meet us there,' Gabby said. 'As he lives virtually opposite the hotel, it seemed silly to drag him over to us and for him to have to walk straight back.'

'Lulu's happy with her toys in the basket in my room,' Harriet said. 'So let's go and... what's the expression? I know – today we're ladies who lunch.'

They were soon on the Promenade du Soleil, walking past La Pinède and then further along the road, the flags at the entrance of the Belles Rives could be seen fluttering in the gentle breeze. Gabby looked across the road at the Hotel le Provençal still behind its hoardings but once again beginning to emerge as the grandiose symbol of yesteryear, casting an air, not of glamour yet, but definite promise of good times around the corner.

Philippe was standing outside the entrance appearing to be holding an animated conversation with Jack and Gazz. The three men turned as the three women approached.

'I guess Gazz introduced the two of you?' Harriet said.

'We introduced ourselves just five minutes ago in the Fitzgerald Bar,' Jack said, smiling. He turned to Gabby and courteously held out his hand. 'We were supposed to meet many years ago. It's a privilege to finally meet you, Madame Jacques.'

Gabby smiled as she shook his hand. 'Well, you know the old saying, better late than never. And please call me Gabby, everyone else does, apart from Philippe, who insists on using my full name.'

'My mother is waiting at the beach restaurant, shall we go through.'

Passing through the foyer of the hotel towards the beach restaurant, Elodie caught her breath. Scott Fitzgerald was one of her literary heroes and there were photos of him, his wife, Zelda, and their daughter, Scottie, everywhere. There was a glimpse of the Fitzgerald Bar off the lobby with its original Art Deco styling. Elodie could see herself and Gazz enjoying a cocktail in there together. They walked on past a wide patio with palm trees in pots, down a flight of steps to the beach restaurant with its comfortable wooden director chairs placed around tables overlooking the blue Mediterranean rhythmically lapping at the shore just a few feet away.

Martha Ellicott was waiting to meet them at a table down by the shoreline and stood up as she saw them approaching. Elodie, lagging at the back of the group, unsure of how this elegant woman was going to react to having a grown-up granddaughter thrown into her life unexpectedly, watched as Jack introduced Gabby and Philippe. Stepping back slightly as the three of them chatted politely, he caught hold of Elodie's hand and urged her forward, saying quietly, 'Don't look so worried. Your American grandmother is longing to meet you.'

Seconds later, she was enveloped in an expensively fragrant hug. 'Elodie, I know we're going to have fun getting to know each other. And this is your boyfriend, Gazz? The two of you must come and lunch with me one day, yes?'

Elodie nodded. 'I… we would like that very much, thank you.'

Harriet, watching Elodie and Martha together, and wondering whether Martha would remember her from the gallery, gave a startled jump as Jack appeared at her side and took her hand.

'Finally time for you to meet my mom, come on.'

When she tried to pull her hand away, Jack grinned at her but didn't relax his grip, so she found herself hand in hand with him as they moved forward for him to introduce her to his mother. She saw Martha's eyes linger on their linked hands, a knowing look passing swiftly across her face.

'Mom, this is Harriet, Elodie's mother.'

Martha looked at her. 'Haven't we met before?'

'Yes. I served you in the art gallery the other afternoon,' Harriet said. 'I have to admit your name didn't register with me until you had left. I did wonder then whether you were Jack's mother and whether you knew who I was.'

Martha shook her head. 'No, I didn't. I would have spoken up if I had – nicely, of course. Jack only told me the truth about why he was here in France a couple of days ago.' She shook her head at her son.

The maître d' arrived at that moment with a bottle of chilled champagne and suggested they might all like to take their seats. Once they were all settled, each with a glass of sparkling champagne, Jack stood up to give a toast.

'To my daughter, Elodie, Harriet, her mother, Gabby, her grandmother and last but not least my mother, Martha. Here's to the future and to being a proper united family.' Jack caught and held Harriet's gaze as he finished speaking and raised his glass in her direction. 'Families.'

Harriet raised her glass and, along with everyone else, echoed, 'Families', all the time wanting to break away from Jack's penetrating gaze but totally unable to even blink to shatter the connection.

* * *

'I really enjoyed the lunch today, hope you did too,' Elodie said that evening as she and Gazz walked along La Croisette in Cannes, having ridden Gazz's scooter along the bord de mer. 'Talk about a memorable first ever family lunch. I do like the Belles Rives too. Can we go there on our own sometime, when we've got something special to celebrate? It's got such a lovely atmosphere and all the Scott Fitzgerald mementoes are amazing.'

'End of the season we'll treat ourselves,' Gazz promised. 'I had a great time. You and your new grandmother seemed to get on well?'

'She's lovely and I'm so pleased she and Gabby really hit it off. I was worried that Gabby would feel pushed out, but they are both so different. Grandma Martha wants me to visit her. She's making plans to show me all her favourite places in New York. Says I'll get lots of ideas for stories and features out there.'

'And Jack? Are you feeling happier about having him in your life now you've got to know him a little?'

Elodie nodded. 'It still feels weird, though. We've so much to learn about each other. I've barely got to know my mother properly and now my father wants to be in my life too.' She shook her head. 'It's going to take time to adjust to having parents. Can I tell you something terrible that worries me?'

'Of course you can,' Gazz said.

'I find it really hard to even think about calling Harriet mum. I've not managed it once yet and she's been back in my life for several months now. We're slowly getting closer for sure but...' Elodie hesitated. 'After such a short time of knowing him, I'm already thinking of Jack as my dad. Which I feel is wrong somehow. If I start calling him dad without calling Harriet mum, I think it will upset her.'

Gazz didn't speak and Elodie looked at him anxiously.

'I know I'm a horrible, horrible person.'

'Don't be silly, you're not horrible at all. In fact, I think you're rather lovely,' Gazz said, putting his arm around her shoulders and giving her a tight squeeze. 'The fact that you're worried about upsetting your mum is proof that you care.'

'I've been trying to analyse myself. All I can think of is that it's because he never knew he was my dad, so didn't have to choose whether to stay or go, whereas Harriet clearly did know she was my mother but chose to leave me. But then, I can understand in a way why she did what she did, although it turned out to be an even bigger mistake.'

'I think you should stop worrying,' Gazz said. 'By the time Jack returns to America, you'll probably be calling Harriet mum without a second's thought.'

'Hope so. Jack wants me to go back with him. He's even suggested I move over for six months.'

'Are you thinking about doing that?'

'No.' Elodie's reply was instant. 'My life is here now. I'd like us to go for a holiday, or even several holidays, but not for months at a time.'

Gazz gave a sigh of relief. 'For a moment there I thought I was about to lose you to a life in America.'

'You don't get rid of me that easily.' Elodie turned and gave him a quick kiss. 'Have you thought any more about us moving in together?'

'It's not going to be as easy as I thought. Permanent rental apartments used to be fairly easy to find, if expensive, but now people are offering them as Airbnbs all year round. They make more money and they don't have the possibility of having difficult tenants long term.'

'We will just have to keep asking around,' Elodie said. 'Something will turn up eventually. Maybe Philippe will hear of something. He seems to know a lot of people.'

38

'Has your muse turned up to help now you're painting again?' Hugo asked during a lull in serving customers the following Saturday.

Harriet smiled. 'Yes, she has and I'm really enjoying painting again.'

'That's great. So how many paintings have you managed so far?'

'Six complete and another one almost there.'

'I was thinking of the first week in December for the exhibition I promised to hold. It's still a few months away, so aim for another eight maybe. Is that doable, do you think?'

'I think so, but I honestly do not know,' Harriet said. 'Life should settle down for me now that Jack has finally met Elodie.'

'What? When and where?' Hugo raised his eyebrows. 'Details please.'

Harriet quickly told him about Elodie and Jack's accidental meeting on the beach, 'And Jack treated us all to lunch at the Belles Rives the following day.'

'Nice. And the two of you? Are you friends again?'

'Not sure we've reached the friends stage quite yet. I suppose the best way to describe it would be to say it is all very civilised and grown-up. For Elodie's sake mostly.' Harriet pushed away the memory of Jack holding her by the hand to introduce her to Martha. That hadn't been a grown-up action and it had definitely given Martha the wrong impression of the state of their current relationship.

Hugo looked at her thoughtfully. 'You still like him, don't you?'

'I did like the younger Jack very much,' Harriet admitted. 'But right now it is our shared history, including Elodie, that has brought us back together.'

To Harriet's relief, the gallery door opened and a couple walked in and she moved away from Hugo with a smile of welcome for them, pushing all thoughts of how much she liked the older version of Jack away.

* * *

Gabby walked Lulu on Sunday morning and called in at Colette's, wanting to tell her about lunch at the Belles Rives and meeting Jack and his mother.

'He seems desperate to do the right thing by Elodie now he knows about her. And even more so now that he has met her in the flesh,' Gabby said. 'And the way he is around Harriet is interesting too. I get the feeling that it's not just Elodie he cares about.'

'Has Harriet said anything to you?'

Gabby shook her head. 'No. But she did blush when I teased her about him.'

'Fingers crossed then. Now, I've got some news about the brush pot.'

'Good or bad?'

'Definitely good. My friend says the last seven figure valuation is now too low. At auction today, it would sell for significantly more than that figure.'

Gabby was stunned. 'Truly? I thought it was already an amazing amount.'

'The thing is, do you want to sell it?'

Gabby took a deep breath. 'I'm terrified if it is so valuable that it's going to get chipped or broken, and since I have lived without it for so long, I think I will sell it. Besides, with that kind of money, I could help a lot of people.'

'There's an auction coming up in about ten days that they can squeeze you into. The next one for Chinese artefacts won't be until next year. I'll email them today and tell them so they can begin to advertise in the catalogue. If you bring the pot here tomorrow, I'll pack it up for transporting and courier it to Paris. Okay?'

Gabby nodded. So much about her life had changed in the last year that she hadn't thought it possible for it to change again. But if the brush pot did fetch the kind of figure it was expected to in the auction, then life would inevitably change again, not only for herself but also for Harriet and Elodie.

* * *

That evening, when everyone was conveniently home at the same time for once, Gabby told them what Colette had said. 'The value that appears to have been placed on it is staggering.' She hesitated. 'If you two are in agreement, I think we should sell it. If we keep it, it will have to stay down in the cave – and what is the point of doing that – because I'd hate for it to get broken.'

'Mum, it was left to you, you can do whatever you like with it,' Harriet said.

'I know that, but it's also part of your inheritance, so I want to make sure the two of you are in agreement with selling it. Elodie?'

'I think sell because, like you say, we'd never forgive ourselves if it got broken, right, Harriet?'

Harriet nodded. 'Yes.'

Gabby breathed a sigh of relief. 'Good. Come on. I need to go back down into the cave and get it. Colette has offered to pack it up and courier it to the auctioneers in time for the next auction if I get it over to her tomorrow.'

An eager Elodie led the way down into the garage. 'I'm so excited to finally see this cave.'

Gabby reached up for the piece of stiff wire she'd left on the top shelf of the unit and carefully locating the flower she needed in the pyrography artwork running down the side of the unit, pushed the wire in and heard the satisfying movement of the latch. As she stretched out her arm to reach the left side of the shelf unit, Harriet went to help her and together they pulled the unit towards them and folded it back while Elodie watched in disbelief. 'That is amazing.'

'Take care on the steps,' Gabby said, switching the light on, and they all made their way down into the cave.

Elodie looked around her and moved towards the brush pot on the table. 'This is the pot? It doesn't look like much, does it? I mean, it's obviously very old, but that's it really. It's not a real thing of beauty, is it? Love the wine rack. What's in the boxes?'

'Haven't really looked yet,' Harriet said. 'We could have a quick look now?' She glanced at Gabby.

'Why not,' Gabby replied. 'I suspect it's just *vide-grenier* stuff, oh and maybe some family mementoes,' she said, staring down at the box in front of her. 'This one has photos and what looks like the old family Bible. Shall we take this one upstairs when we go? Take our time going through it?'

'This one is full of books,' Harriet said, bending over a wooden crate. 'They look like French classics – Proust, Balzac and Victor Hugo are on the very top. Do you think they could be first editions? They look very old.'

'China ornaments in this one,' Elodie said. 'And this one definitely looks like boot-sale stuff.'

'I'll ask Colette to come and take a proper look in the boxes,' Gabby said. 'She might take some of the stuff for the brocante.'

'Right, I'll carry the brush pot upstairs carefully, can you manage the box of photos, Harriet? Choose a bottle of wine, Elodie, we can enjoy a glass while we look at the photos.' Gabby picked up the pot carefully. 'I want to put this pot safely on the dresser out of harm's way.'

'We'll close the cave up,' Harriet said, once they'd climbed the steps, putting down the box. Elodie placed the bottle of wine carefully on the top of it and together they pulled the shelf unit back across the cave entrance and pushed it closed with a satisfying click.

Once back up in the garage, Gabby carried on up into the villa and breathed a sigh of relief as she placed the pot safely well back on the dresser. Harriet took the box out to the terrace table, while Elodie fetched three glasses and opened the wine. Outside, Gabby reached into the box and took out several packets of black and white photographs and she went through them slowly before looking up at the others.

'These are so full of memories for me,' she said quietly. 'Look, this one was taken with my maman when we had a day out together in Cannes to see the newly opened Palais des Festivals. We're standing on the new steps that are famous now all around the world. I think Colette must have taken the photograph because she was with us that day.' She handed the photograph to Elodie as Harriet had started to lift the heavy family Bible out of the box.

'Gabby, you look so much like her,' Elodie said.

'Do I? I don't mind that at all. Maman, she was lovely,' Gabby replied, reaching for another photograph.

Harriet, who'd become engrossed in the family Bible, looked up. 'This is fascinating. Entries go right back to the 1800s. So many people died young, they rarely seemed to live beyond forty. If they'd all lived, there would have been quite a clan of Jacques in Juan in the early twentieth century. There's a Thibault Jacques who was lost at sea when he was thirty-eight, leaving a wife and two young children, one of whom died six months later. So sad. Do you think he could have been the one on the clipper ships who brought the brush pot home?'

'We'll never know, but it's certainly a possibility, I suppose,' Gabby said. 'Oh look, here's a postcard from the early 1930s showing the Provençal dominating the skyline and towering over Juan-les-Pins. I do wish I'd known it in its heyday,' she said wistfully. 'The Jazz Age and the years before the Second World War. And the fifties and sixties were a really glamorous time too with the Film Festival. The Provençal Hotel played a big part in it all, but really when I went to work there its glory days were well and truly over. So sad.'

'May I see?' Harriet said and Gabby handed her the postcard and turned to pick up her glass of wine.

Harriet looked at the postcard thoughtfully, an idea forming in her mind. 'Would you mind if I kept this card out? I'd like to do a copy of it for the exhibition.'

'Of course you can,' Gabby said. 'And I shall come to the exhibition and buy the painting. I can see it now hanging in the sitting room.'

39

The next morning, immediately after breakfast, Gabby carefully wrapped the brush pot in a large towel before placing it in a strong tote bag and walked down to see Colette.

Colette opened the door of the cottage and Gabby handed her the tote with a relieved sigh. 'I have never been so afraid of dropping and breaking anything as much as this pot.'

'Coffee? Then we'll pack it up. The courier arrives here at ten o'clock.'

While the coffee brewed in the Moka pot on the stove, Colette unwrapped the brush pot and placed it in the middle of the table.

'I know it's the sensible thing to do,' Gabby said, looking at it. 'But I can't help feeling a bit guilty that, after all these years in the family, I'm the one selling it.'

'Tch,' Colette said as the coffee pot hissed and she moved across to the stove. 'You'd feel even guiltier if you chipped it or broke it. Better for it to be seen by more people. And, like you said the other day, you can help people with the money.' Colette poured the coffee and handed a cup to her. 'You can always use some of the money to buy something valuable to replace it. Something you really like but would never have bought without selling the pot.'

Gabby nodded. 'I'll maybe do that. The three of us spent some time in the cave yesterday looking at the boxes. It was quite a trip down memory lane for me, so many photographs. You're in quite a few.' She took a sip of her coffee. 'Come to supper soon and we'll have a nostalgic time going through them together? You need to have a look in the boxes too in case there's anything there you'd like for the brocante.'

'Thanks. Right now I'd like a few more customers.'

'You're not doing so well?' Gabby said.

'It's summer.' Colette shrugged. 'It's normally quiet, people are too busy enjoying themselves, but it's quieter than usual. Hopefully, come September, things will be busier as the locals have more time and money in their pockets after the season.'

Once the coffee had been drunk, Colette placed a wooden crate-like box on the table and a large bag of wood wool.

'Right, time to get to work,' and she began to fill the bottom of the crate with the wood wool. Then, she cut a strip of bubble wrap and spread it on the table. Gently, Colette placed the brush pot on it and wrapped it up in several layers before placing it in the crate. More wood wool was put around the sides of the pot and then on top before the lid was closed. Once it was closed, Colette went around the lid screwing it closed with a handful of tiny screws. 'There, all ready for a safe journey to Paris,' she said.

* * *

Back at the villa, after Gabby had left for Colette's, Elodie went for a swim and Harriet took a shower before coming downstairs to ready to walk Lulu before she got on with her painting. She seemed to have slipped into the role of principal dog walker, not that she minded, she adored the little dog. As Harriet bent down to put Lulu's collar on, Elodie walked in from the terrace. Wrapped in a towel, she was talking animatedly into her phone.

'No, I'm sure it will be fine. We'll see you later,' and she ended the call and looked at Harriet.

'That was Jack. We are both invited to have lunch with him today. I told him yes on your behalf. You're not working at the gallery this morning, are you?'

'No, but...' Harriet protested.

'Jack seems to think you've been avoiding him?' Elodie said. 'He also said it's time just the three of us had a family meal together. So we're to meet him at twelve o'clock down at the brasserie in Juan. I'll be in town this morning anyway, got to get some info for a feature, so I'll see you there.' She went to go upstairs but stopped on the first stair and turned back to Harriet. 'If you can't make it or don't want to go, just ring and tell him,' and with that Elodie bounded up the stairs.

Harriet took a deep breath. She hadn't been avoiding Jack deliberately, it was just that their paths hadn't crossed since the Belles Rives. It didn't mean that he hadn't constantly been in her thoughts. He had. But she wasn't about to admit that to anyone, and that included Jack himself.

Besides, there had been no effort on his part either to contact her before this summons-like invitation to lunch. She toyed with the idea of turning her phone off and simply not turning up at the brasserie. He would have good reason to accuse her of avoiding him then. Harriet smiled to herself. She wouldn't give him that satisfaction. She'd walk Lulu, come home, change and then walk into town to have lunch with her ex boyfriend and their daughter.

* * *

Two hours later, as she approached the restaurant, Harriet saw Jack sitting alone at a table. Damn, she'd been hoping that Elodie would be there already.

Jack had spotted her approaching and was standing up to greet her, which he did with two cheek kisses that once again she wasn't quick enough to dodge. He grinned at her knowingly.

'I'm glad you could make it,' he said. 'And I'm glad Elodie isn't here yet. It gives me a little time to talk to you and try to sort us out.'

'There is no us,' Harriet said as she sat down on the chair he'd pulled out for her.

'There was once and I believe there can be again. I still have such powerful feelings for you, Harriet.'

Harriet opened her mouth to speak and closed it again as a waiter arrived with a chilled bottle of rosé in an ice bucket and proceeded to pour them both a glass.

'Merci,' Jack said.

Before he could continue the conversation, Elodie arrived. She went straight to Jack as he stood up and happily accepted his greeting cheek kisses. 'Hi, Jack.' She was about to sit down when she hesitated and moved across to Harriet and awkwardly kissed her cheek. 'Hi, Harriet.'

Harriet's eyes widened in surprise. Cheek greeting kisses had never happened between the two of them before.

'Hi. Have you had a good morning?' she asked in an attempt to cover her shock.

'Yeah,' Elodie nodded. 'And I saw Gazz for ten minutes or so before I came here. I nearly invited him to join us and then I remembered you said just the three of us. A family meal,' Elodie said, looking at Jack. 'So I didn't.'

Jack poured her a glass of rosé. 'Santé.'

'I still can't quite get my head around having lunch with "my parents",' Elodie said. 'Who'd have thought that would ever happen?'

'We can only apologise that you've had to wait so long,' Jack said. 'But I promise you that this is the first family lunch of many that the three of us will have in the future. Right, Harriet?'

'Whatever you say, Jack,' Harriet said, deciding to play along with his 'happy family' version of the future.

The waiter returned at that moment, notebook in hand, ready to take their orders. Harriet quickly picked up the menu. Jack, she knew, would choose a meat dish of some description, Elodie would go for mussels and frites and today she'd have... 'A salad Niçoise please,' she said, smiling up at the waiter.

Once the waiter had taken their order and left, Harriet sat back and sipped her wine, listening to the light-hearted banter between Jack and Elodie. She was glad that the two of them had already established a friendly relationship.

'So what do you think, Harriet?' Jack said.

Hearing her name, she realised she'd zoned out of their conversation. 'Sorry, I was miles away. What do I think about what?'

'The two of us visiting Jack in America in the autumn – I mean the fall,' Elodie smiled. 'It could be fun, the two of us going together, a bit of mother and daughter bonding.'

Harriet looked at Elodie in surprise. Was she serious and offering a tentative olive branch? It was a nice thought but then Harriet remembered the exhibition and the paintings she had to complete and she shook her head. 'Sorry, no can do. I'm committed to my exhibition. But there's nothing stopping you from going.'

She immediately regretted her words as she saw the look of disappointment flash across Elodie's face. 'But maybe we can go together another time? I'm told spring in New York is wonderful.'

40

A week later, Gabby and Philippe were sipping their after-lunch coffees in Gabby's favourite Juan-les-Pins restaurant. The one where Philippe had first taken her to lunch last Christmas and where he had organised the party for her seventieth birthday on New Year's Eve. The walls of the restaurant were covered with black and white photographs of Juan-les-Pins dating from the nineteen thirties through to the sixties and included several of the Hotel le Provençal when it had been one of the most famous hotels on the French Riviera.

Gabby had just finished her coffee and replaced the cup on its saucer, when her mobile pinged with a text from Colette.

'Sorry, I need to read this,' she said. 'It's important.' Today was the day of the auction in Paris of the brush pot. She hadn't told Philippe about the auction and Colette had promised to let her know as soon as the pot was sold. She was going to watch the auction live on the internet.

Gabby let out a short gasp as she read the text:

Sold for two million euros above the estimate

And struggled to contain her emotions as the phone shook in her hand.

'Are you okay?' Philippe asked anxiously. 'You've gone pale.'

'I'm fine,' Gabby said shakily. 'I do need to talk to you later about something that has happened, though.' She gave him a smile. 'It's something good, something very good in fact, so don't worry.'

'You sure I shouldn't be worried?'

'It's good, so no, please don't worry.' Gabby stood up and took a deep breath, needing to come back down to earth. 'I feel so special at being able to have a look at the show apartment in Le Provençal,' she said. 'I know you told me the tickets were limited, do you have any idea how many people will be at the open viewing this afternoon?'

Philippe shook his head. 'No. Does it matter? Come on, I've settled the bill, let's go.'

Gabby looked at him. That was a bit snappy for Philippe, he was normally so placid. 'It's my turn to ask, are you okay? You seem a bit tense.'

'I'm fine. I just want to get there on time.'

Gabby was surprised minutes later when, instead of going to the main entrance, Philippe opened the door of a building alongside and ushered her in. She looked at him curiously.

'This is the office of the developers. We register here and then they will take us into the apartments.'

The office, with its thick carpet and highly polished desk, an Apple computer placed in the centre and a large banana tree plant in a terracotta pot, felt more like the study of a very successful person to Gabby. A woman behind the desk looked up as they entered and was immediately on her feet to welcome them.

'Bonjour. Monsieur Vincent and Madame Jacques?'

'That is us, yes,' Philippe answered.

'Monsieur Roget will arrive immediately,' and she pressed a discreet button under the desk. Seconds later, a door behind her opened and a well-dressed middle-aged man came out to greet them. After shaking hands, he picked up the two brochures from the desk and ushered them towards the door. And then, for the first time in forty years, Gabby was once again entering the building that unknowingly had played such an important part in her life.

Walking in through the main entrance of Le Provençal took Gabby's breath away. Everything was so pristine and of the highest quality. The chandelier hanging over the reception desk was dazzling in its brightness. The marble floors, the leather Chesterfield placed at an angle to the highly polished oak desk with another high-tech computer, an array of glossy brochures on its surface, another receptionist with a welcoming smile standing behind it to welcome them.

Gabby was transported back to those far-off days when it had been her standing in the shabby hotel foyer as a lowly receptionist greeting guests who still came to stay in the famous hotel. So many celebrities had stayed in Le Provençal down through the years its registers had read like a Who's Who of politicians, actors, singers, jazz musicians and the rich. Now of course, it was no longer a hotel but a block of luxury apartments with several high-class boutiques on the ground floor. Once the apartments were occupied there would be a full-time concierge rather than a receptionist sitting behind that oak desk, to help residents with anything they might need.

Monsieur Roget ushered them into the waiting lift and as he pressed the button for the seventh floor Gabby stared at her reflection in the mirrors that lined the spacious elevator.

Gabby turned to look at Philippe. 'I would have expected the show apartment to be on a lower floor. And there doesn't appear to be anyone else looking. I thought it was going to be busy.'

Monsieur Roget gave Philippe a puzzled look. 'The show apartment is on the first floor, madame, but you and Monsieur Vincent have been booked to see this empty and unfurnished one.'

As the lift came to a gentle silent stop and the doors opened, they stepped out into a hallway with an open door into an empty apartment.

Gabby walked straight through to the window. 'Oh, what a view. I never came up to this floor when I worked here. Strictly out of bounds.'

Monsieur Roget gave a visible start. 'Madame Jacques, you knew the old Le Provençal?'

'Yes, I was a young receptionist here in the late sixties and very early seventies.'

'May I ask,' he hesitated. 'Do you happen to recall a woman called

Agnes Roget? She worked here during that time also,' the man asked quietly.

Gabby looked at him and smiled. 'Yes, I remember her well. Agnes was very kind to me at a difficult time in my life. She had a son who had a Saturday job as a bellboy. I think his name was Clovis.' Gabby stopped as she saw the smile cross the man's face. 'Is that you?'

'Yes.'

'You worked with Old Henri, the oldest bellboy in the business I always thought.'

Clovis laughed. 'Taught me a lot did Old Henri. Mind you, some of it was stuff that my mother wouldn't have wanted me to learn.'

'So how have you ended up here?'

'Long story. Went off to Paris, trained as an architect. Worked all over the place, eventually landing up with the developers that bought this place and here I am.'

Philippe cleared his throat.

'I'm so sorry, Philippe, for the trip down memory lane, but isn't it great that Clovis here still has a connection to the place?'

Philippe nodded and smiled.

Clovis handed them both a brochure. 'These are for you to keep. Please take your time looking around. I'll see you back in the foyer when you're ready.'

Gabby opened her brochure with its stunning colour photographs of the furnished show apartment and computer-generated photographs of how the pool and the landscaped areas would look once finished. 'Did you know there is a pool as well?' she said as she began to wander from room to room. 'This is a big apartment. The kitchen is a lovely size, a bathroom and a shower room, two bedrooms, a study and this wonderful sitting room. I can just imagine it furnished, but I dread to think how much it would cost to buy.'

'Gabriella? I have a confession to make.'

Something in the tone of Philippe's voice made Gabby turn and look at him.

'There is no open day for locals. I – we – are here as prospective purchasers.' He took a deep breath. 'What would you say if I asked, do you think you could live in this apartment with me?'

Gabby stood stock-still. 'Are you serious?'

'Never more so.'

'You are able to buy something like this?'

Philippe gave her an enigmatic smile. 'Yes, I am, but I wouldn't – not without you wanting to share and live in it with me.'

'I'm stunned.' Gabby shook her head. 'Can I think about it? Can we have a proper talk about it later?'

'Of course.'

Gabby wandered around the apartment again, looking at the bathroom with its marble and gold fittings, the kitchen with its hand built units. 'It's truly a beautiful apartment,' she said. 'It's even got a few Art Deco fixtures from the old building around the ceiling.' With one final glance, Gabby completed the tour of the apartment. 'I think I've seen enough,' Gabby said. 'I'd quite like to leave now and find somewhere to sit and have a serious talk.'

'D'accord.'

They rode the lift back down to the foyer in silence. Gabby acknowledged Clovis with a smile and an absent wave as Philippe went over to the desk to the receptionist.

'We'll be in touch. Thank you.'

Once outside, they made their way slowly down to La Pinède, where Gabby headed over to a bench in the shade under a pine tree. She needed to sit down and gather her thoughts.

Philippe sat down beside her and together they sat in silence for several moments, each deep in their own thoughts, until Philippe took a deep breath. 'Gabriella, there was another question I wanted to ask you back there in Le Provençal, one I intended to ask you first, but I was so anxious about you liking the apartment, I got the order of speaking wrong.' He took hold of her hand. 'I long for us to live together in the Provençal apartment, but I want it to be as man and wife. Gabriella Jacques, will you please marry me?'

41

Gabby looked at Philippe, shocked. 'You want to marry me?'

'Yes, don't look so surprised, *ma cherie*. You must know how I feel about you. And I think you're quite fond of me too?

Gabby nodded. 'Yes, of course I am, but I never dreamt...' She shook her head. 'At our age you think it's not...'

'Think it's not what, Gabriella? Not possible to find love again? Life is what you make it and you've made me happier in the last year than I've been for a long time. I want us to be happy together. And yes, I do love you. Very much."

'Before I give you my answer, I have to tell you something,' Gabby said. 'That text earlier? It was from Colette. Ten days ago, she couriered the brush pot to an auction house in Paris. Remember a year or two ago, there was an old Japanese vase found in an attic in Brittany that turned out to have religious significance and it sold for millions?'

Philippe nodded.

'Well, my old Chinese brush pot, whilst not of religious importance, has turned out to be a very rare item. It was auctioned today and sold for two million over the estimated price, which was much more than I ever expected in the first place.' Gabby rubbed her face with her hand. 'I can't quite believe it.'

'Do you have any plans for the money?' Philippe asked quietly.

'Nothing definite, but obviously Harriet and Elodie will benefit and I was thinking of setting up some sort of charity foundation but...' she shrugged. 'No idea what though. It will all have to sink in first. It'll be a week or two anyway before any decisions can start to be made.'

'Why did you want me to know about it before you gave me your answer?' Philippe asked.

'Mainly because I want to be open and honest with you about everything and I thought you ought to know about such a momentous happening. Having so much money is bound to change our lives – it's like a lottery win.'

'So you've told me. We are prepared for our lives to change. Now please tell me – are you going to marry me? And do we get to live in the Provençal? Or would you prefer somewhere without the memories?'

'There's only one answer I can give you to both questions – and that's yes.' And Gabby moved happily into Philippe's embrace as he put his arm around her shoulders and drew her towards him.

'Thank you, my darling. That makes me so very happy.' Philippe stood up. 'Come on, there's a bottle of champagne in my fridge. We need a glass to celebrate and then we go choose a ring, yes?'

* * *

Gabby was bursting to tell everyone her news but had to wait until after supper that evening when the three of them were finally sitting out on the terrace together, listening to the cicadas getting quieter and quieter, until finally the garden was empty of their noise.

Gabby took a deep breath, wanting to have their full attention. 'I have news. Important news.'

Both Harriet and Elodie looked at her and waited.

'Philippe has asked me to marry him. I said yes and we're going to live in the Provençal when the apartments are all finished.'

Elodie flew out of her chair and gave her grandmother a tight hug. 'Gabby, I'm so pleased and happy for you. Philippe is so lovely. You so deserve to be happy.'

Harriet too got up and hugged her mother. 'Congratulations. Like Elodie says, you deserve to be happy.'

'When are you having the engagement party?' Elodie asked.

Gabby shook her head. 'Oh, I don't know that we need one.'

'Of course you need one,' Elodie said. 'We'll work out a date and have it here. We'll organise it, won't we, Harriet?'

'Of course,' Harriet agreed, laughing.

'Thank you,' Gabby said. 'But that's not all my news. The next news is somewhat even more mind-blowing. The brush pot was auctioned in Paris today and it made rather a lot of money.' Both Harriet and Elodie gasped when she told them the sum and sat down quickly. 'Of course, you two will each get a large sum and then I'd like you to think about charitable causes we could help. Set up a foundation or something. I also have to talk to you about the villa, Elodie. There's something I haven't told you. I was waiting until the time was right and this seems like the moment,' Gabby said. 'When I inherited it ten years ago, I signed it over to you. You are the owner of Villa de l'Espoir, not me. I never expected to come and live here ever again, but I always planned for you to inherit the villa.' Gabby glanced up at Harriet. 'Your inheritance is the Dartmouth house. Since we sold it, and moved over here, the money has been invested for you.'

'Mum, I'm speechless,' Harriet said. 'It's almost too much to take in.'

'I know how you feel,' Gabby said. 'But it's all rather wonderful, isn't it?' And she smiled at them happily.

42

A few days later, when Elodie had taken Lulu for a walk and Gabby was out with Philippe collecting the engagement ring Gabby had chosen which had needed adjusting, Harriet was at home alone trying to paint. Last Saturday when Hugo had asked her how many paintings she was likely to have ready for the December exhibition, she'd felt ashamed telling him about the meagre amount she'd managed so far. She was so lucky to have met Hugo. Other artists struggled to find someone willing to exhibit their work and here she was prevaricating. If the exhibition was to ever happen, she had to get painting. The fact that she was also trying to get her head around the events of the last few days and sort her thoughts and emotions out didn't help.

Now that Jack and Elodie had met, whatever happened in the future would be down to them. They were both adults; they could sort everything out between themselves. There was no need for her to be involved, but she couldn't stop thinking about Jack's toast at lunch for a united family. Just how united a family did he have in mind?

Absently, she looked at her latest effort on the easel that she'd finished yesterday. Propped up on the easel ledge was the photo she'd used as inspiration. An old wooden door, set in an ancient stone wall, in one of the narrow lanes of Antibes old town, was hanging open at a drunken angle half off its hinges, its olive green paint faded and peeling. A flowering blue plumbago plant was running rampant over the top of the wall and down the side of the door.

Standing there, comparing the painting with the photo, she felt happy that she'd got the light and the shadows right and had created an atmospheric and nostalgic painting. Now to put it safely out of the way and make a start on the next painting – one that would go into the exhibition already marked as sold.

Harriet had already decided that this one, the painting of the Hotel Provençal as depicted on the postcard they'd found in the box from the cave, would make a more than suitable wedding present for Gabby and Philippe.

The gate buzzer startled her. Jack's voice came over the intercom. 'Hi, Jack here. May I come in, please? I'd like to talk to Harriet.'

For a fleeting moment, Harriet debated about staying quiet and letting Jack believe that everyone was out. He'd only come back though. It would be easier to see him without company.

Harriet put her paintbrush down, slowly walked through to the hallway and pressed the entry button. She was waiting by the front door as the gate closed behind Jack.

'Hello, Jack. I'm not sure what there is left to talk about now that you've met Elodie and the two of you are happy to be in each other's life.' Harriet smiled at him, hoping to indicate that she was pleased for the two of them.

'Elodie and I are only one part of the equation – you and I are the other part,' Jack said. 'We need to talk. No Elodie? Gabby?' he asked, looking around.

'I'm home alone and I should be painting. Can whatever you want to say wait for a few days?'

Jack shook his head. 'No. I want us to have an honest, open conversation with each other. A proper discussion about what happened in the past – and what happens now, in the future.'

Harriet took a deep breath before she turned and walked back through the villa to the veranda, where her easel stood. Jack followed her and she gestured at him to sit at the table and sat opposite him.

'This is lovely,' he said, looking around the garden. 'The pool looks inviting right now it's so hot.'

'Jack! Please get to the point of why you are here – or I'll push you into the pool! And don't think I'm joking.'

There was a pause while he looked at her. 'You and I have unfinished business,' Jack held up his hand as Harriet went to speak, and his eyes stared into hers. 'It's the truth and you know it. We – and let's not forget our wonderful daughter – have all missed out during the last twenty-four years. The future will include the three of us and in time I hope and pray we can become the family we are meant to be.'

Harriet felt herself deflate. She did know it was the truth, but admitting it was hard.

'That night the two of us had supper on the beach was like old times. It felt so good to be back with you. And lunch the other day, just you and me with our daughter, was surely a special family moment for you. I know it was for me.' Jack paused. 'I'd like us to see if the love we shared all those years ago is still there, that it's just been buried by our separation.' Jack looked at her. 'For my part, I feel it is – I'm not sure whether you feel the same, though.'

Harriet gave a helpless shrug. 'How can I not? What we had in the past was wonderful. But we're both different people now. Life has hurt us both. And for that, believe me, I blame myself, no one else.'

Jack reached out and picked up her hand. 'But deep down we are still those two kids who met, fell in love and, I suspect – believe even – we never truly fell out of love with each other. Life took us down separate forks in the road, but now we get a second chance to join our lives together again. And this time we've got Elodie too. We can be a proper family. I know my own feelings are refusing to stay buried any more now that we've met up again.'

Harriet gave a deep sigh. 'I agree with everything you've just said, but it's not that easy. Oh, I know we're both single and we have Elodie linking us together forever, but for a start, you live in America and I live here in France. As do both Gabby and Elodie. I can't leave either of them. They haven't been back in my life that long. And we both know long-distance relationships are difficult.'

'I've thought of that already. I'll buy somewhere over here and we make France our base – our home. We can spend the majority of our time here and visit America whenever we want to or are needed. Next problem?'

Harriet swallowed hard. Jack had clearly anticipated her reaction to his words and had the solution ready and waiting.

'This exhibition Hugo is arranging for me at the end of the year, it could be the start of me finally finding my place in the art world,' she shrugged. 'On the other hand, it could be a complete flop. I just need to give it my all and find out once and for all whether I'm good enough for other people.'

'It won't be a flop. Your paintings are excellent. The house we buy will have to have a studio for you, obviously.' Jack looked at her. 'This Hugo – I need to know, do you have feelings for him?'

'I've told you before, Hugo is a friend, a good friend. We are not, and never have been, involved emotionally, although I think Hugo had hopes in that direction before...' her voice trailed away.

'Before I turned up,' Jack said with a smile. 'So there is really nothing to stop us from getting to know each other again.'

Harriet looked at him and laughed. 'God, you are still the same. Make up your mind over something and you want it quicker than instantly. You are so impatient.'

'Maybe,' Jack said, a serious look on his face. 'But be warned, I'm not losing you this time round. We should have been together for the last twenty-four years – I'm determined to spend the next quarter of a century – the rest of my life in fact - with you. And I have the very best of reasons for that.'

'Really? And what is that?'

'Because I am, have been and always will be, deeply in love with you.'

Before a stunned Harriet could react to his words, Jack had pulled her into his arms and, holding tight as if he'd never let her go, was kissing her in such a way that left her in no doubt at all about how much he loved her.

43

After Jack had left, Harriet sent a text to Jessica inviting her to meet up for lunch. She needed to talk to someone. Gabby and Elodie were too close, she needed someone who could view the situation dispassionately. A minute later, her phone rang.

'Hi. Lunch would be fun. It is ages since we caught up. Meet you in ten minutes down by the casino,' Jessica said. 'We can go to the restaurant next door.'

Jessica was waiting for her when Harriet arrived and the two friends quickly found a table and ordered moules and frites and a bottle of rosé.

'Come on then, spill the news,' Jessica said, pouring them each a glass.

'First, I'm sorry we haven't seen much of each other since the party. Summer seems to be disappearing fast. Life seems to have got busy and somewhat complicated and I'm in need of some unbiased advice.'

'No worries, summer is always full on down here, and this year I've been busy with doing the Airbnb, which, if I'm honest, I'm not sure is worth the hassle. Anyway, Hugo tells me you're painting again and that there's an exhibition planned?'

'Yes, I am. Desperately behind with producing enough paintings, but there's several weeks yet until December. The thing is, one of my complications is that Elodie's father has turned up.'

Jessica gave her a wide-eyed look. 'Hugo did tell me an ex-boyfriend had shown up, but that was all. I can't believe you haven't told me this before.'

'Yes, I'm sorry about that. Life has been a bit full on. Jack was understandably cross with me when he found out about Elodie. And Elodie...' Harriet sighed. 'Well, she took her time to meet him, which was stressful, but that side of things has worked okay now.'

'So, what do you need advice on?'

'Jack, like me, he had an unhappy marriage, is now divorced and says he's never forgotten me. And he wants us to get back together.'

'Had you forgotten him?'

'No.' Harriet said without hesitation, touching the silver bracelet that Jack had given her.

'So what's the problem?'

'He's American and lives there. I live in France. He is full of plans for relocating, living half here and half in the States. He seems to forget I've only just been reunited with Gabby and Elodie. I can't just desert them again.'

'I don't think it sounds like he's asking you to do that,' Jessica said slowly. 'Anyway, Elodie has Gazz now – I love that girl by the way, she's perfect for my son – and now Philippe has asked Gabby to marry him, I don't see there's a problem there either.'

Their moules and frites arrived at that moment and they both tucked in. It wasn't until they were both mopping up the cream sauce with slices of baguette that Harriet looked at Jessica.

'I'm just putting up obstacles, aren't I?'

Jessica nodded. 'I think you're frightened of it going wrong a second time. But from what you've told me, it didn't go wrong so much as you made a bad decision and took the wrong road years ago. If you want my advice – go where your heart tells you.'

'Both you and Jack make it sound so easy.'

'It is. Just say yes and do it.'

* * *

Harriet left Jessica after lunch, both of them promising to get together more often, and was making her way home when her mobile beeped with a message from Hugo:

Could really do with you this afternoon if possible? The world and his wife seem to have descended in the gallery

Harriet quickly replied:

In town. I'll be there in five minutes

The gallery was packed with more people than Harriet had ever seen in the shop at one time. She put her bag out in the office and went to help Hugo behind the counter. It was another hour before things quietened down and things returned to normal.

'Where did they all come from?' Harriet asked.

'I think there were a couple of coach tours in town today,' Hugo replied. 'Clearly full of art lovers. Thanks for helping out.' He paused and looked at her. 'So, how are things with Jack?'

'Settling down, thankfully. Have you heard the news about Gabby and Philippe?' Harriet asked, not ready to talk to Hugo yet about the direction things with Jack actually seemed to be going in. 'They're getting married. The engagement party is tomorrow evening and if you'd like to come you'd be more than welcome. Not a large party, just family, the Vincents and Jack and his mother.'

Hugo raised an eyebrow. 'His mother?'

'Yes, she's a lovely woman. She's actually a customer of ours too, so you're sure to like her. I'll make sure she knows who you are.'

'Thanks. I'll be there. Here we go again,' he muttered as the door opened and group of half a dozen or so walked into the gallery.

'Smile and think of the money they're spending,' Harriet said.

44

Harriet and Elodie, having insisted that Gabby and Philippe had an engagement party, did the organising together. With just twelve people expected, there wasn't a lot to do. Once again, finger food from the super-market and boulangerie was the easy option - sliced baguettes with cream cheese, jambon or smoked salmon, savoury pastries, crisps, stuffies and olives. All followed by a selection of miniature desserts – lemon-curd tarts, bite-sized meringues and tarte tatin.

By seven thirty on the night of the party, the food was laid out on the terrace table with plates and champagne glasses. Two bottles of the cham-pagne from the cave, plus three bottles of pink champagne in case the older champagne wasn't drinkable, were in the fridge. Lulu was shut safely away in Harriet's bedroom until everybody had arrived, when Harriet would let her out, and Harriet and Elodie were now both down on the terrace, waiting for Gabby to join them.

'Don't think we've forgotten anything, do you? We don't need music until later, do we?' Elodie said.

Harriet shook her head. 'No. All we need now is for Gabby to come downstairs and for Philippe and everyone to arrive.'

'Well, I'm here,' Gabby said. 'It all looks fantastic. Thank you so much. Come here both of you and let me give you a hug.'

The two of them moved towards her and as Gabby put an arm around each of them, they put their arms around her and each other. Gabby sighed happily. A proper family group hug.

'To be standing here in the garden of Villa l'Espoir with my daughter and my granddaughter, waiting to celebrate my engagement, is something beyond my wildest dreams,' she said, her voice trembling. 'I am so happy to have you both in my life,' and she planted a kiss on Harriet's forehead before doing the same to Elodie.

As they moved apart, the ring on her hand flashed in the last rays of sunlight. Harriet caught hold of the hand and held it.

'That is one beautiful ring, Mum.' A two-stone diamond twist ring with smaller diamonds set in the platinum twist, it was stunning in its design.

Gabby bit her lip. 'It is, isn't it? I didn't want a modern ring and we both loved this vintage one the moment we saw it. And the fact that the provenance describes it as Art Deco makes it perfect in the circumstances, don't you think?'

'Definitely,' Harriet said.

'It's beautiful. I'll open a bottle of champagne and we can have a private toast before everyone gets here,' Elodie said, and went to fetch a bottle from the kitchen. 'I've brought one of the cave bottles seeing as how they're vintage too,' she remarked as she carefully placed a cloth over the top of the cork and began to twist and manoeuvre it out of the bottle. A tight fit, it was a minute before she'd finally released it with a satisfying 'pop' and began to pour them a glass each.

Their three glasses clinked together.

'Congratulations to you,' Elodie and Harriet said before they all took a sip. There was silence as they looked at each other.

Harriet was the first to speak. 'I have never tasted champagne like that before. It's wonderful.'

'Let's hope the remaining bottles are as good,' Gabby said, laughing.

The gate buzzer sounded at the moment.

'Party time,' said Elodie. 'I'll go and let people in.'

Philippe, Mickaël, Jessica and Gazz all arrived together, followed within minutes by Jack and Martha. By the time Hugo, Colette and Lianna arrived, the second bottle of champagne had been opened.

Elodie was at the table picking up a plate of savoury tartlets to hand around, when Harriet whispered in her ear, 'We forgot something.'

'What?'

'We need someone to do the toast to the happy couple.'

'Oh, you can do that,' Elodie said.

'Are you sure you don't want to?'

Elodie shook her head. 'I don't mind doing it, but I think you're the person who should do it. In about ten minutes I think would be perfect timing.'

'Okay.' Harriet picked up the champagne bottle and went round topping everyone up ready for the toast. Once she was sure everyone had some in their glass, she clapped her hands.

'Toast time. I'd just like to say how happy we are for you as we celebrate your engagement with you. Mum, I'd like to personally say how happy I am that you have found someone to love and who clearly loves you back. Please raise your glasses to Gabriella and Philippe. Congratulations.'

'Your turn, Papa. Speech. Speech,' Mickaël called.

Philippe, standing next to Gabby, took hold of her hand. 'Merci, everyone, for coming to celebrate with us tonight. And merci to Harriet and Elodie for organising everything. Both Gabriella and I feel incredibly lucky to have met each other at this stage of our lives, but when that *coup de coeur* hits there is no escape, however old you are. Some of you have asked when is the wedding. Well, it is already booked for three o'clock the thirty-first of December - New Year's Eve and Gabriella's birthday. Which gives me just one date to remember for both important *anniversaires*. You are all, of course, invited. Thank you.'

As the evening grew darker and the moon became a round ball of silver up in the sky, and the solar lights were lighting up the garden, Harriet moved towards the open doors of the veranda. Time for some music. She'd set up the laptop earlier and now she pressed the button for the playlist she'd chosen. She'd deliberately chosen some Ella Fitzgerald and Frank

Sinatra tracks, knowing that Gabby liked that kind of easy music. As Ella's voice singing 'Begin the Beguine' drifted on the evening air, she watched Gabby slip into Philippe's arms and the two of them swayed together.

'Now, that is a good idea,' a voice alongside her said, and before she realised what was happening, Jack's arms were around her and they too were moving together to the music. Knowing it was useless to protest, and not wanting to either, Harriet gave in and stayed willingly in Jack's arms.

Elodie, dancing with Gazz down by the pool, glanced up and saw her parents in each other's arms. Was the undreamed of actually going to happen? Was she finally, at nearly twenty-five years of age, going to have a proper set of parents?

When she looked again a few moments later as the music changed, the two of them had drawn apart and were simply standing there looking at each other before they turned and walked hand in hand back to the party.

Colette and Lianna were the first to say goodbye to Gabby and the others at eleven o'clock. As Harriet saw them out and went to close the gate behind them, Hugo appeared at her side.

'Time for me to leave. Thanks for a lovely evening,' he said. 'Gabby and Philippe make a great couple. And you were right, Martha is a lovely woman.'

'See, I said you'd like her,' Harriet said, smiling at him.

'I like her son too,' Hugo said quietly. 'I realised something tonight that makes me sad, but I have to face facts. You and I can only ever be friends, as much as I'd have liked more.'

'Hugo, I'm sorry too. I really like you but...'

'But you love Jack more.' He sighed. 'It is what it is. See you Saturday as usual. Be happy.'

45

The three of them were all at home the next morning. Gabby was just pottering around the villa doing bits and pieces waiting for Philippe, Harriet was getting ready to walk Lulu, and Elodie was up in her room writing her Sunday magazine feature when an agitated Jack pressed the buzzer. Harriet, standing near the intercom as she clipped on Lulu's lead, answered.

'Harriet, I need to speak to you urgently, alone if possible,' he said.

'I was about to take Lulu for a walk, want to come with me?'

'Yes, that would be perfect.'

They'd barely left the impasse when Jack told her his news.

'I have to return to the States. Something has cropped up that Nathan can't deal with and I can't do it remotely. I have to be there personally. Will you come back with me? Three or four days, a week at the most.'

'No. I can't, there's too much going on here at the moment,' Harriet said instantly.

'Please, Harriet, just think about it. I'm sure Gabby and Elodie can spare you for that short time. You can stay in my house, and I can show you around a little, and then we can travel back together.'

'No, it's not possible. I can't take a week off painting. I'm way behind producing stuff for the exhibition as it is. I promise, though, I'll be here waiting for you to come back.'

Jack's shoulders sank. 'If you're sure I can't persuade you, I'll get back to the hotel then. I need to organise a few things. I couldn't get a direct flight from Nice to the States. My flight to Paris leaves at ten o'clock tonight. I'll pick up a connection to New York in the morning.'

'I'll walk back with you,' Harriet said, her heart heavy at the thought of him leaving.

As they reached the Pinède Gould, Jack pulled her to one side where they were hidden from curious glances by a large shrub before taking her in his arms. 'I love you, Harriet, always have, always will. But you haven't said those three little words to me that I long to hear. I need to know before I leave this time: do you feel like that about me?'

Harriet stood on tiptoe and gave him a kiss that would leave him in no doubt about how she felt. As they drew apart, she said, 'I have always loved you too and I always will.'

'Finally, the answer I've longed to hear. I'll see you next week,' Jack said, releasing her. 'And we'll make plans for a future where we are together all the time.'

After leaving Jack at the hotel, Harriet walked home slowly with Lulu and went straight to her room. She didn't want Elodie or Gabby asking questions, she simply wanted to be alone. Saying goodbye to Jack outside the hotel and realising how much she did still love him, her mind had flashed back to the last time he'd been called home urgently.

Not going with him that time had changed the whole course of her life – for the worse. Sensibly, she knew not going with him tonight would not have the same result. She wasn't pregnant for a start; his father was now dead; there was no reason for him not to return to her. And Martha was still here. And it was true, too, she had to paint at least three pictures this week to still be in with a chance of being ready for the exhibition. But she felt bereft at the thought of him being thousands of miles away.

She picked up her phone and idly scrolled through the photos of the paintings she had done to show Hugo. She could see that they were good, that her confidence was returning. The summer season would finish soon and things would calm down, there would be time to do more, to catch up.

Taking a week off wouldn't truly be a problem. She was the problem. What had Freya said to her at the supper that evening – 'Not everyone gets a second chance. If you do, you should grab it with both hands.' And then Jessica's recent words popped into her mind too. 'Just say yes and do it.'

Harriet went down for lunch when Elodie called to say it was ready. She sensed the other two were treading carefully around her and her feelings and lunch was a subdued affair. Philippe arriving to swim with Gabby that afternoon brought some light-hearted relief, but Harriet soon escaped back to the silence of her room.

It was six thirty when she finally gave in to her feelings. On her laptop, she pulled up the web page for Nice airport. She'd just check and find out whether the ten o'clock flight to Paris was fully booked. Full or not, it would be a sign.

Harriet stared at the page. Three seats were still available. She grabbed her credit card from her purse and started to type in her details. As she filled everything in and waited for it to be verified, she could hear Philippe downstairs and she opened her door and called out, 'Philippe, I have a favour to ask you. Could you please drive me to Nice airport right away? Jack is flying to Paris tonight – and I need to catch the flight too.'

'Of course,' came the reply.

Hurriedly, Harriet threw some clothes, underwear and shoes into a small carry-on case. Anything else she needed she'd buy in America. She remembered to grab a coat from the wardrobe – New York would be cold after the south of France – made sure she had her phone and her passport before running downstairs. This time she wasn't letting Jack leave without her.

Downstairs, she found Elodie and Gabby standing with Philippe waiting for her. 'We're coming too. Just in case,' Gabby said. Harriet didn't ask in case of what, she knew. If she missed the flight, she would be desolate.

Philippe made for the A8 autoroute slip road and soon they were speeding towards the airport. Nearly eight thirty, half an hour and they should be there. Philippe drove straight to the 'Kiss and Fly' outside departures.

'Gabby and I will find somewhere to park. You go with your mum,

Elodie, we'll see you in there.' Turning to look at Harriet, he gave her a smile. '*Bon chance*. You're doing the right thing.'

Elodie was out of the car, leading the way into departures. 'You check in and I'll see if I can find Jack while you're doing that.'

Minutes later, she spotted him in the queue for the departure lounge. 'Dad,' she shouted. Heads turned towards her, including Jack's, and she shouted, 'Wait' and waved frantically.

Harriet reached her side at that moment. Wordlessly they looked at each other before moving into a tight hug.

'Go on, Mum, Dad's waiting,' Elodie said as they separated and Harriet started to walk towards Jack.

Elodie caught her breath. She'd just called them Mum and Dad in a perfectly natural way without even thinking about what she was doing. She stood there watching as her dad opened his arms and her mum walked into them.

Just before they went through the doors into the departure lounge, Jack and Harriet turned and waved and both mouthed the words 'We love you' at her. She waved back, wiped the tears from her cheeks and mouthed the words 'Mum and Dad – I love you both too.'

EPILOGUE
31 DECEMBER

Life had become extremely busy for Gabby and Philippe after their engagement party. Both of them wanted a small intimate wedding, but it didn't take long for Gabby to discover that even a small event took a lot of organising. It was a huge relief when Philippe suggested they hired a wedding planner. Not only did he suggest it, he found an excellent one, and from then on Amelia was in charge of everything. She organised dress fittings for Gabby, Harriet and Elodie. The photographer, the flowers, the cars – everything was taken care of. The civil ceremony in Antibes would be followed by a reception in the Belle Rives and a month's honeymoon touring Italy.

The buying of the apartment in Le Provençal was set in motion, but it would be a few more months before they could actually move in. When they returned from honeymoon, Philippe would move into Villa l'Espoir until the purchase was complete. But today was Gabby's birthday and they were getting married...

* * *

Life became extremely busy for Harriet and Jack too after they returned from that first visit together to America. Harriet, amazed by how much she'd enjoyed New York, happily agreed to dividing their time between France and America. Jack's house there was put up for sale and they were looking for somewhere on the coast with a view of the ocean. In France, Harriet was thrilled to find a lovely villa with a studio in the hills above Cannes, not far from Mougins, the village she'd adored when Hugo had taken her there. Harriet had met Nathan and Kelly, his wife, and got on well with them, which was in direct contrast to Sabrina, Jack's ex-wife, who couldn't have been more disdainful of the fact that she was an artist. Martha, though, told her to ignore her. 'Jack's a different man since you came back into his life and she's jealous.'

They'd had several family outings with Elodie and Gazz and had settled into their role of parents of a grown-up woman happily.

The December exhibition in Hugo's gallery was a success, many of the paintings had sold and Harriet accepted several commissions for the new year. And today Harriet would be a witness to her mother marrying Philippe...

* * *

Elodie had several features published in the run-up to Christmas and editors had started to approach her with their requirements. Gazz had had a good first season on the beach and was looking forward to next year. The news that the villa belonged to her had been a shock to Gazz, but he'd happily agreed to move in with her when Gabby and Philippe finally moved out to their apartment in Le Provençal in the New Year. And today she was being a proper bridesmaid, even though bridesmaids weren't really a thing in France...

* * *

Standing on the steps of the Antibes Town Hall, and now known legally as Madame Gabriella Vincent, Gabby held the hand of her new husband and smiled happily as the wedding party threw rose petal confetti over them both. Returning to live in France had been the best decision she'd made.

Her fractured family had become whole again, with Harriet and Elodie reunited, and France had given her an amazing new husband.

The New Year that would be rung in at midnight promised to be filled with so much love and happiness with Philippe at her side. Together they walked down the steps to the waiting wedding car with its ribbons and balloons. Philippe helped her in before getting in himself, holding her hand tightly as the car set off for Juan-les-Pins and the Belle Rives. As the cacophony of car horns started and the wedding procession moved through the streets, Gabby gave a contented sigh. Life was wonderful.

ACKNOWLEDGMENTS

So many people to thank. Team Boldwood you are amazing and I thank you for having faith in me and my stories. Big thanks to my editor, Caroline, and Jade and Rose – the three of you are wonderful! This time too I have to thank the developers of the Provençal Hotel, Caudwell Investments, in particular Franck Jurquet who patiently answered my questions. My husband too has been a huge help acting as a sounding board and technical advisor. And big thanks must go to Rachel Gilbey and all the bloggers out there who do so much to help authors. Lastly, but by no means least, a huge thank you to my readers who make it all worthwhile. I hope you enjoy this one.

Love, Jennie.

xx

MORE FROM JENNIFER BOHNET

We hope you enjoyed reading *Summer on the French Riviera*. If you did, please leave a review.

If you'd like to gift a copy, this book is also available as an ebook, hardback, large print, digital audio download and audiobook CD.

Sign up to Jennifer Bohnet's mailing list for news, competitions and updates on future books.

http://bit.ly/JenniferBohnetNewsletter

Explore more gloriously escapist reads from Jennifer Bohnet.

  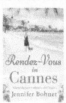  

ABOUT THE AUTHOR

Jennifer Bohnet is the bestselling author of over 14 women's fiction novels, including *Villa of Sun and Secrets* and *The Little Kiosk By The Sea*. She is originally from the West Country but now lives in the wilds of rural Brittany, France.

Visit Jennifer's website: http://www.jenniferbohnet.com/

Follow Jennifer on social media:

    facebook.com/Jennifer-Bohnet-170217789709356

    twitter.com/jenniewriter

    instagram.com/jenniewriter

    bookbub.com/authors/jennifer-bohnet

Boldwood

Boldwood Books is an award-winning fiction publishing company seeking out the best stories from around the world.

Find out more at www.boldwoodbooks.com

Join our reader community for brilliant books, competitions and offers!

Follow us
@BoldwoodBooks
@BookandTonic

Sign up to our weekly deals newsletter

https://bit.ly/BoldwoodBNewsletter

Ingram Content Group UK Ltd.
Milton Keynes UK
UKHW042058030423
419500UK00002B/2

9 781801 622837